EMBRYO

EMBRYO

a novel by
Daniel M. Klein

DOUBLEDAY & COMPANY, INC.

GARDEN CITY, NEW YORK

1980

All of the characters in this book are fictitious,
and any resemblance to actual persons, living or dead,
is purely coincidental.

DESIGNED BY LAURENCE ALEXANDER

Library of Congress Cataloging in Publication Data

Klein, Daniel M
 Embryo.

I. Title.
PS3561.L344E47   813'.54
ISBN: 0-385-15797-5
Library of Congress Catalog Card Number 80–709

For FREKE VUIJST
whose ideas, perceptions, and criticism
made this book possible.

ACKNOWLEDGMENTS

I want to express my profound gratitude to Dr. Robert Desnick, Chief of the Division of Medical Genetics at Mt. Sinai Medical School in New York. Not only did he offer me a personal crash course in genetics, but his fecund imagination provided solutions to innumerable puzzles that cropped up in the writing of this story.

I also want to thank Sihanoush Djamdjian of the Division of Medical Genetics and Dr. Leslie Schweitzer of the Department of Pediatrics, both of Mt. Sinai, and Eleanor King and Dr. James Haddow of the Foundation for Blood Research in Portland, Maine, for their generous and patient instruction.

Several other people helped me in a variety of ways: Tana Ross of Mt. Sinai, Thomas Cathcart of Mercy Hospital, Portland, Dr. Herbert Klein of the University of Pittsburgh School of Medicine, and Dr. Mansour Zandieh of the Long Island College Hospital; Pat Kemer, my typist, Mel Berger, my agent, and Susan Schwartz, my editor. My heartfelt thanks to you all.

Finally, I again want to express my appreciation to Freke Vuijst, my wife, for her invaluable contributions at every step of the way.

D.M.K.

Beware of what you desire, for you will surely get it.

—BEDOUIN PROVERB

EMBRYO

PROLOGUE

IT HAD been a perfect pregnancy from the start. No nausea in the first trimester, no constipation in the second, no backaches or leg cramps in the third. Not a single varicose vein had surfaced on her calves. Her ankles and wrists had not swelled once. Her weight gain averaged an ideal three pounds per month until the ninth when it increased to a healthy four. The baby's head engaged in her pelvis like clockwork at the beginning of the thirty-seventh week. And the fetal heartbeat remained strong and regular throughout. All things considered, her obstetrician was extremely pleased. Franny Hollander was a very lucky woman, indeed.

Ten days before her expected due date, just as she had finished delivering her three o'clock lecture in Modern American Literature, Franny felt her first contraction. By five, she was in the Labor Room of Hebron Hospital, fully effaced and three centimeters dilated. At nine-thirty her water broke and at ten, completely conscious and puffing back her instinctive urge to push, she was pronounced ready for delivery.

Her husband, Sydney Hollander, scrubbed and costumed in the mandatory green smock, slippers, cap and mask, helped the maternity nurse lift Franny from her bed onto the rolling stretcher and then to guide it into the Delivery Room. There, they were joined by the obstetrician, a tall, muscular man, also in green, and together they lifted Franny onto the delivery table. While the maternity nurse fitted Franny's legs into the chrome stirrups, the obstetrician removed a pair of thin rubber gloves from a sterile paper pack and pulled them on. The nurse told Franny that she was again going to be doused with antiseptic and proceeded to splash the cold, brown liquid onto her belly, vagina and inner thighs. The obstetrician reached his hand through her vagina into the birth canal, touching the crown of the baby's head. He said that everything was going well and told her to bear down hard with the next contraction. The nurse placed Franny's hands on the cold metal handles at each side of the table and Sydney cupped the back of his wife's head in his hands.

Franny waited until the contraction built to the moment before climax, then curled her back, resting her chin on her chest, and pushed hard, took two quick breaths, held the third and pushed again. The obstetrician felt the baby's head slip almost an inch down the canal. He told Franny that she was doing an outstanding job, that a half dozen more good pushes might be all that was needed.

Sydney slipped out of the Delivery Room, raced across the hall to the Labor Room and returned with his Pentax fitted with a close-up lens and loaded with Kodacolor film. When he re-entered the Delivery Room, Franny was again pushing, her face flushed and damp, her eyes pinched shut, the arteries in her temples pulsing visibly. As Sydney walked behind the doctor, he could see an oval patch covered with wet strands of raven-black hair just inside her vagina. Beaming, he set his camera down on a stool, picked up a cloth and mopped his wife's forehead. He told her that she was the most wonderful woman in the world.

When the contraction subsided and Franny was leaning back, breathing deeply, the obstetrician again told her that she was doing a first rate job, that it would all be over in a matter of minutes. He asked her if she felt she needed a local anesthetic for the episiotomy, and she shook her head, no. The obstetrician patted her thigh, smiled, and nodded to the nurse. The nurse walked across the room to the wall inter-com, pressed the red speak button and said, "We're having a baby in Delivery Room Two." She walked back to the sterilizer, removed a pair of surgical scissors, and handed them to the doctor. Although he knew his wife could barely feel the doctor snip her perineum, the sound of the blades going through her flesh made Sydney wince. He busied himself with his light meter until it was over.

Franny felt another contraction coming and took two deep breaths in preparation. At its height, she pulled herself by the handles almost upright and pushed for a full thirty seconds, panted, and pushed again.

"He's crowning," the obstetrician said, grasping the baby's head. "Gently now, Franny. He's here."

Sydney, tears in his eyes, positioned himself just behind the nurse. He had the camera in his hand, but did not lift it.

Reading each feature with the nerves in the rim of her vagina, Franny felt the forehead of the baby slip out of her, then the slight curve of the nose, the mouth, the chin. She felt a warm rush as it turned and then a soft tug as first one shoulder, then the other, passed out of her. And finally she felt the baby's warm, wet arms against her thighs as the rest of its body slithered out, wriggling and soft.

"What a beautiful baby boy," the nurse said.

The obstetrician cradled the newborn child in his arms as the nurse put a stethoscope to its chest.

"One fifty," she said.

"Excellent," the obstetrician said.

The nurse quickly brushed the vernix from the baby's face, inserted catheters into each nostril and sucked out the mucus while the obstetrician completed his evaluation of the baby on the Apgar scale. He noted that the baby was pink to the soles of his feet, that his respiration was strong and regular, that his deep blue eyes blinked when turned to the light, that his limbs were active and flexible.

"Apgar, ten," the obstetrician said to the nurse.

"Perfect," she said. "A perfect baby."

Sydney stared, overwhelmed, as the nurse took the baby from the obstetrician's arms, its umbilical cord still pulsing. It was indeed an extraordinary looking child, perfectly proportioned, its skin unwrinkled and glowing, its fine, oval-shaped head covered with coal-black fuzz, its face serene and lovely, like an infant in a pre-Raphaelite painting.

The obstetrician placed two clamps on the baby's umbilical cord, snipped between them, then quickly tied it off with ligatures two inches from his navel. He lifted him up and over Franny's knees and brought him to rest on her bare abdomen, the infant's perfect little head against her breast.

Sydney put the camera to his eye, framing the baby boy with Franny's face as she lifted her head to look at him. And before the camera dropped from his hands to the Delivery Room floor, his finger tripped the shutter, capturing his wife's gaping mouth.

Two weeks later, when Sydney Hollander developed the roll of film that had been in his camera, he was no longer shocked by the expression he saw on his wife's face. It was the same look of total revulsion that he saw every time he brought the baby to her.

PART

1

"I FEEL like a pornographic ad in a medical supply cata-logue."

Marie Preston lay completely naked on top of the king-sized bed in her bedroom, her long, well-turned legs crossed at the ankles, an electronic thermometer jutting almost jauntily from her mouth with a thin white wire connecting the end of the thermometer to a digital display on her bedside table. It read, "99.2."

"Keep your mouth closed, dearie," her husband, David said. Grinning, he sat down on the end of the bed and ran his hand from her knees to her ankles. "Or else we won't know when you're done on this side."

"Hmmm?"

"I said, two-tenths of a degree more and you're in busi-ness."

Marie took the thermometer out of her mouth and smiled at her husband. "I'm very sorry, hon, but I can't hear you with your clothes on."

David laughed. He kicked off his loafers, pulled off his argyle socks, stood and walked over to the window. Out-side, a light snow had begun drifting down on Central Park. David began unbuttoning his shirt, and Marie propped her-self up on her elbows to watch him.

"Mild-mannered psychiatrist David Preston slipped out

of his blue oxford shirt to reveal that underneath it all he was really—"

"Twenty pounds overweight. Hey, Marie, why can't you keep that thermometer in?"

"It broke. Ran off the scale. I was too hot for it to handle. Give me a break, will you, David? I've been over ninety-nine all day now."

"Me too."

"Is that a fact?" Marie laughed. "Maybe that's our problem. Maybe you're the one in this family who ovulates."

"No, the thermostat in my office went phlooey again. Half my patients thought the sweat on their brows meant they were on the verge of a breakthrough."

"Maybe they were. Maybe the heat makes their unconscious rise."

"By George, I think you've hit on something, woman. Analysis in a hot house. We'll call it thermal therapy. Let's move to California and open up a clinic."

"I've got a better idea. Let's make love."

"I knew you were after something."

David kicked off his pants and lay down next to Marie on the bed. They looked at one another quietly for a moment and then rolled on their sides, facing each other, and kissed. They held each other tightly and kissed again.

"This is nice," Marie said.

"Yup. And this will make it the third time this week. I call that coverage."

Marie closed her eyes and sighed deeply. "Not funny, David," she said. "Not funny at all."

"Sorry."

Marie opened her eyes and looked at him. Her eyes were sad. "Well, let's get on with it. Number three," she said.

They snuggled up against one another and again began kissing, David's hand caressing her back, then moving down to her buttocks, his middle finger slipping in and out of the crease between them. Suddenly, Marie pulled back from him.

"To the casual observer, we would be making love, correct?"

"Marie, please."

"But no, we are not making love. We are making a baby. Correction, we are attempting to make a baby. We're probably making nothing at all."

"Marie, cut it out, would you? Why do you always have to break the goddamn mood?"

Marie sat up, putting her back against the bedboard. "What kind of mood are you talking about, David? A getting-the-old-job-done mood? Coverage?"

David sat up beside her. "It was a bad choice of words," he said. "Forgive me. I already said I was sorry. And in case you hadn't noticed, I was in an altogether different mood anyhow. A very pleasant mood. A very sexy mood. Jesus!"

Marie turned her head and looked at David for a full minute, then she sighed.

"Oh, God, I'm sorry. Who the hell do I think I'm kidding anyhow? You walk in here and see your fetching wife with a thermometer sticking out of her kisser. What kind of a mood do I expect you to be in?"

David suddenly smiled. "But, honey, haven't I ever told you? When I see that thermometer in your mouth it turns me on. I imagine that I am that thermometer lounging under your tongue, registering every gentle fluctuation of your temperature. Hmmm."

Marie laughed, then impulsively grabbed his hand and pressed it against her bosom. "You really are a sweetheart, did you know that?" she said.

"I happen to love you." David leaned over and kissed her cheek. "I also happen to think that making love and making babies just might happen to have something to do with one another."

Marie slid down in the bed and kissed David's thigh. "I certainly hope so," she said, grinning. "Or else we've been wasting an awful lot of valuable time for nothing."

Marie imagined the sperm swimming past her cervix, through her uterus and up into her fallopian tubes. Immediately after David had ejaculated, she had slipped two thick pillows under her buttocks. She wanted to give the squiggly little fellows the advantage of gravity for their long upstream marathon. Go, boys, go! You can make it! Don't give up now, please! All it takes is one of you. Just one. Marie smiled to herself. She was thinking of Woody Allen in the film, "Everything You Ever Wanted To Know About Sex But Were Afraid To Ask." In one sequence, Allen had played a sperm in a white raincoat and hat poised for a dive into the vaginal canal. He didn't want to go. It was a suicide mission and he knew it.

Marie gently tugged her arm out from under David's sleeping head. For someone who had needed the combined efforts of every biology major in Holmes Hall to get her to pass her natural science requirement at Radcliffe, Marie now knew just about everything there was to know about sex and reproductive biology.

Nothing like real-life motivation. Let Professor Weston test her knowledge now, fifteen years later. She could take a summa in sperm motility, do an honor's thesis on fallopian cilia. She looked over at the clock radio on David's bed table. A quarter to one. A full hour had passed. If it was going to happen, it had probably happened by now. The single survivor of David's forty million spermatozoa had reached and penetrated her ovum. Fertilization had occurred; mitosis had begun. Baby was on the way. If it was going to happen. If.

Marie swung her long legs over the side of the bed. She pulled open the drawer of her bed table and removed a long sheet of paper, her basal body temperature chart. Under

"December fourteenth," she put a little dot at 99.2 degrees, then connected that dot with the previous day's dot—97.9. The day before that her temperature had been 98.6. Great. Yesterday's drop could have been the ovulatory dip. Her chart was definitely biphasic. Maybe the clomiphene was doing its stuff after all. Marie put an "X" under the fourteenth. There were "Xs" under the thirteenth and twelfth. David was right, it was good coverage. She put the chart back into the drawer, stood, and walked to the window. The cold air pushing through the window frame felt good on her body, bracing. She had almost climaxed this time, but the thoughts had stopped her again just when she was about to let herself go. Baby thoughts. Biology thoughts. Sure, making love and making babies had something to do with each other—unless you thought about it. She hadn't had an orgasm in months, not a full-fledged one. Not like the good old days when making love was making love and she didn't have a thought in her head. Not that she was complaining. She would trade a year's orgasms for a baby. Two years. Do you hear that, God?

There was a thin patina of snow covering the trees in Central Park. Few people were still in the street. A lovely night. Maybe the snow would hold until Christmas. Wouldn't it be nice to be pregnant by Christmas? Marie felt a chill pass through her. *Déjà vu.* When had she had that thought before? Last Christmas. Or was it the Christmas before? She went to her closet, removed her blue corduroy robe and pulled it on as she walked into the living room. Sometimes her womb felt like a winter night.

Baby, no baby, charts, wombs. Wasn't there anything else to think about anymore? My God, what was the big deal after all? It wasn't as if she had spent her whole life wanting to procreate the species, for crissake. In high school and college, when she wasn't worrying about a late menstrual period, she hadn't given her reproductive apparatus a thought. Marie sat down on the sofa, stretching out her legs.

She felt some of David's semen oozing out of her and, although she knew it didn't really matter now, she wanted to keep it inside her. In her college group, the notion of marriage and babies had been the stuff of television detergent ads, the unimaginative dreams of lesser women. Now, all but one of her clique were married and had children. Marie had held out until she was thirty-three, and only then she had consented because David assured her that they could maintain independent lives, that they wouldn't fall into the airless traps the others had. And for two years it had worked that way. David's private practice had flourished; he had been published four times in the *American Journal of Psychiatry*. Marie had been promoted twice, from circulation manager of *City Life* to business manager and now to vice-president of Hamilton Publications. Children hadn't fit into their career plans, into what the editors of *City Life* were forever referring to as their "mobile lifestyle."

But by the time both David and Marie had reached their thirty-fifth birthdays—she was just one month younger than he—they both had had to admit that they were actually tiring of the four-day jaunts to Paris, the parties, the Hampton summers. It had developed a breathless, directionless feel, as if the "mobile" lifestyle were attached to some forever-spinning Calder contraption. And they had started to talk about having a child. Just talking about it. Just about one child. At first, every time the subject came up, they would look at each other and laugh in disbelief. A child? Whatever for? Hadn't you seen that survey in *McCall's?* Eighty-some percent of parents said that if they had it to do over, they wouldn't have a single baby. Not one. What did Marie and David want to ruin it all for? Their lives were perfect, better than either of them had ever imagined life could be. Between the two of them they were making more than eighty thousand dollars a year. Their co-op on Central Park West was roomy and beautiful. They had a large circle of bright, exciting friends. They had a greater variety of interesting things to do on any given day than 90 percent of the people in the country. And they wanted to give all that up for two o'clock feedings?

Even now, Marie could not remember how the decision to have a baby had been made. Or even if it actually had been made. What had happened was that once, just as they were beginning to make love, instead of slipping away to the bathroom to insert her diaphragm, Marie had whispered to David, "Hell, let's forget it this time." That was it. They had made love, wonderfully, beautifully, with more feeling than they had in some time. They hadn't said a word about it afterward. Marie had even used her diaphragm the next time they had made love, later that week. But two weeks later, when her period had come, she had felt a little pang of disappointment. And when she had told David, she could see that he was disappointed too. The following month, she hadn't used the diaphragm at all. And when her period had come at the end of that month, it was more than a pang she felt. It was an ache. Marie had felt that ache at the onset of every menstruation for a little more than three years now.

One year after that first diaphragmless night, at the end of her routine annual checkup, Marie had mentioned in the most casual way that she hadn't been using contraception for the past twelve months. Her gynecologist, Ralph Lowenstein, an old classmate of David's from Columbia Medical School, had put down his folder and looked at her directly.

"Do you want to have a baby?" he had asked.

"That's the idea, I guess."

"Let me put it another way," Lowenstein had said. "How badly do you want a baby?"

"On a scale of one to ten?" Marie had laughed.

"Sure. On a scale of one to ten."

"Well, on a scale of one to ten, I'd say—"

Marie had intended to say, "Nine-point-five," but she never finished the sentence. She gulped back a sob instead.

And when that didn't hold, she simply let out the tears that had been welling inside of her for the past six months. Lowenstein had let her cry for a while, patting her hand from time to time, and then he stood up and said, "Look, why don't we start this examination all over again. Sometimes we can put our finger on the cause of infertility right away."

Infertility! It was the first time anyone had used that unfortunate word in connection with Marie. She would hear it and use it again at least once a day for the next two years, and every time it would conjure up a bone-dry, wind-swept desert. Infertile. Nothing growing. Lifeless.

Marie had again undressed and Lowenstein had repeated every examination procedure he had just finished, listening to her heart and lungs, taking her blood pressure twice, feeling her breasts, putting her up on the table, her feet suspended by stirrups, and inspecting her pelvic organs for size and position. He had even taken a second Pap smear so he could definitely rule out early cancer as the cause of a "hostile" uterus. He had examined her fingernails for signs of anemia, checked her arms, legs, and abdomen for abnormal hair growth—a possible indication of a male/female hormone imbalance. He took four vials of blood from her arm—one for anemia tests, another to spot thyroid irregularities, and the other two to check for other hormone deficiencies.

Marie had said not a word until she was dressed and again seated across from Lowenstein's desk.

"Healthy as a horse, right?"

"You seem to be in excellent health for a woman your age, Marie."

"Ouch."

"Thirty-six is young in terms of your life expectancy. In terms of child-bearing, I'm sure you know it's a little on the old side."

Marie grinned. "My hygiene teacher warned us against teen-age pregnancies."

"Marie, most women your age have teen-age children."

Marie looked back at Lowenstein coldly.

"What the hell are you trying to tell me, Ralph? That it's too late in the game for me to be thinking about playing mama? That I ought to consider sublimating my late-blooming maternal drive with volunteer work at a day-care center?"

Lowenstein's expression remained calm, patient. "Marie, I'm just telling you that it might take a little work. That it might not be easy. Your chances, statistically speaking, were certainly a lot better for conceiving and carrying to term twenty years ago, whatever your hygiene teacher told you. But your chances now are still very good, especially with the tests and aids we can afford you these days. Your chances are really quite good, Marie, if you're willing to be patient. Very patient."

Marie remained silent for a moment, then she took a deep breath and let it out slowly.

"Forgive the outburst, Ralph. It looks like the old girl is a little tense, doesn't it?" She smiled. "That's probably part of the problem, huh? An uptight womb or something?"

Lowenstein smiled. "Not long ago, I would have agreed with you. In med school they told us that half of infertility problems were psychogenic. We were supposed to recommend hot baths, cocktails and serene thoughts. I'll bet that most gynecologists around the country are still offering that advice, not that it could hurt. But it was just an easy way out for things we didn't know yet. For problems we didn't know were treatable."

"I don't know whether to be relieved or not," Marie said. "I guess I'm relieved. I don't think I could have lived with the idea that it was all in my head. That it was my fault."

"It might not even be *your* body's fault," Lowenstein said. "David will need some tests too."

"Jesus! The thought never entered my mind."

"It's probably entered his. It's not a very pleasant thought for a man, I can tell you. For a lot of men, infertility is tied up in their minds with sexual inadequacy."

"Let's not start feeling sorry for David yet, okay? I'm still busy feeling sorry for myself."

Lowenstein walked to his file cabinet and removed two printed sheets from one of the drawers.

"Let's not start feeling sorry for either of you just yet, Marie. Let's just get to work. I'm going to need a detailed history from you, from both of you. A lot of it is personal stuff. Sexual habits, that sort of thing. You can fill these out at home, together or separately, whatever makes you more comfortable. Drop it off here tomorrow. I'll also need a urine sample from you from all you pass in the next twenty-four hours. Miss Watkins will give you a container for it. And do try to relax, Marie. It's not the end of the world. It's probably not even the end of your family tree."

Marie stood up and offered her hand to Lowenstein.

"Thanks, Ralph," she said. "You're a real prince. I didn't mean to abuse you. I guess it's just going to take me a little while to get used to my new status as a barren woman. Oh, God, that does sound horrible, doesn't it? 'Barren woman.'"

Lowenstein put his hand on the door of his office.

"And it may not even be accurate." He smiled. "Just remember, warm baths, cocktails, and serene thoughts, okay?"

Marie laughed. She took the printed forms Lowenstein had given her and stuffed them into her handbag.

"And I'll write you the juiciest history you've ever read. I'll have to deliver it to Miss Watkins in a plain brown wrapper. Good-bye, Ralph. And thanks again."

Marie had walked home from Lowenstein's Park Avenue office, cutting across Central Park at Seventy-ninth Street. The Park had seemed filled with young mothers carrying infants in bright-colored harnesses, pushing them in

strollers, walking hand-in-hand with toddlers. She could
barely look at them.

Now, Marie stretched and lifted herself up off the sofa.
She wandered into the kitchen, opened the refrigerator door
and stared inside. She took out a plain yogurt and sprinkled
it with brewer's yeast—her friend Marybeth's surefire fertility potion. Magic. Well, why not? As far as Marie was concerned, the whole business of conceiving a child was pure
magic anyhow. When you looked at all the events that
could possibly go wrong in that process—the insufficient
hormones, the blocked tubes, the inflamed endometriums,
the lazy sperm—it was a wonder the species had survived
three generations after Adam and Eve. She took her dish of
the bitter yogurt back into the living room. Magic, indeed.
It couldn't be any less effective than medicine.

At first, the very notion of their being infertile had
struck both Marie and David as totally preposterous.

"It simply can't be," David had said, laughing. "We
both come from long lines of perfectly fertile people."

It did seem like something that only happened to other
people, people on poor diets or something. Everything else
either of them had ever done, ever even tried, had come so
easily. Radcliffe, the job, money. And here was something
that any fool could do, any neighborhood dog in heat. For
godssake, some women got pregnant off of public toilet
seats, didn't they?

And, of course, what really struck them both as ridiculously ironic was the lengths to which they had gone in the
past to *avoid* pregnancies. One evening, about a week after
Marie's first discussion with Ralph Lowenstein, she and
David spent hours recalling their "close calls." Their favorite, by far, was the late night in Rome when they had raced
from *farmacia* to *farmacia* in search of a douche bag. The
Italian word for that apparatus had been deemed unessen-
tial by whomever compiled their phrase book, and Marie

had been reduced to a pantomime which scandalized the pharmacists of the Holy City. Anecdotes from the Age of Birth Control. There was another misnomer, birth control. The only thing that could be controlled with any certainty was quite the opposite of birth.

After the jokes and bawdy reminicences, it was finally time to get down to business. David had had a sperm count done by Bill Ferguson, another friend from Columbia Med, a Park Avenue urologist. The results were inconclusive: forty-million sperm per ejaculation, borderline sufficiency. When David had come home with this news, he had been despondent and angry, just as Lowenstein had predicted.

"Since when is forty million of anything borderline sufficiency? Good God, it only takes one to do the job, doesn't it? I could give twenty-million of them to the IRS, another ten mill to charity, and still have enough left over to populate every borough in New York." David had poured himself a drink and swallowed it in a single gulp. "Jesus, Marie, I should have known it was my fault."

"He said, 'borderline,' didn't he? That doesn't sound like anybody's fault yet."

"Thanks for the condolences, pal, but I'm in the mood for facing facts. And the fact is, I've been shooting blanks for years now."

"Come on, David, let's not get maudlin."

"If you don't mind, I'll get any damn way I please."

Bill Ferguson had conferred with Ralph Lowenstein. Ferguson maintained that under optimum conditions, David's sperm count should be sufficient for conception. Lowenstein had his doubts, but proceeded with further tests, tests that stretched out over months, leaving Marie feeling less and less like a woman, let alone a human being. She began to feel like a curious object of scientific scrutiny, and a faulty object at that. At times, the whole process seemed to have nothing whatsoever to do with the baby Marie wanted so much, the sweet little child she was now dreaming about almost every night only to wake into a world of hysterosalpingographies and endocrine vaginal cytologies.

The first test, the Huhner post-coital analysis, turned out to be a comedy on the order of looking for douche bags in Rome. Adam Collier, a colleague of Lowenstein's who specialized in fertility problems, had given Marie detailed instructions: she and David were to abstain from sexual relations for one week prior to the fourteenth day of her cycle and on that morning they were to make love no later than nine o'clock; Marie was to remain on her back for one hour afterward and to appear in Collier's office at exactly eleven. By nine-thirty, David still didn't have an erection.

"I think he's dead," David had said, looking down at his flaccid penis. "Look at him. It looks like a suicide. He's finally surrendered to this cruel world."

Marie grinned. "Well, the least we can do is give him a decent burial. In his day, there was none better."

"I wish he were still here to hear that."

"David, look. I think he did."

"Well, well. There's life in the old boy yet."

They had made love quickly and while Marie remained in bed for the requisite hour, David had dressed and left for his office, already late for his first patient. At a quarter to eleven she was dressed and in front of their apartment building. There wasn't a taxi in sight. At five of eleven, she flagged down a passing police cruiser.

"This is an emergency," she told them. "I have to get to my doctor's office immediately."

They delivered her, no questions asked, to Collier's office at eleven on the dot. Collier immediately ushered her into his office where she undressed and hopped up on the examination table, slipped her legs into the stirrups and waited stoically while Collier inserted a vaginal speculum and sucked the mucus from her cervical canal. The results were good: Marie's mucous lining was "friendly," David's sperm remained motile inside of her. Collier had even commented that they appeared to be having sexual relations with positive effectiveness.

"My husband will be glad to hear that," Marie had replied, deadpan.

The tests that followed during the next several months were considerably less amusing. To determine whether or not Marie's tubes were blocked, Collier had performed two tests, one more unpleasant than the other. The first, a gas insufflation, required Marie to lie still on the table while a gas-tight nozzle was inserted into her cervix and carbon dioxide was blown from a tank up inside her. Collier watched the manometer; the needle did not rise. "Fine," he said. "You can sit up now."

"What's fine?" she asked.

She didn't hear the answer. The moment she sat up an excruciatingly sharp pain pierced her shoulders and she fell back onto the table. Collier had neglected to tell her that if her tubes were clear the gas would pass up into her thoracic cavity. The pain was a harbinger of good news. Terrific.

As a double-check, a few weeks later Collier had recommended a hysterosalpingography, an X ray of her uterus and fallopian tubes. This time, Collier had warned her that the injection of iodine into her womb might cause her some discomfort. In truth, by now Marie welcomed the pain. If she was beginning to see all gynecologists as sadists, she was also beginning to see herself as some sort of masochist. The more the pain the better. It was all expiation, punishment, the dues she had to pay. Perhaps, if the pain were great enough, the powers, whomever they may be, would finally grant her a baby. If they wanted her to, she would bleed for a baby.

The hysterosalpingographs showed no irregularities.

By now, almost two years had passed since her first visit to Lowenstein, and Lowenstein was convinced that their problems lay with David's sperm count. Ferguson, on the other hand, contested that Marie's basal temperature charts suggested that she was not ovulating. And so, like surrogate lovers quarreling, David's urologist and Marie's gynecologist wrangled over who was to blame for their infertility. Finally, Ferguson offered a compromise: They would put Marie on a three-month course of clomiphene, a drug which induced ovulation, and David and Marie would have sexual intercourse as frequently as possible between the twelfth and seventeenth days of her cycle. Beyond that, the two good doctors had no definite plans. The three-month clomiphene treatment expired on December twenty-fourth.

The snow was swirling at her living room window. Marie watched as the wind tossed clusters of flakes against the window pane. She reached out and traced one, a beautiful six-pointed star, with her finger tips. It was a good sign, she was sure. Maybe she would be pregnant by Christmas.

"DR. KINGSMILL, I presume."

Paul stopped and turned. Standing in the doorway of Genetics Lab 2 was an extraordinarily beautiful woman. And she was smiling at him. Paul smiled back.

"How did you guess?" he said.

"You walk like an Englishman," the woman said. She stepped out into the hallway and offered Paul her hand. "I'm Eva Persson."

"Ah, yes." Paul took her hand. It was pleasantly warm. "Dr. Fine has just been singing your praises to me. He says that you are the one who keeps the genetics department afloat. But he didn't tell me that you were also an expert on international walks."

Eva laughed, her hand still lingering in Paul's.

"It's only a hobby," she said. "Now I, for example, have a typically Swedish walk."

She removed her hand and walked away from Paul with an exaggeratedly stiff gait, then turned and walked back to him. She was really quite lovely from all sides.

"Yes, indeed," Paul said, "an altogether different walk. Much more dignified than my Anglo slouch. I really should make an effort to walk more Swedishly. Perhaps you could give me lessons."

Eva smiled. "I'm sorry, Doctor, but I'm afraid it's not an acquirable trait."

"Genetically determined, eh?"

"Like everything else."

They both laughed.

"Sam, uh, Dr. Fine asked me to escort you down to GYN for the amnios. If that's agreeable with you."

"Most. I'll slouch beside you."

Eva led him to the elevator and pressed the down button. She looked at Paul appraisingly while they waited. "You've already caused quite a stir here, you know, Doctor. The famous Paul Kingsmill from the Elmwood Clinic. It's quite a coup for Fine. You've done wonders for our reputation at Hebron just by coming here."

The elevator arrived and they stepped in. Eva pressed the button for the fourth floor.

"Was it sagging?" Paul said, smiling. "The genetics department's reputation, I mean."

"Let's just say it's been a little limp. All we have is Bernstein stretching chromosomes, and I can't really say that looks like prize material."

"Oh, yes, the ever important prizes."

"They say around this time of year you can hear them caroling in the laboratories, 'No-o-bel, No-o-bel.'"

Paul laughed. He was surer by the minute that he was going to like it here at Hebron. The elevator arrived at the fourth floor and they got off.

"I trust everyone knows I'm no prize-winner myself," Paul said. "I simply happened to have worked in the same lab as a Nobel Laureate. Accident of circumstance. I'm not even sure any of it rubbed off on me."

Eva looked at him. "Rumor has it that Sir Edmund owes a rather large slice of that prize to your work."

Paul stopped for a moment. He wondered what other rumors had preceded him from London on the international genetics grapevine, rumors from the hallowed Elmwood Laboratories.

"To tell the truth, Doctor," Eva went on, "we've all been dying to know why you left Elmwood for little old Hebron."

Paul looked into the Swedish woman's aqua-blue eyes. It hadn't taken her long to get around to that, had it? Laboratories Stateside were probably no less gossipy than British ones. Worse than business offices, really. Not that it wasn't a reasonable question. But what did one say? That there was something uncomfortable-making about working for a man, Laureate or not, once you discovered that he fudged his data to beat out the competition? That even though you shared in his knighted glory, you could not restrain yourself from confronting him, lecturing him on the noble calling of scientific inquiry, reducing the distinguished old man to pleas and tears? That in the end, both humiliated, you had no choice but to keep your mouth closed, pack up your notebooks, and relocate as far from London as possible? Paul sighed. Put that way, it sounded more virtuous, so ever much more upright than it had probably ever been. Surely Theresa had been right and there was more than a little self-destructiveness involved too. He smiled.

"Well, to be perfectly honest, Miss Persson," he began, "I came to New York for the chromosomes. You have a much better mix here, you know. Just what I needed for my study of the inheritance of funny walks."

Eva smiled, the touch of a blush rising in her cheeks. "Forgive me, Doctor, I'm afraid I was out of line."

"It was really quite a natural question," Paul said. "And do call me Paul, please. Whenever anyone addresses me as Doctor, I still look behind me for a wise old fellow with a medical bag."

"And I am Eva."

They shook hands with mock formality, the second

time their hands had touched since they had met. Then, Eva leading, they continued walking on through a pair of swinging green doors marked with the letters "OB/GYN," and down a long, yellow-tiled hallway. On the walls, spaced twenty or so feet apart, were small attractively designed posters. The headline on them read, "Birth Defects Should Not Be a Surprise," and pictured below were two children's faces, one normal, the other with Down's syndrome—a mongoloid baby. The text below, in both Spanish and English, urged all expectant mothers over thirty-five years old to have an amniocentesis performed on them before their seventeenth week of pregnancy. It ended with the slogan, "You have a right to know." Paul stopped to read one of the posters in its entirety. He looked again at the picture of the Down's child, the mongoloid features, the telltale flap of skin slanting from its eyelid.

"Fifty years ago they thought that if a pregnant woman so much as looked at a picture of a child like that she would have an abnormal baby," he said. "Now, it's an advertisement."

"I'm afraid the Americans were never known for their subtlety," Eva said from behind him.

"I don't know. The poster never once mentions the words 'therapeutic abortion.' That's rather subtle," Paul said, and they continued down the hallway.

They entered a small office vestibule where a black attendant greeted Eva and told her that Dr. Bouchard was expecting them in the Ultrasound Room, that they should go right in. Almost by reflex, Paul buttoned up his white coat before entering.

Bouchard, a short, plump man in his fifties who appeared to have hair everywhere except on his head, was seated at a metal desk. Across from him sat a Puerto Rican woman in her late thirties wearing a T-shirt emblazoned with the words, "Julio Did It," and an arrow pointing down to her four-month pregnant belly. She looked apprehensive.

"Hello, René," Eva said. "This is Dr. Kingsmill. He's come to observe our amnio techniques before we lock him away in a laboratory."

Bouchard extended his hand to Paul without rising.

"That is, if you don't mind, Doctor," Paul said.

"Please. It would be my pleasure, Kingsmill. You're from Elmwood, aren't you?"

Paul nodded.

"Good. I'd appreciate your comments."

Paul smiled. "I'm just observing, but thank you."

Bouchard looked at the sheet in front of him.

"Well, let's see what we have here then. A thirty-nine-year-old woman. Ten pregnancies, starting from the age of, uh, sixteen, so she says. Probably more like fourteen. Four different fathers. This one is the fifth, actually. And eight live births, two with congenital hearing impairments. Dr. Kaplan sent her to us from the Bronx. Among other things, he wants us to figure out how far along she is. The lady can't remember when she did it, although she seems to be certain of with whom."

Paul looked at the patient. She had sat impassively while Bouchard gave her history. Doctors and social workers had probably talked about her in her presence most of her adult life.

"I'm Dr. Kingsmill," Paul said, extending his hand to the woman. "I'm going to watch while Doctor Bouchard performs the amniocentesis, if that is all right with you."

The woman looked back at Paul frightenedly, then looked away, her arms remaining stiff at her sides. Bouchard smiled. "I'm sure it's perfectly all right with Miss Garcia," he said. "Let's get started, shall we? Miss Bailey?"

A middle-aged nurse led the patient to the table in the center of the room, helped her up onto it, and undid her maternity jeans, tucking them down under her buttocks. Then she lifted the woman's T-shirt to just below her large breasts, fully exposing her bulging abdomen. The nurse then swabbed her belly with a thick gel and pulled the ultrasound arm to where it was poised just over the woman's middle. Bouchard had positioned himself on the other side of the table; Paul and Eva stood near the patient's feet.

"Okay," Bouchard said. "Let's take a peek at the little fellow, shall we?"

He flipped a pair of switches on the console next to him and the nurse began moving the ultrasound arm back and forth over the patient's slippery belly. Immediately, an image floated into view on the screen, looking like a murky underwater photograph. The nurse continued manipulating the arm and the image became clearer: a baby curled in its mother's womb.

"Excellent. Very good, Miss Bailey. Punch up a Polaroid of that, okay?" Bouchard smiled at Paul. "What do you think, Doctor?"

Paul was staring at the patient. Her eyes were fixed on the ultrasound screen which was suspended just above her head and to her right, looking for all the world like a ward television set. Her eyes had widened, full of wonder and fear. Good God, the Americans aren't particularly subtle, are they? The woman was looking at a picture of the baby inside her.

"Yes, very good," Paul murmured, now looking down at his hands. He reminded himself that, of course, they did things differently here, that it was his first day and he was just observing, that this wasn't even his department. "Very good," he repeated, more loudly.

Dr. Bouchard turned to the real-time ultrasound console, the scanner which showed the image in motion. "It's supposed to be state of the art," he said, smiling as he flipped it on. "It better be with that price tag."

"Is my baby good?"

Everyone turned to look at the patient's face. Other than Paul, it was the first time any of them had done so since they started the procedure.

"Yes, we think so, Miss Garcia. As far as we can tell now, your baby is just fine." Bouchard looked up at the screen: The fetus was moving, one of its arms arcing up and down. "Why, look, Miss Garcia. I think he's even waving at you." Bouchard winked at Paul.

Paul stared back at Bouchard incredulously. "Aren't you concerned about bonding?"

"What about it, Doctor?"

Paul again looked down at his hands. Good Lord, would he never learn to keep quiet? He looked up and, choosing his words so that they could not be understood by the patient, he said, "I was only thinking that it might be premature to personalize the fetal image. You know, maternal attachment might be chancy at this stage of your testing."

Bouchard ran his tongue deliberately across his upper lip. "Yes, I've heard that at Elmwood you keep the screen out of the patient's sight." He smiled at Miss Garcia. "But we like our patients to know everything we're doing. I guess we just aren't too much for the old medical mystique over here."

"Yes. Yes, of course," Paul said. He looked past Bouchard at the wall behind him, and sighed. Oh well, he supposed he had deserved that. Why even as far back as medical school when a physician asked for comments, he usually was asking for something else. Praise would be nice. Adulation better. Once again, Paul remembered why he had opted for the laboratory. He really didn't like doctors. Out of the corner of his eye, Paul saw Eva looking at him. She winked. Paul smiled quickly and looked again at the ultrasound screen. Using a knob to maneuver two dots superimposed over the fetal image like some video game, Miss Bailey was measuring the width of the unborn child's head. A digital display on the console showed the results: "40 cm." Bouchard touched another button. The display flashed: "20 wks."

"Well, well, what do you think of that, Miss Garcia? You're twenty weeks pregnant. Halfway there. Now, if you'll just tell your little fellow to stop moving around in there, we'll be done with you in a minute."

Keeping his eyes on the screen, Bouchard ran his finger across Miss Garcia's belly, looking for a "window," a point in the amniotic sac where he could insert his syringe without contacting the fetus or placenta. In a moment, he found it, wiped the gel away with tissue paper, and marked the spot with a dot of antiseptic. The patient had not once taken her eyes off of the screen.

"Syringe."

The nurse handed Bouchard a long, slender needle.

"Will it hurt the baby?" Miss Garcia asked.

"It will barely hurt you," Bouchard said. He tipped the syringe up over the dot.

"Please, don't hurt the baby," the patient said.

"He won't. I promise you," Eva said, and a second later the doctor had slipped the needle through Miss Garcia's abdominal wall into her womb and began to withdraw the pale yellow fluid. He took twenty milliliters, removed the syringe's barrel leaving the needle inserted, and poured the contents into a sterile vial, then held it up against the light, like a winetaster. It was clear. He took a second twenty milliliters. This time, when he made the transfer to the vial, a couple of drops fell on the patient's belly. For the first time, she looked down over her breasts and saw the needle sticking out of her womb. She flinched and looked again at the screen. In a matter of minutes, the vial was full and the needle had been withdrawn. The nurse swabbed the patient's abdomen, helped her dress, and showed her to the door.

"Well, good luck, Miss Garcia," Bouchard said.

She left.

Bouchard had put a stopper in the vial and attached an identification label to it. Eva put out her hand.

"I'm going back to the lab, René," she said. "I'll save somebody a trip." She took the vial from him and then turned to Paul. "Are you staying?"

"No, I think not." Paul smiled cordially at Bouchard. "Thank you, Doctor. I look forward to seeing you again."

They shook hands.

"Come again on a Thursday or Friday," Bouchard said. "That's when we do private patients. They're usually more interesting."

"Yes, of course."

As Paul and Eva walked out through the door, Miss Bailey was ushering in a black woman who was easily in her mid-forties. She looked four or five months pregnant.

"Well, I'm afraid I put my foot in it," Paul said, once they were out in the hallway.

Eva grinned at him. "I think you're refreshing. And old Bouchard is and always has been a horse's ass."

They were at the bank of elevators now. Eva pressed the "Up" button.

"I've got an idea," Eva said. "Why don't we just drop this off at the lab and then I'll take you for lunch at a place I know where doctors never go."

"Perfect. Especially the part about no doctors."

"Miss Persson. May I see you a moment?"

Paul looked up. A tall man with muscular arms extending from his green operating smock was standing in the hallway where it intersected the elevator gallery. Eva had turned her head and was looking back at him. Suddenly, she handed Paul the vial.

"Take this up, would you, Paul? And let's take a rain check on lunch, okay?"

Before Paul could answer, she had turned and began walking toward the green-clad doctor. The elevator opened and Paul stepped in, alone. He pressed the button for floor six. In his hand, the vial was still warm with Miss Garcia's amniotic fluid.

THE CURSE!

The damned bloody curse!

Marie sat in a stall of the women's room on the eighteenth floor of the Hamilton Building examining the tissue in her hand. It was stained pink with flecks of crimson at the edges. Blood red. Rhymes with dead. Oh, dear God, why? What did I do wrong?

According to her chart, she had been two days late as of this morning. She hadn't said anything to David. She didn't have to. He watched the calendar more closely than she did. When they had parted in front of their apartment building at ten, he had been all smiles. He told her to have a great day. Enjoy the office party. But take care of yourself.

Sure, David. But what for? Whatever for?

For the last twenty-four hours she had been sure she was pregnant. Yesterday, in the middle of the night, she had tip-toed into the bathroom to examine her breasts. They had felt heavier. In the mirror, they had even looked bigger. Rounder. Fuller. A sign.

A sign that she was willing to believe anything.

A sign that her period was coming.

Someone opened the women's room door and she heard the chatter and laughter outside. Someone was singing, "Good King Wenceslas" in drunken off-key. The door swung

closed and all was silent again except for the click of high
heels coming toward the stall next to her.

"Hello? Who's there?"

"Kate. Kate Cochoran. Is that you, Marie?"

"Yes."

"Too much to drink?"

"No."

"Is something wrong, Marie? You sound funny."

"No. Do you have a Tampax?"

"Sure do. Never travel without them. Like good luck
charms, my Tampax and my diaphragm. As a matter of fact,
I just came in here to slip in the little Betsy. Saperstein in
promotion has been whispering amorous things in my ear all
afternoon. And after a few cups of that punch, he starts
looking like Joe Namath. Ha! I wonder who I look like to
him. Faye Dunaway, I hope. Open the door. I'll give you an
extra for good luck."

For a second, Marie could not move. Then she said,
"Just slip it under the door, Kate."

"Sure. Here."

Marie took the two tampons from Kate's hand.

"Are you sure you're all right?" Kate asked.

"Yes."

"I guess I'm funny. I never get the monthly blues.
Whenever my little friend comes, I go out and celebrate. To
me it's just—"

"Kate. Put in your diaphragm and get the hell out of
here, would you, please?"

"Jesus, I'm sorry."

Marie heard Kate's heels click toward the door.

"Hey, I'm sorry," Marie called. "I'm really sorry, Kate."

"That's okay. I understand, I guess. Well, Merry Christmas."

"Yes. Merry Christmas, Kate."

After she had put in the Tampax, Marie went to the

sink and splashed cold water on her face. She looked at her reflection in the mirror and sighed. Where had this morning's bloom gone?

"Merry Christmas," she said.

To avoid the merrymakers, she took the back stairway up to the twentieth floor. Not a soul was there. She went over to her secretary's desk, opened the top drawer and removed a cigarette from the pack of Parliaments. Why not? It's too late to die young. She lit it, walked into her office and sat down. There was a note clipped to her calendar. It said, "Your mother called at four o'clock." Marie took a deep inhale on her cigarette and let it out in little spurts. Not exactly the person she wanted to talk to right at this moment. Nothing personal, Mom. Or was it? Marie peered down her side window to the Christmas lights strung along Fifth Avenue. Is it self-destructive to resent your own mother for having been fertile? She dialed the Connecticut area code and number and waited.

"Hello?"

"Hi, Mom. Merry Christmas."

"Oh, hello, darling," Marie's mother said. "I'm glad you caught me. The taxi's on the way. I did so want to talk to you before I left for Brenda's. How's David?"

"Terrific. We're both terrific, Mom."

"Oh, that's nice. Did my package come?"

"No, Mom. Not yet. I can hardly wait."

"Oh, it's really nothing much. Just something I saw in Pandora's Box that I thought you'd like. It's from China. Some sort of ancient good luck—"

"Don't tell, Mom. Please. Let it be a surprise."

"You always were one for surprises, weren't you?"

"Yes."

"Look, darling, the taxi will be here any second now. Shall I call you Christmas morning or will you call me at Brenda's?"

"Either way, Mother."

"I just didn't know. I mean, Brenda says you haven't called there in months."

"I've been busy."

"I don't want to get involved, but it causes her such pain, darling. She's always looked up to you, you know."

"I know."

"She's all alone with those children. They're the only comfort she has."

"Mom, I'll call on Christmas morning, okay? I've got to go now. I'm still at the office."

"Of course. Sorry to keep you. Good-bye, darling. And love to David."

"Thanks, Mom."

"Honey?"

"Yes?"

"Is there anything else you wanted to tell me? Any news?"

Marie swallowed. "No, Mother."

"Oh. Well, I think I hear the taxi honking. Bye, sweetheart."

"Bye, Mom."

As Marie put down the receiver, she noticed that her hand was trembling. She pulled the cigarette stub out of the ash tray, dusted it with her fingers, pulled it straight and lit it again. She felt inordinately tired. She drew twice on the cigarette, stubbed it out again and dialed David's office.

"David Preston."

"Hi. It's me."

"I'm just finishing a session. Can I call you back?"

"I just wanted to tell you I'm going home."

"I thought you were going to meet me here."

"I'm going home, David. I'm exhausted and I'm not going anywhere tonight. Give my apologies to Tom."

"Marie, can we discuss this later?"

"David, we can discuss it any damned time you like. I'll be home in bed. You can reach me there."

"Marie, wait a second. I'm going to take this on the other phone."

Marie kept the receiver to her ear, listening as David said some words of apology to his patient and went out into the reception room. The patient must never hear the psychiatrist dealing with his hysterical wife. Bad for business.

"Marie, now what's the matter?"

"Three guesses."

"Oh, God, I'm sorry. Really."

"It's not your fault," Marie said, without thinking. Who knows? Maybe it was.

"Honey, I think you should have yourself a drink and come over here, okay?"

"No, not okay, David. I don't want to see anybody just now. Possibly not even you. Look, why don't you go over to Tom and his wife's, whatever her name is, and decorate their tree and drink eggnog and have a jolly time. Tell them I've come down with the grippe or something. I'll see you when you get home."

"Marie, you can't just lock yourself away and—"

"Oh, get off it, will you, David? I'm not locking myself away. I just can't face another person today. Aren't I entitled to that, for crissake? Or are you afraid I'll offend your new buddies?"

"As a matter of fact, I was thinking of Tom and Bonnie. They've had this planned for a long time. And anyway, I think it will do you some good. If you go home, all you'll do is lie around thinking morbid thoughts."

"I feel like thinking morbid thoughts."

"No you don't, honey."

"Then I'll take a sleeping pill."

David paused for a moment. Then he said, "Marie, I'm not giving up, you know. And you can't either. Not yet."

Marie felt the tears start to fill her eyes, then to slip down the corners onto her cheeks. Damn! She hadn't been going to do this. Not over the phone. She wiped the tears from her face before she spoke again.

"You'd better get back to your patient. She's going to think you aren't interested in her problems."

"Are you coming?"

"Maybe," Marie said. And she hung up the receiver.

Marie had met Tom Roundtree a few times at the office which he had started sharing with David three months ago. In a way, she had been impressed with him. Unlike others of David's colleagues she knew, Tom had an ingenuous, extroverted manner. No beard, no mumbling. A man who truly seemed to like people. Very peculiar for a psychiatrist. Midwestern is what he was. When David had told her that Tom was from Ohio she had said she didn't know they needed psychiatrists out there. He probably was an excellent therapist, but Marie had never felt the same desire to make him a friend that David had. Too cheerful for this point in her life. These days all she could take were other low-grade depressives like herself. And if Tom Roundtree was brimming with Midwestern good cheer, as Marie could have guessed, Bonnie Roundtree was virtually overflowing with it. A sweet woman, no doubt. And certainly abounding with what Marybeth called, "positive life energy." But if nobody minded, Marie wasn't feeling too positive about life tonight. Not at all. This was a bad idea, David. Very bad. Marie wanted to go home the minute she walked in the door.

By way of fortification, Marie downed two eggnogs before she even sat down. Bonnie, a pleasant-looking woman with a broad-featured, open face similar to her husband's, tried gallantly to spark a conversation with her. She told Marie how eager she had been to meet her, how few friends they had made so far in New York, how much they enjoyed it here even though the City was so overwhelming. Marie did her utmost to keep her end up, to say something friendly, but she had this ache to contend with. And she felt like she could barely breathe. What had begun in the office as a sense of fatigue now felt like a spreading paralysis. Maybe the drinks hadn't been such a good idea after all. With a great deal of effort, she rose and was about to excuse herself for the bathroom, when a black maid entered the room hand-in-hand with the most stunning-looking tow-headed little boy Marie had ever seen.

Marie didn't move. This was absolutely more than she could take tonight.

"Adam, this is David and Marie Preston," Bonnie said, smiling. "David works with Daddy."

Adam was no more than two years old, but he already had the exquisitely-defined features one could only expect to see on a somewhat older boy, perhaps an English school-boy from someplace like Eton. The shape of his head alone, a perfect oval, was reminiscent of the boys pictured in the royal family portraits Marie had seen at the Tate. But it was Adam's eyes which overwhelmed her, large, bright, deep-blue eyes surrounded by long, thick, straw-colored lashes. Dazzling eyes.

The boy smiled beautifully and said, "Hello, David and Marie."

Marie felt her heart thumping away in her chest. This is what real heartbreak was all about—a two-year-old boy. She wanted to look away, but she couldn't take her eyes off him.

"Come here, Bozo," Tom said, stooping down. The boy let go of the maid's hand and ran to Tom, who scooped him up and lifted him onto his shoulders. "This is just a hello and good-bye, you know, kiddo."

"I know, Daddy. Hey, look. I'm as big as the tree." He reached his hand out toward the Christmas tree that stood by the window.

"He's the most beautiful child I've ever seen in my life," Marie said finally.

Tom bounced the boy up and down on his shoulders. "He's the heartbreaker in the family. That's for sure."

"What a wonderful ambition for your son," Bonnie said in a mock-scolding tone.

"May I hold him a moment?" The question came out before Marie could check it. What was this now, some new kind of masochism? She looked at David helplessly.

David winked.

"Careful," he said. "I bet he's heavier than you think."

The boy was reaching out his hands to Marie. She hesitated just a second more and then took him in her arms, pressing him against her bosom, his face just below hers. He had a marvelous, buttermilk smell. He looked up at her and grinned and Marie smiled back, holding back her breath, afraid that if she breathed tears would come and there would be no stopping them.

"Time for bed, Bozo," Tom said. "We've got a big week coming, you know."

"Should I take him, Marie?" Bonnie asked.

"No, I will. If that's all right," Marie said quickly.

"He can walk, you know," Tom said, grinning, but Marie was already following Bonnie down the hallway, the boy snug in her arms.

"Did you brush and scrub?" Bonnie asked when they arrived in the boy's bedroom.

"Yup."

"Then it's off to beddy-bye. Can you manage, Marie?" Bonnie had let down the side of his crib.

"I think I can."

Marie set Adam down in his crib, then pulled the blankets up to his chin. The boy's eyelids fluttered. "Sleepy," he said.

"You don't mind if we skip the story tonight?" Bonnie slid the side of the crib back up.

Adam closed his eyes and sighed contentedly, the two women looking down at him. Suddenly, he reopened his eyes, said, "Good night, Mom. Good night, Marie," and closed them again. He was asleep.

"What a wonderful boy," Marie said, still staring down at him. "And so incredibly gorgeous."

Bonnie laughed. "Heaven knows where he gets it from. Neither Tom or I ever looked like that."

"I don't know. I think I see some of Tom around the eyes," Marie said. She didn't, really.

"That's what Tom says. Every once in a while he pulls out this old brown photo of his great uncle Knut to prove which side of the family Adam gets his good looks from." Bonnie laughed again. "But you could fool me. Knut must have been eighty when the picture was taken."

Marie smiled.

"I only hope our new baby is half as sweet-looking," Bonnie said.

Marie straightened up and looked at Bonnie. Her heart was racing again and again the fatigue was overtaking her. She had just gotten used to the idea of Adam. Only a moment ago, she had even told herself that, pain or not, she must no longer deny herself the pleasure of other people's children. But one lesson a night was enough. Especially tonight. She put one hand on the crib railing to steady herself.

"Are you expecting?"

Bonnie beamed, her brown eyes sparkling. She looked down at Adam, then put a finger to her lips. "We haven't told big brother yet," she whispered.

This time there was no holding back the tears and, although she cried silently, they flooded out of Marie's eyes as if she were bawling out loud. Her whole body quaked with it. Bonnie immediately put a hand out on Marie's shoulder, but Marie pulled back and Bonnie's hand slipped away. Right now, Marie hated this well-meaning, good-hearted woman beyond any reason. She couldn't help it. This woman already has one child, one wonderful, beautiful, loving child. Why another? Why not one for me? Who the hell is in charge of distribution anyhow? Is it because she's more maternal than I am? Because she never wanted anything else besides babies? Well, damn it, that's all I want now. Just one. And I'll give the world for it.

Perhaps a full minute passed before Marie stopped crying and lifted her head. Bonnie reached over to the top of the bassinet and removed a clean diaper.

"Here, use this," she said.

Marie managed a weak smile, took the diaper from Bonnie and wiped her eyes and nose. Amongst other things, she felt terribly guilty.

"I'm really very happy for you," Marie said. Part of her meant that too. "I hope you can believe that."

"Of course, I do," Bonnie said. "I bet you'd like to use the bathroom, huh?"

"Yes, that'd be a good idea."

Bonnie led Marie into the bathroom, a large, high-ceilinged room with bright, countrylike curtains. She took a towel and washcloth from the closet and handed them to Marie, then turned to leave. At the door, she turned back, seemed to hesitate for a second, and then said, "It took us five years before I could have Adam."

Marie stared at her, her mouth slightly open. She wasn't going to ask any questions. Whatever the story was, she didn't want to hear about it. Not tonight. She'd had enough tonight. More than enough.

"We had just about given up hope," Bonnie was saying.

"I already have. Around four o'clock this afternoon." Marie turned the water on loudly in the sink.

"I don't think you have to," Bonnie said, looking at her warmly.

Marie stiffened. Won't you please leave me alone, woman? Don't take liberties just because you saw me fall apart.

"I'm afraid I really don't have too much choice about it," Marie said, flatly.

"I think you do," Bonnie said, seating herself on a low stool next to the hamper. "Do you mind if I sit down?"

Marie said nothing. She only wanted to get out of here, go home, anywhere. She looked down at the floor as Bonnie again began to speak.

"Seventeen doctors told me I couldn't have children. Ten just in Cleveland. Most of them said I didn't ovulate. The rest said they didn't know what was wrong. Which was even worse, if you know what I mean. I had every test there was—the Huhner test, X rays of everything, half a dozen D and Cs. Even a laparoscopy. I can't remember how many times I was in the hospital. Or in what cities. I've probably had my tubes blown open more times than any woman in America."

Marie had turned off the water while Bonnie spoke, but she kept her eyes half-closed and down, looking at the diamond pattern of the tiles on the floor. Now, as Bonnie paused, she looked up at her and Bonnie smiled.

"And then I found Dr. Raymond McPartland here in New York," Bonnie said. "And I was pregnant with Adam in less than four weeks."

Marie shrugged. This wasn't the first time she had heard about one miracle fertility doctor or another. She had even seen a couple of them recommended by other friends. All with the same results.

"Bonnie, this has really been very thoughtful of you to share this with me. I mean that. I didn't even know David had told you about our . . . our difficulties."

"He told Tom and Tom told me."

"Yes. Well, anyway, I really do appreciate this. Don't misunderstand me, please. But I'll tell you the truth, I don't think I can see another doctor. Not even the latest expert. I'm just . . . I'm just too tired or something." Marie wiped her hands on a towel and turned toward the door.

Bonnie nodded. "Of course. I can understand that."

"And anyhow, all of our problems are different," Marie went on, although she hadn't intended to. "I mean, it may be David. His sperm count is a little low."

"Yes," Bonnie said. "So is Tom's. Thirty million."

Marie looked at Bonnie incredulously. "Thirty million?"

"Yes. You'd think that would be enough, wouldn't you?"

"No," she said. Marie took a step toward Bonnie. "I wouldn't. Not from what I've read. That sounds pretty low, if you don't mind my saying so. I mean, what did this doctor—"

"McPartland."

"What did this Dr. McPartland say?"

"Oh, he said it was very low. Below borderline, really. But he thought it could be enough once he unblocked my left tube. That's what was really wrong, Marie. That's what seventeen doctors had somehow missed."

"My God."

"Yes," Bonnie said, standing. "You know what my first thought was when I heard that I was pregnant with Adam? You'd think I would have just been happy, wouldn't you? But I was furious. Really. At all those doctors. All those sloppy examinations. All those years. All that waste."

Marie stared at Bonnie. She had certainly underestimated her. In the mood she'd been in, she had probably been underestimating a lot of people lately. "I can certainly understand that," she said.

Bonnie looked at Marie sincerely. "He's more than just the latest expert, Marie. McPartland's a wonderful, understanding man. And he's a specialist in women like us. You know, the over-thirty-five set. That's all he sees. And from what I've heard, his batting average is just about a hundred percent. And those are mostly women who've already seen half a dozen doctors who told them to start thinking about adoption."

"That's quite a reputation," Marie said. She played her lower lip under her teeth for a moment. "I suppose he's impossible to see."

"Very," Bonnie said. Then she smiled broadly, "Marie, I hope you won't be put out with me. But, well, I've been seeing McPartland often lately. I needed a few little adjustments before I could get this one going." She patted her belly. "And, well, I told him about you."

Marie stiffened. "But, Bonnie, you hadn't even met me yet."

"I know. I'm sorry if I spoke out of turn, Marie," Bonnie went on quickly. "But it just came up so naturally, I didn't think about it. I hadn't planned on saying anything to him about you, at least not until I asked you. But there we were, having our after-examination chat and out it came."

"Well," Marie said, smiling, "it's just as well that you did, Bonnie. I would have probably walked out of here and put off contacting him for another thirty-eight years."

"I told him he might hear from you soon," Bonnie said.

Marie laughed. "You really are something, lady. You don't waste any time, do you? Do you mind if I give you a great big hug?"

Bonnie smiled shyly, almost girlishly at Marie. "I think I'd like that," she said.

The two women embraced warmly, then Marie pulled back, leaving her hands on Bonnie's shoulders.

"Why have you done all this for me, Bonnie? You don't really know me?"

"I didn't do much," Bonnie said. "And if you really want to know, I had a selfish reason—I wanted somebody to be pregnant together with. You know, it's so much more fun that way."

"You really are confident of this doctor, aren't you?"

"Marie," Bonnie said. "I'll bet you anything you'll be pregnant in a month."

"Well, if it isn't the Bobbsey Twins," Tom said, as the two

women came back into the living room, both smiling broadly.

Marie walked over to the couch and sat down next to David. He had been right, they didn't have to give up hope yet. Not by a long shot. She leaned over and kissed his cheek. "I've got some news, friend," she said.

"I think I just might know what it is," David said, putting his arm around her waist. "Tom, here, has already been lecturing me on the advantages of private schools over public. What do you say, hon? Do we want our kid to be a snob?" He laughed.

Marie looked at David quizzically. "You know?"

"Yes," David said. "Tom has been doing jigs about this Doc McPartland ever since you left the room."

"Not exactly jigs," Tom said, deadpan. "More like a soft shoe."

Tom, Bonnie and David burst into laughter and Marie looked from one face to the other, at their bright, happy eyes, at their open mouths. For one moment, they all looked terribly far away, like players on a stage, and Marie felt curiously lonely.

"He even showed me McPartland's bio in the GYN Directory," David was saying, catching his breath. "You'll like this, hon. He's a Harvard man."

Now Marie smiled. She really was very happy.

"Too bad," she said. "I was hoping he'd be a quack with a Sears Roebuck degree. You know, something a little different for a change."

"Careful," Tom said, grinning. "I went to Sears."

At dinner, and afterward, back in the living room with their Irish coffees, the talk was about everything except babies. But it was, of course, the only thing Marie could think about—being pregnant, having her baby, even decorating its room. From time to time, a thought would obtrude warning her not to get her hopes up too high, that she couldn't take another disappointment. But she found she could push the thought away easily. This time it just felt different. She was sure it was.

Before they left, Marie asked if she could take a last look at Adam. Bonnie went with her into the bedroom and they looked down at the boy. Even asleep, with those magnificent eyes closed, he was enchanting to look at. The women tip-toed out into the hallway and Bonnie put her arm through Marie's.

"Won't it be lovely to be pregnant together," she said.

Marie beamed. "Absolutely lovely."

After they had seen Marie and David onto the elevator, Bonnie threw her arms around her husband's neck.

"I feel just like Santa Claus," she said.

Tom smiled. "A regular gift from the Magi."

HAPPY CHRISTMAS, old boy.

Eva Persson lay stretched out on her back on Paul's bed looking, this Christmas morn, like the most bountiful gift Father Christmas had ever delivered. Paul, up early and feeling wonderfully refreshed, took a long gaze at her sleeping body. She was, indeed, an extraordinarily lovely woman. From head to toe. From her thick, hay-colored hair to the delicate articulation of her ankles. From the sublime scoop of her breasts to the elegant turn of her hips and thighs. And skin, good Lord, she had skin that glowed. Not even the thin surgical scars on her abdomen marred the total glorious effect—they were perfectly neat and symmetrical. Paul pulled tight the sash on his dressing gown. Great genes, he thought, smiling. Magnificent genes.

He wandered out of the bedroom, down the hall and into what the rental agent had described as a Hollywood kitchen. Never having been in California, he had wondered from the start what connection this closet of a cooking area had with the fabled open spaces of that state. He put up a kettle of water and looked out of the window. Across the airshaft, not more than fifteen feet away from him, he could see a small boy and girl sitting near a Christmas tree unwrapping packages. They looked wonderfully happy.

Paul wondered what he would do today. Would he and

Eva spend it all together or, after breakfast, would they both begin to feel a bit awkward and one of them would speak of an engagement that had to be kept, some chores that had to be done. It was really quite impossible to tell. Last night at eight o'clock, as he switched off the light source on his photomatic microscope, his plan had been to walk home along Madison Avenue, stop for a light dinner at the Sechuan House, and perhaps read an article or two in *Heredity* before going to bed. No sentimental activities for Christmas Eve. Too chancy for a recently divorced man in a strange city. It could make a man moody.

Eva had been standing in the hallway just outside his laboratory door when he had come out pulling on his coat. Had she been waiting there? He still didn't know. He rather hoped she had. They had had dinner together and then, in the most friendly, natural way, she had suggested that they spend the night together. "To keep away the ghosts of Christmas past," she had said. Like the proper, Oxford-bred fool that he was, Paul had been bothered by the idea of mixing up workmates and bedmates. He had even quoted Eva one of his father's absurd old Welsh epigrams on the subject: "Never wear your pajamas to a duck shoot."

"I promise not to wear pajamas," Eva had said.

They had laughed as they left the restaurant arm-in-arm. The very idea of denying oneself such a lovely prospect for the sake of some antiquated protocol was patently ridiculous. New York was so much freer than London in such ways. What a good move that had been.

The lovemaking had been nothing short of spectacular. So very different than it ever had been with Theresa. With Eva, all was spontaneous, avid, and so very graceful, an erotic *pas de deux* from start to finish. And then, from start to finish again. And again. Thank you, Father Christmas. I swear, I'll never doubt your existence again.

Paul poured the boiling water into his teapot and brought it out to his eating table in the living room. There had been something missing, of course, but that was to be expected. He and Eva barely knew one another, in fact had only eaten together for the first time last night. One didn't create intimacy overnight. That took years, eh, Theresa? And anyway, intimacy and passion are inversely related, as you so cleverly used to put it. Paul brought the cup to his lips and sipped his tea. Much heat, but little warmth. That's what had been missing, of course. Warmth. Bernstein had said that Eva was typically Scandinavian in that respect. It comes from all that skiing, Paul's labmate had said, all that coolly gliding over things. Paul set down his cup and smiled. Somehow, he doubted very much that Bernstein would have turned his back on last night's invitation had it been directed at him, however coolly. It is really quite remarkable how little we geneticists know about the real power of sex.

And perhaps Bernstein was wrong, anyway. Certainly, there was a cool efficiency about Eva. That's what made her so effective as supervisor of laboratories. But Paul had also detected a childlike sentimentality about her as well.

Earlier in the week he had overheard her and a technician discussing an amniotic culture that was growing too slowly. Eva had lifted the small flask of microscopic cells and held it up against the window. "I think she's hungry," she had said. "Give her more glutamine at the next feeding and I think she'll be okay." Last night, Paul teased Eva for using such affectionate terms for fetal cells.

"Why not?" Eva had said, blushing, her eyes twinkling. "I think of them all as my little babies."

Now, Paul turned in his chair. Leaning against the archway to the hall was Eva wearing his blue-flannel pajamas and his lambskin wool hat. And she was grinning.

"And where do you think you're going?" Paul said, smiling.

"To a duck shoot."

GYNECOLOGISTS' WAITING rooms always reminded Marie of the vestibule outside the Headmistress's office at prep school—rows of silent, sullen females, their ankles crossed and an almost palpable sense of guilt in the air. Dr. Raymond McPartland's was a delightful exception. Here, the patients—ten of them when Marie arrived some twenty minutes early—were actually talking to one another. And some were even laughing. The decor certainly had something to do with that. It more closely resembled a tasteful and warmly done Park Avenue living room than the chrome-and-vinyl neo-McDonald efficiencies that Lowenstein and Collier favored. McPartland's waiting room consisted of tan Sloane section pieces on a red and green oriental carpet, potted rubber plants and hanging ferns, a marble-topped serving table containing an urn of piping hot espresso—decaffeinated, the receptionist told her—with a revolving supply of cups and saucers, and a low, iron-and-glass coffee table covered with magazines, mostly *New Yorkers* and *Vogues*, although Marie was pleased to see that Hamilton Publications was represented with *About Town*.

But, of course, it had to be more than just the furnishings that accounted for the positively convivial atmosphere in here. These women, all well-groomed, intelligent-looking people in their thirties, were happy and they were decidedly happy to be here. Half of them, by Marie's estimation, had an obvious reason for being so—they were in varying stages of pregnancy. But the other five, like Marie herself, seemed to have an equally valid reason for their happiness—they anticipated being pregnant in the near future. Expecting expectancy.

David arrived, a bit breathlessly, only a couple of minutes before the receptionist called their name.

"Am I late?"

"Nope." They kissed. "What's that on your tie?"

"Ooops. Oyster stew. I had a bowl for lunch." David leaned toward her. "It does wonders for my sperm count."

Marie laughed and so did the woman next to her.

"My husband swears by chicken livers himself," the woman said, patting her pregnant belly. "I've learned never to argue with success."

"How nice to enjoy the company of pregnant ladies again," Marie whispered to David as they were ushered into the maze of dressing, examination, and interview rooms that lay beyond the waiting room. "It was no fun hating strangers."

They were separated almost immediately, David to have his sperm counted yet again, and Marie to have her blood and urine tested.

"I already gave at the office," David said as the nurse led him down the hallway.

"You better not have," Marie called after him. "See you later."

Marie always wondered what David thought about while he masturbated into a paper cup for this test. He claimed he couldn't afford to think about anything other than his aim. Marie grinned. That's all she thought about when she gave a urine sample.

Twenty minutes later, they met again in the office of a nurse who took a detailed medical and sexual history from each of them—they could recite these intimacies by rote by now—and then they were taken to the genetic counseling office where an attractive young black woman took what she referred to as their "pedigree," a tracing of their respective family trees in search of possible inheritable defects and diseases. Neither David nor Marie could think of any.

"Isn't it a bit optimistic to be doing this at this point?" Marie asked.

"That's exactly what it is," the black woman replied, smiling.

Then she led them back to the corridor where, almost two hours after they had left the waiting room, they met Dr. Raymond McPartland.

"Dr. Preston, Mrs. Preston, it's a pleasure to meet you." McPartland, a tall, muscular man with thinning hair and a sensitive, angular face, shook Marie's hand first, then David's. "I hope everybody's been treating you well so far."

"Yes, they have," Marie said. Bonnie hadn't told her what a sympathetic face he had.

"Why don't we go right into the examination room and then we'll talk in my office."

"Do you want me to come too? I mean into the examination room?" David asked.

"I don't see why not. Unless it would bother you, Mrs. Preston."

Marie smiled. "I've got nothing to hide," she said.

"Good," McPartland said, opening the door to a large examination room. "You can change over there." He pointed to a screen on the far side of the room. "Shall I call someone to help you on with the smock?"

"That's okay. At this point I could do it in my sleep."

McPartland smiled. He was pulling on a pair of rubber gloves. "I understand Tom and Bonnie Roundtree recommended me to you," he said to David.

"Funny, Bonnie said she recommended us to you," Marie called from behind the screen. Then she shook her head. What was all this giddy wise-cracking about? She wanted to make a good impression on the man. "What I mean is, we feel very fortunate to be able to see you. I know how busy you are."

"Good," McPartland said.

Marie padded back to the examination table in her bare feet, sat on its edge and swung her long legs over and into the chrome stirrups in a single motion.

"They ought to make this an event in a rodeo," she said. "I could take first prize."

She looked up. David had his "doctor" look on his face, which meant humorless. Neither man was even smiling.

"Just relax," McPartland said. "This won't take more than a couple minutes."

Quickly, expertly, he probed her pelvic organs, from time to time, saying, "Good." Then he removed his hand, adjusted his lamp, inserted a speculum and looked up into her vaginal canal. Again, he said, "Good." He peeled off his gloves and dropped them into a waste pail.

"All right," McPartland said, reaching his hand down to Marie's and pulling her upright. His arm was impressively strong. Definitely the kind of gynecologist whose patients have naughty fantasies about him, Marie thought.

"Everything's in the right place, right?"

McPartland smiled. "I think so," he said. "Why don't you get dressed, and we'll meet you in my office. It's just across the hallway from here."

"Don't start without me," Marie said. She hopped off of the table, went behind the screen, and dressed as quickly as she could. There was certainly something about this man, a sureness, a seriousness, that would have given her confidence in him even if she had heard nothing about him.

When she entered McPartland's office, David was seated in a Harvard armchair leafing through a copy of *Lancet* and McPartland was clipping X rays to a light box on the wall behind his desk. Marie immediately recognized them as the hysterosalpingographies she had asked Collier's office to send to McPartland.

"A good likeness, don't you think?" Marie said, as she sat down next to David.

"Yes," McPartland said. He sat down at his wide, oak desk, opened a folder, and took out a sheet of paper. "Well, let's see if we can fit this picture together," he said. "Is it all right if we use first names in here?"

"Of course," David said.

"Well, let's start with your half of the picture then, David. Today's analysis shows a spermatozoa count of between forty and forty-five million. That's rather low, as I'm sure you know. But motility is excellent. And I think if you made an effort to get more rest—I often find that a nap for an hour or so before dinner can bring a borderline count up into a more productive range. I'm afraid, other than a multiple vitamin supplement, that's all I can recommend for you."

David nodded and McPartland removed several more sheets from the folder and spread them out in front of him. Marie sat forward in her chair and looked at them.

"Now, Marie, as is usually the case, the female half of the picture is a bit more complex. But that is also an advantage. It usually presents more options for treatment." He cleared his throat and lifted one of the papers in front of him. "Let's start with your basal temperature charts. I had an opportunity to go over some of your material last night and—"

Marie had stood up and now came around to the side of McPartland's desk to look at the chart with him.

"Excuse me," she said. "You don't mind if I look on with you, do you?"

"Please," McPartland said, bringing the chart over to Marie's side of the desk. "Well, as you can see, your cycle has been rather consistent for at least the past three years. More consistent, I'd say, than many women who have no troubles conceiving at all. I'm rather inclined to agree with Dr. Lowenstein. I think the clomiphene has probably been superfluous. I have little doubt that your ovulation is normal. See this here?" He pointed at the graph.

"You mean, the ovulatory dip?"

McPartland smiled. "Yes."

"Don't you think it's a little more pronounced since I've been on clomiphene?"

"Maybe we should let him finish," David said.

"No, please," McPartland said. "It's always a pleasure when a patient is this knowledgeable. But in answer to your question, I think not. Look here, this chart is from well before you were taking the drug and the difference is negligible, don't you think?"

"I guess so."

McPartland stood and turned on the light behind the hysterosalpingographies.

"No," he said. "My first guess is that you have hydrosalpinx in your right fallopian tube. A single blocked tube, in other words." He pointed to a white line on the X ray with his pencil. "Right here, to be precise."

Marie stared. She had looked at these pictures at least twenty times in Lowenstein's and Collier's offices. They all looked like Rorschach tests to her. David had risen too and was squinting at the negatives.

"It's been a long time since I've tried to read one of these," David said. "I'm afraid I can't see it."

"It's not the obstruction that's evident," McPartland said. "It's the dilation, here at the outer edges, that concerns me. It appears to be distended with fluid. And that's usually a pretty sound indication of blockage."

"Is it treatable?" Marie's heart had begun to beat more quickly.

"Let's take one thing at a time," McPartland said, turning off the light box. "Why don't we sit down and talk some more."

Marie perched herself nervously on the edge of her chair. "Okay, I'm sitting," she said.

"Marie, I can't be absolutely sure of my diagnosis until I take a closer look. I think a culdoscopy is advisable. You know what that is?"

"Yes," Marie said.

"And then, if my diagnosis does prove correct under the culdoscope," McPartland went on, "my guess is that your condition could be corrected rather easily with a non-surgical procedure known as hydrotubation. It's a sort of flushing out of the obstruction. I probably can do that at the same time as the culdoscopy if it's indicated. And I do think it is."

"Are you telling me I can have babies?"

"Well, probably just one at a time," McPartland said, smiling.

Without thinking, Marie clapped her hands together. "Thank God," she said. "Thank God."

McPartland leaned forward. "I'm glad I could give you some optimistic news," he said. "Why don't you work out a good time for the culdoscopy with Miss Gold at the reception desk. I do them right here, usually in the evenings or in the mornings before office hours. Do either of you have any questions?"

Marie was beaming. Somehow, she wasn't really surprised by this news. It was as if she had been expecting it for years. Even before Bonnie had told her about McPartland, she had suspected that her real problem was something ridiculously simple, that one day some doctor would say just what McPartland had, that her condition could be corrected quite easily.

"Only one," Marie said. "Do you accept kisses of gratitude?"

McPartland smiled as he stood and extended his hand to Marie. "I'll take a raincheck on that," he said. "For the day we know you're pregnant."

He shook hands with each of them and walked them to the door.

"I hope everything works out well for the two of you," he said at the door. "What are you hoping for? A boy or a girl?"

"Just a baby," Marie said. "Any flavor will do."

"Well, let's see what we can do," McPartland said. "Good-bye now."

Marie virtually danced down the hallway toward the door to the waiting room. She felt a kind of lightness, a gladness, that she could only remember feeling when she was very young. In fact, she felt very young altogether.

"David?"

She stopped and turned. David was walking slowly behind her, shaking his head. She waited until he had caught up with her.

"David? What's wrong?"

"I know it's ridiculous," David said. "But I just can't stop thinking about Ralph and Collier. Those damned idiots. Somebody ought to take away their licenses."

"Oh, come on, David. Why even think about that now? Who cares?" Marie threw her arms around him and kissed his cheek. "I've got better things to think about. Much better. Hey, look!"

On the wall next to the door to the waiting room was a large bulletin board covered with snapshots of babies ranging from three months to almost a year old. Most of the photos were Polaroids and all of them were in color with the names of the children handprinted along the borders. Marie and David stopped and looked silently from picture to picture. All but a very few of them were very beautiful babies. Exceptionally beautiful. The wispy-haired blond babies with their bright-blue alert eyes and glowing pink skin. The shining, raven-haired babies with their almond-shaped hazel eyes and rich Mediterranean complexions. The cocoa-colored babies with their soft, jet-black fuzz and warm, intelligent eyes.

"Oh, Christ, I think I'm going to cry," Marie said, finally.

"I know what you mean."

"And look. There's Adam up there." Marie pointed to a little blond boy with dazzling eyes near to the top of the bulletin board.

David stood on his toes to read the name on the photograph.

"Nope," he said. "It's Raymond Alan Ross. Nice looking little fellow, huh?"

"Are you sure?"

"That's what it says. Will you look at all the boys named Raymond in honor of the good doctor?" David grinned.

"Well, I think that's a perfectly wonderful idea," Marie said, smiling too. "I think we ought to consider it."

"Not my son," David laughed.

"Why not? Or do you want a Joshua or Jonathan or Jonah like everybody else?"

"As a matter of fact, I've always favored Prescott."

"Prescott? Prescott Preston? It sounds like some kind of kitchen appliance."

"You've got to admit, it's got a ring to it."

And David and Marie Preston walked arm-in-arm out into the waiting room, laughing.

On her way back to the office, Marie bought herself a bouquet of silver-colored roses. And in the elevator, holding the flowers to her nose, her face radiating happiness, she looked like a woman in a Vermeer painting. Several people in the car could not help themselves from looking at her and smiling. Impulsively, just as the car left the seventeenth floor, Marie pressed the button for the eighteenth. When the door opened, she got off and walked to Kate Cochoran's office in the circulation department.

"Hi, Kate."

"Marie. What happened to you? Did you win the lottery or something?"

"No. Listen, Kate, I want to apologize for the other day. You know, in the ladies'. I was a little out of sorts, I'm afraid and I took it out on you."

"Forget it. I have."

Marie sat on the edge of Kate's desk. "Thanks," she said. "Kate, could you do me a favor? Could you send out a gift subscription of *City Life* and, let me see, how about *Soma* to a friend of mine?"

"No problem. What's the name?"

"Here, I'll write it down for you." Marie wrote Raymond McPartland's name and address on a piece of paper.

"Do you want me to send one of those gift letters with it?" Kate asked. "You know, dear Mr. Whoha, for the next twelve months lucky you will be receiving blah, blah, blah."

"Why not?" Marie said, standing again. "And sign it, 'An Admirer.'"

Kate grinned slyly. "Why Marie Preston, I thought you were a happily married woman."

"I am," Marie said. And she danced out of the door.

ABRAHAM BEGAT *Isaac; and Isaac begat Jacob; and Jacob begat Judas and his brethren.*

He was crying again. She heard him through the bathroom door. He always cried around now. He sounded like a cat trapped in a box. Franny slipped the bolt through the lock in the door and turned back to the mirror.

And Judas begat Phares and Zara of Thamar; and Phares begat Esrom; and Esrom begat Aram.

Louder.

And Aram begat Aminadab; and Aminadab begat Naasson; and Naasson begat Salmon.

She swung open the medicine chest door and her reflection slipped away like a ghost. Lying on its side, like a toppled tin soldier, was Sydney's razor.

The crying again. Sharp as a blade.

Louder.

And Salmon begat Boaz of Rachab; and Boaz begat Obed of Ruth; and Obed begat Jesse; and Jesse begat David the king; and David the king begat Solomon of her that had been the wife of Urias.

"Darling, we're putting him to bed now. Do you want to say good night? You don't have to touch him. Mrs. Guerny will hold him. Just a quick good night, okay? It will be good for both of you."

Franny slammed the medicine chest door shut.

"Sweetheart, what are you doing in there? Are you all right?"

And Josias begat Jechonias and his brethren about the time they were carried away to Babylon. And Jechonias—

"Franny, have you locked the door again? We made a promise, didn't we? What if we had to get in there? What if I needed to bring Benny in there? You have to think of that, you know. At least of that."

Louder.

And Eliud begat Eleazar; and Eleazar begat Matthan; and Matthan begat Jacob.

"Listen, honey, he's stopped crying. Mrs. Guerny is putting him to bed, all right? He's fine. He's just fine. He's been a good boy all day. Just open the door, honey, okay?"

And Jacob begat Joseph the husband of Mary of whom was born Jesus, who is called Christ.

"Franny, please! Don't make me break open the door. You don't want that either, do you? It will wake the baby. He'll really cry then."

Franny set the razor down on the sink, rinsed her face and hands and turned to the door. She pulled the bolt and opened the door.

When Sydney caught first sight of his wife on the other side of the door, he made a little whimpering sound, like a small animal makes when it is threatened.

"Oh, my God, Franny . . . What have you done to yourself? What have you done with all your hair? All that beautiful hair . . . Franny, please, God, tell me . . . What is wrong? What is wrong with you?"

Now the birth of Jesus Christ was on this wise: when as his mother Mary was espoused to Joseph, before they came together, she was found with child of the Holy Ghost.

"DOPE ADDICTION has been much maligned. Seriously, David. Those *CBS White Papers* never tell you how absolutely marvelous it feels."

Marie leaned heavily on David as they walked north on Park Avenue from Seventy-third Street. She was feeling simultaneously sluggish—each step took the most determined concentration—and floatingly light. Great dope, really. Much better than that Hawaiian grass she and David had tried when they still thought their problem might be psychological. Two drags of that stuff and they had slept through their well-planned orgy—they hadn't even had erotic dreams. Not that she was feeling erotic now. Just very happily high. Detached and silly. Whatever those little yellow oval pills were that Miss Gold had given her to take every four hours since breakfast, at this moment Marie was quite sure she could contentedly take them for the rest of her life.

"Ah, there it is. A lamp in the wilderness."

Above the sidewalk entrance to Dr. McPartland's offices, a single lantern-shaped lamp shone in the night, looking like a suburban porch light. David pressed the doorbell and after only a few seconds, Miss Gold's voice said, "Is that you, Mrs. Preston?"

"Yeh, Joe sent me," Marie said, using her Cagney voice.

She giggled as the door opened and she and David walked in.

"Good evening, Dr. Preston, Mrs. Preston. How are we feeling tonight?"

"Terrific." Marie leaned toward Miss Gold, a mousy-looking young woman in a heavily starched white uniform. "Great dope, Miss Gold. Really. I'm your slave. Just give me more."

Miss Gold looked quizzically at Marie, not smiling. "Oh. The Pertofrane. Have you taken it all?"

"Just two left. I had a fix before we left the house." Marie winked and this time Miss Gold smiled, albeit weakly.

"Fine. Why don't we go in, then?" Miss Gold turned to David and took Marie's overnight bag from him. "Dr. Preston, I think you'd be more comfortable if you went home right now. Dr. McPartland will call you later this evening. Is that all right?"

"Of course." David put his arms around Marie. "Have a ball, darling." He kissed her ear.

"How come I get to have all the fun?"

They kissed one another on the lips, a lingering kiss, Miss Gold gazing self-consciously around the empty waiting room until they were finished. Then, when David let go of her and turned to leave, Marie felt a little tug of anxiety in her stomach.

"David?"

"What, hon?"

"Uh, next time you see me I'll have fallopian tubes like the Holland Tunnel."

David stepped back and kissed her on the cheek.

"I love you," he said.

"Me too. Bye."

Miss Gold held the door open for David and then locked it after him.

"Just follow me, Mrs. Preston," Miss Gold said. "Can you make it without any help?"

"You bet."

Marie followed the nurse out of the waiting room into the long corridor behind it. The doors to the offices and conference rooms coming off it were all open, but the rooms were dark. Marie watched her shadow bounce along the corridor wall and then disappear at each doorway.

"Miss Gold? I think I may be coming down a little bit. Do you think I could take a couple more of those little pills before I get on the table?"

"We'll have to ask Dr. McPartland. But I'm sure it will be okay." Miss Gold waited for Marie to catch up with her. "You have nothing to worry about, Mrs. Preston. A culdoscopy is a very simple procedure."

"Who's worried?" Marie made a face of mock-fright.

They entered the examination room.

"Good evening, Marie. How are you?" Dr. McPartland, wearing a green operating smock and cap, was washing his hands at the sink. "Forgive me if I don't shake your hand."

"Of course."

"This is Dr. Langerfeld, our anesthesiologist. And you already know Miss Gold. She'll be assisting me."

Marie looked at Dr. Langerfeld, a tall, rather stately woman with steel-gray hair pulled back in a bun.

"I thought all I needed was a local anesthetic."

"Just a spinal block," Dr. Langerfeld said. "You'll be fully conscious. Although another tranquilizer might make it easier for you."

"Now that you mention it," Marie said, smiling.

McPartland was shaking his hands dry in the air. "We'll leave you and Miss Gold in here to get ready. We'll see you later, Marie. And don't look so worried. This will all be over"—he looked up at the clock on the wall. It was a few minutes before eight—"by eight-thirty. Okay?"

"Sure." Thank God for Dr. McPartland.

Marie hadn't realized that she looked worried. Certainly, that high, floating feeling had left her the moment she walked into the corridor. But she knew there was nothing to be worried about. The day after her first visit to McPartland, she had promptly gone to the Forty-second Street library and looked up both culdoscopy and hydrotubation. The first was a minor surgical procedure she had heard about before. All it seemed to amount to was a tiny slit of an incision in the vagina right near the cervix into which they slipped a little telescopelike device and looked around. Seeing is believing. Really a very forthright way of examining the situation. And, the medical encyclopedia said, about as dangerous as having a wisdom tooth extracted. The hydrotubation, she found, wasn't even considered a surgical procedure. No cuts were necessary. Just a squirting of an antibiotic and an enzyme up through her tubes. A kind of flushing out. What could be simpler? She popped her two remaining Pertofrane pills into her mouth and washed them down with a paper cup of water.

"Why do you suppose Dr. McPartland does these things here rather than at the hospital?" Marie asked, as she started to get out of her clothes.

"Mostly for scheduling," Miss Gold said, folding Marie's skirt neatly on a hanger. "You have to wait months just to set aside an operating room for a simple culdoscopy at Hebron. Most of the doctor's patients have waited too long already."

"You can say that again." Marie was now completely naked. "All right, I'm ready. Where's the cake?"

Miss Gold frowned at Marie.

"Nothing," Marie said. "Those pills are doing their stuff again."

"Good. Why don't you get up on the table and we'll wash and shave you."

"Oh, terrific. But try to keep the sideburns even this

time, will you, Giuseppe?" Marie hoisted herself up onto the examination table. Miss Gold obviously had no sense of humor at all. Well, how funny can life seem if you spend a good part of it shaving other people's pubic hair?

"Hold still." Miss Gold stroked the razor across Marie's mons. "There's another reason, too," she said. "McPartland's equipment is more up-to-date than Hebron's."

"That's good to hear."

"Oh, he's the best, Mrs. Preston. But I'm sure you know that."

"That's what I've heard."

Marie looked down at her clean-shaven pubes. They had a pink vulnerable appearance that made her feel uncomfortable.

Miss Gold washed and dried Marie and then slipped a white smock over her head. She then wheeled a rolling stretcher to the examination table.

"Can you get onto this without any help?"

"I think so. Just don't let it roll away before I get on."

Miss Gold braced the table against her hip while Marie rolled onto it. "Now, let's just open up a vein and we'll be ready."

Marie extended her right arm. Miss Gold swabbed it, then tied her bicep with a tourniquet, and jabbed a couple of times with a needle before finding the vein. She inserted it, rolled over an I.V. stand, connected a tube to the needle, and released the valve.

"I'm not really hungry," Marie said.

"Dr. Langerfeld always likes a vein open," Miss Gold said. She left Marie for a moment, walking to the wall on the far side of the examination room. Marie heard her open a door and she wondered why she hadn't noticed before that there was a door on that side of the room. Miss Gold returned with Dr. McPartland. He smiled down at Marie.

"Hello," he said. "I hope you don't mind our informality here." He took a position at the foot of the rolling stretcher. "After hours, Miss Gold lets me do things I haven't done since medical school."

"Fair Harvard, eh?"

McPartland began guiding the table across the room, Miss Gold following alongside pushing the I.V. stand. They passed through the door into the operating suite. It certainly looked up-to-date to Marie, at least from her upside-down point of view. No wonder his bills were so high. Those lights alone must cost a small fortune. She reminded herself to ask David whether they should request professional courtesy.

"Now, we'll just get you onto the table and the hard part will be over." McPartland smiled. He had come around to the head of the stretcher and now put his hands under Marie's arms. Miss Gold was at her feet and together they lifted her onto the operating table.

"Please roll over onto your left side," Dr. Langerfeld said. She was already wearing her surgical mask. With her features hidden, her eyes looked less severe. Marie rolled onto her side. Miss Gold separated her smock in the rear and began washing her back with a very cold liquid. It sent a shiver up Marie's spine.

"Are you done? Can I go home now?"

"I'm going to have to ask you not to talk, Mrs. Preston. We're sterile in here."

Nice choice of words, Doctor.

"Thank you," Langerfeld said. "Now pull up your knees and curl forward. There. That's right. Now, I want you to hold very still, Mrs. Preston. In one moment I will be inserting a syringe."

Marie felt someone brush another cold liquid on her back and then she felt the syringe enter her spine a few inches above her buttocks. It didn't hurt, but it made her feel uncomfortable and more than a little queasy. She had always hated anesthetics of any kind, even at the dentist's. At least they weren't putting her completely out. As long as she was conscious, she didn't have to feel completely vulnerable.

Suddenly, the numbness swept over her like a cold draft. Everything below her waist felt deadened and heavy. Not pleasant at all. Maybe she should have taken a whole handful of those little pills. She tried to think of something else. She imagined she was a magician's assistant and the magician was slicing her in half. Not funny. Think of something else.

Langerfeld had wrapped a sphygmomanometer sleeve around her arm and was pumping, her stethoscope in the crook of her arm.

"One twenty over seventy," she said.

"Good," McPartland said. Marie couldn't figure out exactly where he was standing.

Now Langerfeld put the stethoscope on Marie's chest and listened. She nodded to McPartland and then went to the foot of the table.

"Marie, can you feel this?"

"What?"

"Good," Langerfeld said.

"All right, Marie," McPartland said. "Can you hear me all right?"

"Yes."

"I'm going to have to ask you to do some acrobatics now," McPartland said. "Miss Gold will help you. I want you to turn to your right. Yes, that's good. Now tuck your knees up under your chest. Keep the I.V. clear, please, Miss Gold."

Marie was surprised at how easily her body responded to the doctor's demands, almost as if it were doing so without her willing it to.

"Put one arm out here," Miss Gold was saying. "Now the other here."

"Good," McPartland said.

Marie was now lying face down with her naked but-

tocks sticking up in the air. How civilized we all are, she
thought. Three adults are contemplating my bare ass with
the solemnity of priests. It was humiliating, really. The stirrups. Now this. A kind of rape. What sort of man becomes a
gynecologist anyway? Do they have happy childhoods?
Does it all begin with a little game of "I'll-show-you-mine-
if-you-show-me-yours?" behind the garage? David ought to
do a paper on that. She inched her elbows forward for bal-
ance. Don't forget why you are here, she told herself. You'd
lie like this in Macy's window if you thought it would help
you get your baby.

"Are you comfortable?"

"Very."

"Hold still now, Marie. I'm making the incision."

She felt something on her vagina, like a drop of warm
water. In the position she was in, all she could see was the
cloth on the table just below her face and a band of the
floor over the edge of the table. She felt something else.

"Minor kinking of the right tube."

McPartland was speaking in a clipped, dictationlike
voice. The culdoscope must be in. Kinking?

"Adhesions of right tube, outer edge."

Just what he had said he'd find.

"Left tube clear."

She felt something sliding inside her.

"Hold still just a couple of minutes longer," McPartland
said.

She heard someone walk to the far end of the room,
then a heavy door opening and closing, then steps again.

"Very still," McPartland said. "I think this is even going
to be easier than we thought, Marie."

She felt something warm gushing up inside her, then a
strange tingling sensation that seemed to radiate to her entire body. Electric, almost sexual.

"What was that?" Marie asked.

"Hold still, Marie. Just a minute longer."

Again, she felt something slide inside of her. Was the anesthetic wearing off?

"Right tube clear," McPartland said.

"My God! That was it?"

She had never imagined that he could check his results immediately. But, of course, after the hydrotubation, he was looking again with the culdoscope.

"Yes," McPartland was saying. "That was it." Marie could almost hear him smiling.

"You're not kidding me?"

"No, Marie. I'm not kidding you. The procedure seems to have been successful. But please, don't move."

"Don't I get to kiss you now?"

She could hear McPartland laugh quietly.

"Not yet," he said. "Now I want you to very gently slip down onto your left side. Miss Gold will help you. And careful with the I.V., please. That's it."

Marie was back on her side again. She couldn't believe it was over. She looked at the clock on the wall. Eighttwenty.

"Can I call David now?"

McPartland came over beside her. He was removing his rubber gloves.

"I'll give him a ring as soon as I've washed up," the doctor said. He patted her hair. "Marie, the best thing for you now will be a good night's rest. You don't realize it, but this has been a little shock to your system. We're dripping a sedative in the I.V. to make sure you sleep well. I don't think your stomach could take a pill now. Miss Gold will take you into our little recovery room and she or Miss Armbruster will stay with you until morning. I'll look at you again then."

Marie tried to lift her head, but she was indeed very tired. She smiled.

"Can I have babies now?" she asked.

McPartland looked at the chronometer on his wrist.

"Let's see," he said. "Today's the fifth of January. Why don't you and David plan a quiet evening somewhere on the fifteenth."

Again, Marie smiled, but her eyelids already began to feel too heavy to keep open and her tongue felt thick in her mouth.

"Make baby," she mumbled and fell into a deep and dreamless sleep.

On the evening of January fifteenth, a crisp and cloud-less New York Saturday, after a stroll through the de Kooning retrospective at the Museum of Modern Art, two very dry gimlets apiece at the Algonquin, and a long, sweet and clean-tasting meal at Take Sushi, Marie and David walked slowly back along Fifty-seventh Street to the Plaza Hotel and the ninth-floor suite overlooking Central Park they had taken for the weekend. They had champagne, they undressed, and then, without saying a word, they made love as only true lovers do—sweetly, unhurriedly, moving to-gether as in a slow dance. And when Marie climaxed—the first time in many months—she was not at all surprised. It was as if she had never doubted that making love and mak-ing babies were one and the same thing.

"MAN, SOMETIMES these things read better than *Peyton Place*." Mel Bernstein dropped a sheaf of manila folders on the cafeteria table before setting down his tray across from Paul. "Do you mind if I sit down? Or were you holding out for something better?"

"Oh, please do sit down, Mel," Paul said. "I was hoping someone would come along who could explain to me exactly what this is." He poked his fork into a glistening lump of congealed vegetables on his plate.

"You don't know what that is, Paul? Good grief, man, you haven't lived, have you? That's Hebron's basic dish, the stuff generations of docs have drawn their sustenance from, not to mention generations of mold. It's called American chop suey. The basic ingredient is unborn linoleum." Bernstein leaned his large head across the table and laughed.

"Not that the food at Elmwood was any better," Paul said. "The staple there was a curried potato dish. It was the color we all fancied. Nature's own yellow. Now what was this about *Peyton Place?*"

Bernstein shoveled a soupspoonful of chop suey into his mouth. He tapped the pile of folders beside him. "These," he said, his mouth full. "Messy stuff. Sad business, really."

"May I?" Paul put his hand on the topmost folder and when Bernstein nodded, he pulled it beside him and opened it. Inside were three sheets of karyotypes, the sets of twenty-three pairs of chromosomes that carry a complete human genetic message, the lot, from hair color to the precise curve of the nail on the big toe. To make these sheets, a single cell had been magnified thousands of times and photographed, then each chromosome had been cut out with a scissors like paper dolls, paired and arranged in order, pasted to a sheet and photostated. The result, as Paul had observed when he saw his first karyotype in a slide at an Oxford lecture, looked like hieroglyphics painted on a cave wall. And like the archeologists who spent decades trying to decipher hieroglyphics, word by word, Paul, Bernstein, and several thousand other geneticists around the world were spending their lives trying to read these karyotypes, band by band and characteristic by characteristic. At this point, they could decipher almost a thousand bands, each band containing up to several hundred invisible genes. Humans were thought to carry at least a million. It was like reading Shakespeare with a three-year-old's vocabulary.

Paul examined the sheet in front of him. For all his charmingly crude manners, Bernstein was remarkably meticulous in his work. For several years, he had been working on a method of banding chromosomes at an early point in their development, when they were still, in effect, flexible, and then stretching them so that the results were longer, leaner chromosomes with more bands, more gene loci. He hadn't discovered anything momentous. Probably never would. But his work would make it ever so much easier for those who would. Unsung hero department. No prizes for Bernstein.

"Nicely done, Mel. Not messy at all. On the contrary, they're very clear." Paul closed the folder.

"I know," Bernstein said. He had begun working on another dish, this one a creamy green one. "That's not the point. Look at the others in there. It's a little family. Ha, ha, ha."

Paul again opened the folder and laid all three karyotypes out in front of him. Each had a name and symbol identifying sex and family relationship in the lower left hand corner. The first belonged to one Richard Aiken, male, father, the second to Edith Aiken, female, mother, and the third to Aiken fetus, male. The fetal karyotype had been developed from a cell centrifuged out from its mother's amniotic fluid. Paul's eye ran down the fetal karyotype first. He looked carefully at the twenty-first and twenty-second chromosomes for signs of trisomy, an extra twenty-first chromosome that was the precursor of mongolism. No indications. He looked at number six, his own particular specialty, and counted the bands. Again, he saw nothing unusual. He looked at the last chromosome, the Y chromosome, the one that determined the Aiken fetus as male. It, too, looked perfectly normal to Paul. Then he looked at the other two sheets and his eye went immediately to Richard Aiken's Y chromosome. It had an unusually long tail, like a sea horse. Not abnormal, but nothing at all like the fetus'. They were clearly unrelated to one another. Paul picked up Richard Aiken's karyotype and looked more closely.

"Well hung, isn't he?" Bernstein said, grinning. "Too bad he's not the father."

Two interns, a man and a woman, looked up from the far end of the table and smiled.

Paul leaned forward. "Mel, have you told Eva about this? Someone's mixed up the amnios and that could be serious."

Bernstein laughed loudly. Then he stood up. "That's what I love about you English. A nation of boy scouts. Can I get you some bread pudding? It holds the chop suey down."

"Sit down, Mel."

The two interns looked up again. Paul glared at them and they looked down at their food. Mel was still standing behind his chair.

"Paul," he said, in a patronizing voice. "Nobody's mixed

up any amnios. Not at Hebron. Your ice goddess has a foolproof double-check system to guard against that." He crossed his arms on the back of the chair and rested his chin on them, cherublike. "Tell me, Paul, don't married ladies fool around in jolly old England?"

Paul blanched. Indeed, they do, he thought. Especially while their husbands work around the clock at a laboratory. "But, good God, Mel, this woman is pregnant."

"My friend, if I had a dollar for every one of these non-paternities that turns up on our karyos, I could stop begging for grant money. And that's just the surface, old boy. Not everyone's as easy to read as Mr. Aiken's dangling Y." Bernstein pulled himself up straight again. "Really, Paul, the only thing that pisses me off about these numbers is that it ruins my experiments. It wastes our time."

"Dr. Bernstein, what is this material doing outside of the laboratory?"

Paul looked up. Eva was standing directly behind Bernstein, a tray in her hand. Her eyes were ice cold. Bernstein turned to her, a bored expression on his face.

"I was just explaining American mores to Dr. Kingsmill, here."

"That's confidential material, Dr. Bernstein." Eva's tone was almost schoolmarmish. "It doesn't leave the lab without Dr. Fine's permission. Please return it immediately."

Bernstein looked directly at Eva for a moment, then sighed and lifted the folders off the table. "Yowsuh, boss," he said, winking at Paul. "It was getting a little chilly in here anyhow."

He left.

Paul stood and gestured at the chair Bernstein had vacated. He had planned his lunch break to coincide with hers. Since Christmas, they had only seen one another in the laboratory and Paul was beginning to wonder if she were avoiding him. He smiled. "Don't be too hard on Mel, Eva. He's just another lonely old geneticist."

Eva hesitated a moment, her tray resting on the back of the chair. Then she, too, smiled.

"Poor fellow," she said. "All alone with those chromosomes."

And she sat down.

"IT'S BAD news, David. I just know it is. Listen, if it was good news, he would have told me. He'd at least have gotten on the phone, right?"

"Marie, please. Take it easy, would you? McPartland is a busy man. He must see thirty patients a day in there. He doesn't have the time to make personal calls to everyone. So that proves nothing."

Marie sat quietly for a moment, absently gazing at the Swedish ivy which spilled out of the enameled pot in the corner of McPartland's waiting room. This must have been the fourth time she and David had had that same exchange since they met in front of the office. For a month, Marie had been positive she would get pregnant. And soon. But when she had gone that morning to have her blood taken for the pregnancy test, the doubts had started to creep back again. And by three o'clock that afternoon, it was as if they had never left. That familiar dull ache of apprehension again permeated her bones. Then, at three-thirty, Miss Gold had called. She said that Dr. McPartland wanted to see her and David at five-thirty, after his regular office hours.

"Why?" Marie had asked.

"He wants to speak with both of you."

"Yes, I figured that. But why? Does he have the results of my test? Come on, Miss Gold, I'm going crazy here."

"I'm sure Dr. McPartland will tell you everything when he sees you, Mrs. Preston. Five-thirty, then, all right?"

"Yeh. Terrific."

How do you kill the two hours of limbo before you know what the rest of your life is going to be like? After calling David, Marie tried to busy herself with her work. She dictated memos to the advertising directors of *City Life* and *About Town* advising them to clean up some of the back of the book lingerie ads. Too raunchy, she said. We aren't *Cosmo*. She had her secretary read the memos back to her; the wording was all wrong, so she decided she'd do better to discuss it with them in person. She looked at her watch. Quarter to four. Is that all? She told her secretary she was going downstairs for a cup of tea, but when she arrived there she walked right past the entrance to the luncheonette and out onto Sixth Avenue without a coat, then across the street and into the Americana bar. Halfway through her gimlet she realized that if she were pregnant, this drink could be disastrous. What the hell was she doing? She returned to her office. Four-thirty. She called David again, but he was in a session. Her mother called and she had her secretary say she was in conference. She called Bonnie, but the maid said she was out. For a half hour, she stared out of her window trying to keep her mind blank. Impossible. Finally, at five, she put on her coat and walked all the way to McPartland's office.

"Dr. McPartland will see you now."

David stood up. But Marie remained seated.

"Let's go, honey."

"Just a minute, David. I want to tell you something."

David looked at Miss Gold who was standing impatiently in the doorway, then back at Marie.

"What is it, babes?"

"David, if it's bad news again, I don't think I can take

it. I'm serious. I want you to give me a pill or a shot or something and take me home and put me to bed, okay?"

"Okay, honey."

"Promise?"

"I promise. Let's go, Marie."

Marie stood and they followed Miss Gold out of the waiting room into the corridor behind it. Her eyes immediately went to the bulletin board with the baby photos on it —again, she thought she saw Adam's picture, although this time in a different place—but David tugged her arm and she continued walking. Strange, but after that interminable two-hour wait, she now was in no hurry to see McPartland, to hear whatever he had to say. Miss Gold pointed to the open door of his office and told them to go in, that he would be with them in a moment. They entered and both sat down in the Harvard chairs across from McPartland's desk. Silence.

Then, from across the hallway, from the examination room or perhaps beyond, Marie heard what sounded like a heavy door slamming closed. And the sound sent a cold shiver down her back. She was trying to remember where she had heard that sound before when Dr. McPartland walked into the office carrying a split of champagne in his hands.

"Congratulations," he said, smiling.

Before she could think about it, Marie was on her feet and her arms were around McPartland's neck. She gave him a big, smacking kiss on the cheek even as the tears began streaming out of her eyes. McPartland patted her head awkwardly.

"Hey, what about me? Don't I get a kiss?" David had stood up also. "I guess I had a little something to do with this too."

Her face now covered with tears, Marie went to David and they held one another tightly.

"Oh, David. I'm so happy. So unbelievably happy."

"Me too. Me too."

Behind them, McPartland had popped open the champagne and was pouring it into paper cups. Marie and David turned, their arms still around each other, and smiled.

"Forgive the paper cups," McPartland said, now handing a cup to each of them. "These really aren't very festive, are they?"

"Festive enough," Marie said. "And now, if I can stop crying long enough, I'd like to propose the toast."

They all raised the little cups in the air and touched them to one another.

"To the two most wonderful men in the world," Marie said.

"To you, too, darling."

"And to the two of you," McPartland said. "I think you'll make wonderful parents."

"God bless us one and all," Marie said.

They laughed and all drank down their champagne.

"Is that it?" Marie said.

"I'm afraid the bottle's empty," McPartland said.

"No, you dear man, I don't mean the champagne. I meant, is that it—is there anything more we should know?"

McPartland smiled. "There's not much more I can tell you, Marie. Just that you're pregnant. There's no doubt about that. And you'll have to start taking special care of yourself and your little friend in there. Miss Gold will give you a pamphlet on diet and the like and you can make an appointment with her for your first monthly checkup. Other than that, just enjoy yourselves. Because in about eight and a half months, you aren't going to have much time for anything."

David took McPartland's hand and shook it warmly. "Thank you, Doctor. From the bottom of my heart."

"Just one more kiss," Marie said as she took McPartland's hand. "I promise I won't do this to you every time I see you."

She again kissed him on the cheek.

"It's my pleasure," he said. "Now take good care of yourself. And I'll see you in about a month. Good-bye now. And congratulations again to both of you."

Marie literally skipped down the hall and into the waiting room, David striding behind her.

"Honey, will you be careful, please?" he called.

"I'm pregnant," Marie said to Miss Gold. "Me. I'm going to have a baby."

"I know," Miss Gold said flatly. "Congratulations. Here." She handed Marie a pink-covered booklet. "And I've made an appointment for you for March eighteenth, if that is all right."

"That's just great, Miss Gold."

Marie put her arm through David's and Miss Gold let them out of the door.

"Miss Gold and I are great buddies," Marie said, giggling, as the door closed behind them.

"I can see that." David took a deep breath of the brisk January air. "Well, where to now? I don't know about you, but I feel like celebrating."

Marie grabbed David around the waist and put her head against his. "David, David, David. We are such lucky people."

"Yes, we are."

"And I love you."

Across David's shoulder, Marie saw a remarkably attractive woman of about thirty walking up Park Avenue toward them. She stared at her a moment, then pulled away from David. She felt her face flush.

"David, do you know that woman?"

David turned to look. As the woman came closer, they both could see that she was stunningly beautiful, her eyes a luminous blue, her hair silky and blond.

"No, I'm pretty sure I'd remember that face," David said.

"Me too. But I can't place her."

"Hey, I just had a brilliant idea. Do you think we could get a table at Lutèce? It's a Thursday." David searched the street for a vacant cab.

Marie shrugged, her eyes still on the woman as she came near to them. She was fascinated by her face. But it seemed it was more than her glowing beauty that compelled Marie to look at her, something even more than the persistent thought that they had met before—Marie felt a kinship with her, an almost physical tug toward her from inside. Marie was about to speak to her when the woman turned toward McPartland's door and rang the bell.

"So, that's where you met her," David said, raising his hand to an approaching cab.

It wasn't, Marie was sure.

David opened the door of the cab and guided Marie in. When he was beside her, he said, "Are you okay, honey? You never answered me. Is it Lutèce? Or should we just go home?"

Marie was staring out of the window. Miss Gold had let the woman in.

"The meter's running, Mister." The cab driver was looking at them in his rearview mirror.

Marie started. She felt as if she had been dreaming for a moment, but now the dream had gone. She looked at David and grinned.

"Hebron Hospital," she said to the driver. "And please drive carefully. I'm pregnant."

David laughed. "Marie, what—?"

Marie put a finger to her lips, her eyes sparkling.

When they arrived at Hebron, Marie took David's hand and led him to the elevator, up to the fourth floor, then down the hall through a pair of green swinging doors. A crowd consisting mostly of young men and older couples was standing two and three deep in front of a long corridor of windows—the nursery.

David smiled. "Aha! A look at the final product."

"Aren't they sweet-looking, David?" Marie was on her toes, looking from one baby to another, all of them swaddled in pink or blue in their clear-plastic traylike beds. Marie's eyes were bright and excited. Indeed, babies had never looked so sweet to her.

"I don't know," David said. "They all look like Winston Churchill to me. Without the cigar, of course."

"Oh, David. They're gorgeous."

Beside them, an older woman, undoubtedly a new grandmother, was gazing at the babies with a young nurse.

"Yes, they are gorgeous," she said, smiling at Marie. "Look at that one. Isn't he a beauty."

She pointed at a blue-swaddled infant lying with its eyes open in the right hand corner of the window. This newborn did seem to look even more beautiful than the others, with his well-shaped head, alert blue eyes, and pale yellow hair.

"Oh, yes, he is a beauty," the nurse was saying. She leaned forward and studied the tiny bracelet on the baby's wrist. "Of course, he's a McPartland baby. They're all so lovely. Dr. McPartland only sees the finest people."

Marie and David turned to each other and laughed.

And behind the glass, the tiny flaxen-haired boy blinked his blue eyes closed and went immediately and contentedly to sleep.

PART

2

IT WAS a perfect pregnancy from the start. No nausea in the first month, no bladder discomfort in the second, no sciatic pain in the third. Responding to the flow of estrogen from the placenta, her breasts had swollen a full two inches and her nipples and areola were becoming broader and darker. Her pelvic ligaments had begun to soften and she could feel her walk becoming more fluid, like the rolling gait of a sailor. Her blood volume had increased 20 percent allowing fifteen quarts to circulate through the placenta every day to nourish and cleanse the growing embryo. And recapitulating the evolution of man, the embryo was transforming its fishlike gills and reptilian tail to begin its unique human stages of development, a two-inch fetus complete with head and spine, arms and legs, and a beating heart. By the end of the third month Marie Preston awakened every morning feeling the joy of quickening life inside her.

"I'M SORRY we couldn't have happier news for you," Miss Saint Ambrosio, the staff genetics counselor, was saying. "But believe me, it's not the end of the world. We have every reason to believe that you are fully capable of having normal pregnancies in the future. This one, well, this one was just an accident. Chromosomal abnormalities of this type are not caused by anything that either of you have done. It was simply a rare accident of nature."

Miss Saint Ambrosio paused for a moment and Paul looked up from the folder open in front of him. Across the conference table from him and catty-corner to Miss Saint Ambrosio, sat George and Pamela Swan. Their backs were straight in the hospital standard gray-metal chairs and both were looking thoughtfully, attentively at Miss Saint Ambrosio like eager, intelligent students. But Paul could read the melancholy behind their eyes, the despair born of the knowledge that their deathwatch had begun. Paul could read that look as easily as, just one week ago, he had read Trisomy 18 Syndrome in every cell cultured from Pamela Swan's amniotic fluid.

"Dr. Kingsmill is a physician and geneticist," Miss Saint Ambrosio said. "I've asked him to join us today to explain to you exactly what went wrong."

Paul stood and walked to the blackboard on the wall in

back of him. Nothing like chalk to keep it academic, impersonal. He quickly drew twenty-three pairs of chromosomes
on the board and then numbered them.

"Trisomy 18 Syndrome usually occurs when something
goes amiss in the formation of either an egg cell or a sperm
cell," Paul began. "Normally, a female ovarian cell or a male
testicular cell contains forty-six chromosomes, as you see
here. Now, before conception, each of these cells divides in
half, so each will contribute twenty-three chromosomes to
the next generation." He turned to look at the Swans.
"Please feel free to stop me if any of this is unclear."

"Thank you," Pamela Swan said. "But I think we both
follow you. So far, at least. We've done a little reading." She
tried to smile at Paul, but could not completely manage it.

"Good." From his vantage point, Paul could see that
Mrs. Swan was wearing a maternity skirt below her long
tweed blazer and that her belly bulged under the edge of
the table. She was eighteen weeks pregnant. Most probably
she felt her baby kick every night when she went to bed.
And that baby, as Paul was about to demonstrate with perfect clinical lucidity, was not right. Defective. A bad baby.
Paul rolled the chalk against his palm and then looked from
Mrs. Swan's eyes to her husband's. "I hope you won't mind
my saying that I'm terribly sorry about this," he said. "And I
truly wish there were something I could do to make it less
painful. But I'm afraid there isn't."

George Swan took his wife's hand and squeezed it.
"Please continue," he said to Paul.

Paul turned back to the blackboard and sighed. When
there is nothing to say, not even that can be said. Best to
keep it academic after all.

"Now, if any chromosome pair doesn't separate properly during division, one egg or one sperm cell may get both
of the original chromosomes. In this case, the number eighteen chromosome." He tapped his chalk under the number
eighteen chromosome on the board. "And if such an egg or

sperm cell becomes fertilized, the result is an embryo with three number eighteen chromosomes in each cell instead of the normal two." Paul now drew a third chromosome next to the two at number eighteen. "And this, quite simply, is the cause of Trisomy 18 Syndrome. You see, because the accident, the failure to separate, occurs before conception, each of the baby's cells will have a total of forty-seven chromosomes instead of the normal forty-six. And, as I'm sure you know, that extra chromosome will disturb most aspects of its development. Yes?"

George Swan's hand was raised. No doubt, he had once been a polite and competent student.

"Doctor, that all makes perfect sense, I'm sure. But what Pamela—Mrs. Swan—and I want to know is what makes it happen? What do you mean, it's an accident?"

Paul set the chalk down in the tray below the blackboard and looked at George Swan. He was forty-two, the same age as Paul, and from what Paul could glean from the work-up sheet, from a more or less similar background, American version—Princeton, Columbia Law School, junior partner in a Wall Street firm. Bright, ambitious, methodical. A man who believes in reason. A man who believes there are no accidents, that God does not play dice with Nature.

"What I mean by accident is that I don't know. No one does. And it's quite unlikely we will in the near future. But it also means that this sort of thing doesn't happen very frequently at all. Maybe once in a hundred pregnancies." Paul looked down at the folder opened on the table. "Perhaps a touch more frequently at Mrs. Swan's age. But I assure you it's still quite rare."

"Could there be any mistake?" Mrs. Swan kept her eyes focused on the table. "You know, some laboratory mix-up or something. I don't mean to imply that—"

"That's a perfectly reasonable question, Mrs. Swan," Paul said. "All I can tell you is that I repeated my analysis on every cell we could grow from your amniotic fluid. There were a total of one hundred and nineteen. And every one of them had Trisomy 18. That's considered conclusive. And as far as mix-ups are concerned—let's say of amniotic fluids—that has never happened at Hebron. We have a system of checks and double-checks to avoid that possibility."

Mrs. Swan nodded slowly. That had been her last hope for reprieve.

"Let me repeat that Dr. Kingsmill's analysis of both of your cell samples shows no congenital problems," Miss Saint Ambrosio was saying. "I want to make it very clear that this problem will probably not happen again in future pregnancies."

"Accidents don't happen twice in the same place—is that what you mean?" George Swan said.

Paul detected an edge of sarcasm in Swan's question. Not that he could blame the poor man for being angry. And at whom better to vent it than the doctor who uncovered the problem, the man in the white coat with all the answers but one: Why did it happen? Why to us?

"I'm afraid we can't give you any guarantees," Paul said. "Just probabilities."

"Oh, God."

Mrs. Swan had cupped her hand around her eyes. Her whole body was trembling with an effort to hold back a sob, and Paul wanted to go to her, to put his arm around her shoulder and encourage her to let it out, to cry. George Swan stroked his wife's hair until she regained control of herself. Everyone was still for a moment.

"There's one more thing I'd like to say." Paul walked around the table and stood next to the Swans. "Amniocentesis and genetic analysis are both relatively new ideas. Five or ten years ago, your doctor—uh, Dr. Simon—wouldn't have sent you to us to have them done. You would have had a normal pregnancy and carried your baby to term."

Paul paused a moment. George and Pamela Swan were looking at him uncertainly. Miss Saint Ambrosio had pushed her chair away from the table and was putting papers back into her briefcase. She seemed uncomfortable.

"You would have had your baby and you would have been able to see immediately that it was not normal. And, if it lived, within a very short time it would have become clear that the child was severely mentally retarded. You'd know then that you would have to take care of that child for the rest of your lives and that that would be a terrible burden to both of you. But there is something else, something you may not be able to imagine now." Again, Paul paused. Miss Saint Ambrosio was staring at him coldly. This part hadn't been included in their prearranged script. Paul hadn't even known he was going to say it until just a moment ago when Pamela Swan nearly broke down. The Swans had not taken their eyes off Paul since he had begun his little speech. He looked at them warmly and continued. "What's hard to imagine is that somehow you would learn to live with that burden. It would become a part of your lives. You would do your best for him."

George Swan suddenly stood up. "What in the name of God are you getting at, Doctor?"

Pamela Swan grabbed her husband's hand and tried to pull him down, but he remained upright, staring angrily at Paul.

Miss Saint Ambrosio was shaking her head back and forth. "Dr. Kingsmill, please consider—"

"I'm sorry if I've upset you," Paul said. He felt his hands trembling and stuffed them into the pockets of his coat. "Really, that was the farthest thing from my mind, Mr. Swan. It's just that . . . that we've all been talking here as if . . . as if we'd already made a choice for you. And I just wanted you to understand that the choice of terminating this pregnancy is yours. Both of yours. And no one here, not myself, not Miss Saint Ambrosio, not your private doctor, none of us can presume to make that decision for you. We can only tell you what we've found. Not what to do about it. I just wanted that to be clear."

While Paul spoke, tears had started to fill in Pamela Swan's eyes. Now she rose and extended her hand to Paul. "Thank you, Doctor," she said warmly. "Thank you very much."

Paul took her hand and held it a moment. He could not say anything more. Now, silently, George Swan also took Paul's hand, shook it, and then guided his pregnant wife out of the conference room door.

Miss Saint Ambrosio snapped the latches on her briefcase shut, lifted it off of the table, and walked to the door without saying a word. But just as she was about to leave, she turned and looked at Paul coolly.

"You wouldn't by any chance be a minister's son, would you?" she said.

"No," Paul said. "A coal miner's."

But the woman was already out of the door.

Paul went to the blackboard and began erasing the chromosomes he had drawn on it. What, indeed, had come over him? And what would he say next? That retarded children can lead just as contented lives as the rest of us? Maybe more so? That we're all God's children? He replaced the eraser in the blackboard tray and gathered up the contents of the George and Pamela Swan file. He looked again at the three number eighteen chromosomes on the fetal karyotype. What in hell did he think he was doing all day if he didn't believe in eliminating genetically defective children? Or was it more complicated than that? There was a story Professor Faragiano liked to tell at the Medical College: A doctor was considering the advisability of a therapeutic abortion; the father had syphilis, the mother tuberculosis; of the four children they already had, the first was born blind, the second died after two days, the third was deaf and dumb, and the fourth was tuberculous; the mother

was pregnant again and amniocentesis was not available—
what should be done? Invariably the class voted for abortion—*therapeutic* abortion. "I see," Faragiano would say,
peering out over the top of his glasses. "You would have
murdered Beethoven."

"The Beethoven Fallacy" Faragiano had called it. Paul
grimaced to himself. Such anecdotes would be laughed at
by Bouchard. Only yesterday, Bouchard had personally delivered an amniotic tap to the lab and Paul had overheard
him say amusedly to Eva that he hoped it was a boy this
time because it was the patient's third try for one. Did that
mean the patient already had two girls, Paul had asked, although he could have guessed the answer.

"No," Bouchard had replied, simpering at Paul. "She
has one girl and aborted her next two pregnancies when we
found they were girls too. She only wants two children. One
of each, you know. It does keep the population down, Dr.
Kingsmill."

Indeed, it does. If a couple is only going to have two
children, why not have the exact two they want? The very
best two they can have? Blue-eyed, if they so desire. Tall.
Brilliant. The best genetic mix their heredities can muster.
In the age of consumerism, children can be our finest product. Paul shook his head as he walked slowly down the hallway. Was any of it really different from the therapeutic
abortion of the Swan's Trisomy 18 fetus?

He looked in the door of Genetics Lab 2. Eva was not
there. They had made arrangements to have lunch together
again today, so he walked in and sat at her desk to wait for
her. Next to Eva's appointment calendar was a small,
framed picture of her parents. Paul picked it up and looked
at the attractive Swedish couple. Eva had told him that
they were both in their mid-sixties and still working their
dairy farm south of Gothenburg when the photo had been
taken, but to Paul they looked at least fifteen years younger
and certainly unworn by work. Sturdy people. Good stock.

He put the photo down and absently picked up a file from Eva's "Out" box. Inside were a genetics work-up sheet, a fetal karyotype and a karyotype tally sheet. The last was checked for a systematic search. Five slides were listed. No abnormalities noted. Paul looked at the karyotype. It had been done with standard Giemsa banding, striping the chromosomes with gray and black. Nothing unusual. He began slipping the sheets back into the folder when his eye fell on one pair of number six chromosomes. He turned on Eva's desk lamp and held the karyotype under the light.

Something was wrong.

Something was wrong with a number six chromosome of the fetus inside one Bonnie Roundtree.

"JESUS, DO you look gorgeous! I'd almost be willing to get pregnant if I thought it would make me look half as good."

Kate Cochoran strode into Marie's office and plopped herself in the leather chair in front of Marie's desk.

"Thanks," Marie said, smiling. "I assume that's a compliment."

Kate leaned forward and peered at Marie.

"Listen, just between girls, are you wearing makeup or is that a natural blush?"

"Bloom, Kate, bloom. But I can tell you how to get one just like it. First you find yourself a nice fella and then—"

Kate laughed. "Thanks, but no thanks. I'll stick with Ultima. I never did like nice fellas."

"More's the pity," Marie said, buttoning the jacket of her pants suit. It really was beginning to pull too much across her bosom. She unbuttoned it. "What can I do for you, Kate? I'm afraid I've got a lunch date in about five."

"This will just take a minute." Kate pushed a pair of IBM cards across the desk to Marie. "I need your Joan Hancock on these. The gift subscriptions for your Dr. McPartland. From a secret admirer, remember?"

"Of course, I remember. But that must have been three months ago, Kate. No, four. Is that how long it takes to get

our billings out? No wonder we've got cash flow troubles."
Marie picked up a pen and began to sign the cards.

"Don't blame me. It's your doctor friend. He gave our
computer heartburn. It kept spitting his name back to us.
You don't mind if I smoke, do you?"

Marie scrunched up her face. "It's not me who minds,"
she said, patting her belly. "It's Doodles in here. He's from
this new, clean-living generation." She smiled.

"Excuse me," Kate said, putting her pack of cigarettes
back into her jacket pocket. "Jesus, remember the good old
days when it was parents who told their kids not to smoke?"

Marie's phone buzzed and she picked it up. Her secretary told her that Mrs. Roundtree had arrived. Marie stood
and handed the IBM cards back to Kate.

"Listen, Kate, I've got to go now," she said. "And get
that computer fixed or whatever, would you?"

"Oh, it was just a mix-up. McPartland gets *About Town*
already and we had trouble hooking these others on with it.
His original subscription came to a different office. Different
address, different name. That's what bollixed it up."

"Really? Where does he come from?" Marie was waiting for Kate at her office door.

"Springfield, Massachusetts, I think. He must have
shared an office with someone named Richard Monroe
there. And when he split, McPartland took the *About Town*
subscription with him. Monroe probably got the plants and
paintings. When those practices split up, it's like a divorce:
You take the silverware, I'll take the scalpel."

Marie saw Bonnie waiting in the vestibule. She, too,
radiated that special glow of pregnancy. Marie waved at
her.

"I'll put this through right away," Kate said.

"Great." Marie again buttoned her jacket. "And listen,
send a renewal notice to his old partner. Divorces are good
for business, right?"

"Oh, we did that years ago. But this Dr. Monroe split too and didn't leave a forwarding address. We had to give the computer two Bromos and put it to bed." Kate patted Marie's belly. "Have a nice lunch, you two. Something healthy, like ice cream and pickles."

"Thanks." Marie had instinctively pulled away from Kate. It was amazing how many people took the liberty of thumping a pregnant woman's stomach. She walked over to Bonnie and embraced her. "Hi, are you as hungry as I am?"

"Starved. I haven't eaten for two whole hours." After their hug, Bonnie held on to Marie's shoulders and looked down at their bellies. They were still touching. She laughed. "Look. They're friends already."

During lunch of chef's salads and Perrier at the Promenade, Marie made an effort to talk about at least one or two topics other than pregnancy and babies—a lingering allegiance to her pre-thirty-five self when such talk had been a sure sign of the disintegration of the female brain. But it was a losing fight. The skaters in Rockefeller Plaza rink outside their table window made them both think how nice it would be to have a little girl to dress in tights and short skirts. And a mention of the crisis in Pakistan led very smoothly, it seemed, to a discussion of the advantages of the Lamaze method.

Later, they walked arm-in-arm down Fifth Avenue, two attractive pregnant ladies out for a stroll, and when they reached Saks where Bonnie was going to buy her first maternity evening dress of this pregnancy, Marie decided, what the hell, she'd join her for at least a little while although she had already been gone from the office for an hour and a half. They took the elevator up to the seventh floor and on their way to the maternity department—clever layout, Mr. Saks—they stopped to browse in the infant's and children's clothing department. Marie held up a blue-and-green striped pinafore.

"Oh, boy, this is going to be fun," she said, smiling. "Did you know I never played with dolls as a kid? Too busy reading and being a smarty pants. What a waste. But I'm going to make up for it now."

"It is fun," Bonnie said. "Sometimes I drive Adam crazy with little sailor suits and what all. Already all he wants are jeans and T-shirts."

Marie held up another pinafore, this one a blue-and-white polka dot affair. And looking at it, she felt a little pang of sadness.

"Am I terrible?" she said. "I do so much want my child to be pretty. After all I've been through, is that a sin?"

Bonnie put a hand on Marie's arm and smiled. "Marie, with your looks and David's, you don't have a thing to worry about."

Marie laughed. "You've never seen my Aunt Gladys. She always hated me. It would be just like her to pass her genes on to little Doodles in there."

Marie set the pinafore back down on the counter. In the aisle beyond hers, a man was squinting at her. For a second, she did not recognize him, but when she did, she felt like turning away. It was Ralph Lowenstein. She hadn't spoken to him in months, not since she had called him to send her records over to McPartland. It was too late to disappear now. He was walking toward her.

"Hello, Marie. How are you? How's David?"

"Fine, Ralph. And yourself?" Marie clasped his outstretched hand.

"Not bad."

"Oh, Ralph Lowenstein, this is my good friend, Bonnie Roundtree. Bonnie, Ralph."

Lowenstein took Bonnie's hand and shook it cordially, but his eyes had drifted, almost by reflex it seemed, to Marie's belly. Her coat was unbuttoned.

"Uh, are congratulations in order, Marie?" he asked. His brow puckered.

"That's right. For both of us. As you can see, Bonnie has a little head start on me."

"Well, well that's just wonderful news. Congratulations, Marie. That's just wonderful." Lowenstein again thrust his hand toward Marie. Taking it, Marie could feel that it had now turned cold and a trifle damp.

"Thank you, Ralph," Marie said.

Lowenstein shifted his feet and looked around nervously. "I'm just grabbing a little time on my day off to get a birthday gift for my littlest one," he said.

Marie looked steadily into Lowenstein's eyes. "Are you surprised, Ralph?" she said.

"No," Lowenstein said quickly. Then he smiled. "Well, maybe a little."

"There was really nothing to it," Marie went on, although she had just promised herself to leave it at that.

"No, there usually isn't," Lowenstein said. His smile this time was even less convincing.

"All they had to do was clean out a little junk from my right fallopian tube and I was in business."

Lowenstein's eyes widened and his jaw went slack. He stood that way for a moment and then suddenly picked up the shopping bag he had rested on the counter, mumbled a couple unintelligible words of good-bye, turned, and walked away.

"Who was that masked man?" Bonnie said, smiling.

Marie was watching Lowenstein as he pushed his way onto the first elevator that opened. Now she felt guilty. She couldn't resist a little sadistic gibing at the man, could she? She bit her lower lip. That wasn't it. That's not what was really disturbing her. She had intended to embarrass Lowenstein, but he hadn't seemed embarrassed at all. He seemed stunned. Shaken. She turned to Bonnie who was still smiling.

"That," Marie said, "was my old gynecologist."

"I figured as much," Bonnie said, shaking her head. "How those men hate to be wrong."

Marie looked at Bonnie soberly. "Not half so much as I hate it," she said. Then she brightened and took Bonnie's arm. "Let's buy you a dress, lady."

"I HOPE there's not too much vermouth in it for you."

Marie handed a small plastic jar containing a sample of her first urination of the day to Miss Gold. The nurse nodded, without smiling, and immediately pasted a label onto the jar. If it was the last thing Marie was going to do, she was going to make that woman laugh. Marie took a half cup of coffee from the serving table and sat on the long couch against the wall. She set her cup down on the coffee table and shuffled through the magazines on it. *Soma* was there. And *City Life* too. Better late than never. Did McPartland wonder where they came from? He probably didn't even know he was getting them. And Miss Gold clearly wondered about very little at all.

On the other side of the waiting room three women, all in their fifth or sixth months of pregnancy, were chatting gaily about the relative merits of cloth diapers and Pampers. Pampers were winning. Marie considered joining them. She could tell them what she had read about Pampers being non-biodegradable. But she had had that conversation before. Twice, in fact. And Pampers had won both times anyhow. There were only two other women in the room and both were reading, so Marie picked up the copy of *Soma* and leafed through it. She still hadn't finished the article on disco exercises that everyone in the office was talking about.

Somehow it didn't appeal to her. Why did everything have
to end up being self-improving? Couldn't you just dance
and forget about the size of your behind for a little while?

The entrance bell rang and Marie looked up. A couple
in their mid-thirties entered, checked in with Miss Gold,
and then sat down on the couch, the woman, dark haired
with animated eyes, beside Marie. Marie smiled at her and
the woman smiled back.

"Hi," the woman said. "Expecting?"

"Yes," Marie said. "A third of the way there. And you?"

"I'm already there. Our little boy was four months old
just yesterday."

"Congratulations." Marie smiled at the woman and
then at her husband. He smiled back rather stiffly and
picked up a magazine. "Is it as much work as they say?"

"Not so bad. Once you get used to all that mustard they
squirt into their pants." The woman laughed softly. "Of
course, we have some help."

"That's nice. We're going to do the same. I only get
three months maternity leave from my job," Marie said. "Of
course, my mother thinks that's a horrible idea. Unmaternal
or something."

"She's just jealous," the woman said, smiling. "Jealousy
makes people say awful things."

"I think what she'd really like to do is move in with us
and take care of the baby herself." Marie laughed. "She
could bring it up to be just as neurotic as I am."

The woman's face became quite serious. "Don't let
her." She leaned toward Marie. "She'd just start nosing
around and then there'd be trouble."

Marie looked at the woman quizzically. "Yes, I suppose
so." She pulled herself upright, a little away from the
woman, and returned to her copy of *Soma*.

"It's a miracle," the woman said.

Marie looked up from her magazine. The woman was

scratching her forehead near to her hairline and her nails were leaving marks on her skin. "Excuse me?" Marie said.

"It's a miracle." The woman had moved closer to Marie and Marie could see that the pupils of her eyes were dilated, deep black holes. Marie felt a little shiver pass across her shoulders.

"I'm sorry," Marie said. "I'm not sure I know what you mean."

"You know," the woman said, her face suddenly lightening. "The whole business. Having babies. Feeling them grow inside you. Watching them grow up. 'One generation cometh and another passeth away.'"

"Yes." Marie smiled. Maybe this woman's style was a touch eccentric, but she certainly was more interesting than 'how to disco inches off your hips.' Or the Pamper discussion, for that matter. "It's certainly a miracle for my husband and me. We had to wait over three years to get this one started."

"Yes," the woman said. She had leaned her face next to Marie's again and Marie noticed that there was something different about her hair now. It had shifted somehow. A wig. "My husband and I thank God every day for our little miracle."

"Yes. Yes, we're very thankful too." Marie considered picking up her magazine again.

"I was found with child," the woman said.

Marie picked up the magazine and brought it close to her face. "Yes," she said, puckering her brow as if she were about to tackle a difficult article which required her complete concentration.

"I brought forth a son," the woman said, now more loudly.

The pregnant women discussing diapers stopped for a moment and looked at the woman and Marie. Marie smiled at them. They smiled back and immediately returned to their review of the dangers of safety pins.

"I said, I brought forth a son." She was speaking quite loudly now and directly into Marie's ear.

"Yes. Yes, you told me. A little boy." Out of the corner of her eye, Marie saw Miss Gold stand and go through the door back into the office. The woman's husband had taken her hand and was trying to stroke it, but the woman pulled her hand away.

"Franny, maybe you should let the lady read her magazine," the husband was saying. He winked at Marie nervously.

"My husband is a just man," the woman said. "He doth not wish to make of me a public example."

Miss Gold had returned through the door, leaving it open. And now Dr. McPartland entered, a stethoscope hanging from his neck, and everyone in the waiting room looked up at him and smiled. Before her husband could restrain her, the woman was out of her seat and had rushed up to McPartland.

"Hello, Mrs. Hollander," the doctor said. "How are you doing today?"

The woman suddenly dropped to her knees, grabbing McPartland's hand as she landed, and then put his hand to her lips and kissed it loudly.

Some of the women in the waiting room gasped audibly. McPartland pulled his hand away from the woman and stepped backward. His face was flushed. The woman's husband was trying to lift the woman off of the floor. Miss Gold had taken her other arm and as they brought her to her feet, Marie could see that the woman was smiling broadly. In a second, they were all—the woman, her husband, McPartland, and Miss Gold—through the door and it had closed behind them.

No one in the waiting room spoke. Marie put her magazine back on the table and tried to lift her coffee cup, but she found that her hand was trembling too much to hold it and she immediately set it down. That poor woman, she thought. That poor, dear woman. What pushes someone like that over the edge? Marie felt some movement inside her and she settled her back against a cushion. Perhaps she should have been more sympathetic toward her. The least she could have done was listen to her without sticking a magazine between them. And what about the woman's child? What kind of life could this mean for him? Was she like this even before he was born? Marie suddenly sat forward. Maybe the woman didn't really have a child at all. Maybe it was some kind of mad delusion. How many dreams of holding a baby in her arms had Marie had before she finally conceived? A delusion is just the next step. A waking dream. Marie hoped to God that McPartland could help the woman.

"Mrs. Preston."

Marie looked up, startled. Miss Gold was calling to her, the door open in back of her.

"You're next, Mrs. Preston."

"Yes. Thank you, Miss Gold."

"Please try to relax. Take a deep breath and sit quietly for a second and we'll try again."

Miss Armbruster had taken Marie's blood pressure twice already and both times the systolic reading had been over one hundred and fifty. Marie took a deep breath, but sitting quietly was another thing. She couldn't erase the image of Franny Hollander on her knees, her wig askew, revealing coarse black stubble underneath. And that image clearly was doing Marie's arteries little good. She took another deep breath and let it out slowly. Miss Armbruster wrapped the sphygmomanometer sleeve around Marie's arm just above her elbow, pumped it up and placed her stethoscope over Marie's brachial artery. The mercury column bounced at one fifty-two. Miss Armbruster wrote the figures down on her chart next to Marie's weight, now one hundred and twenty-seven pounds, a total gain of eight pounds since her pregnancy began.

"The doctor will be with you in a moment."

Miss Armbruster left the room, taking Marie's chart with her. Marie stood, wandered over to the examination table and leaned back against it, her buttocks resting against its edge. She pulled at the neck of her smock and peered down through her cleavage to the little mound of belly below.

"Well, Doodles, looks like we've got a little hypertension. Nothing serious. Just don't tell your father, he's a real worrier. In fact, he's a professional worrier. People pay him to worry for them. Ooops, someone's coming. See you later."

She let go of her smock as Dr. McPartland walked into the examination room, carrying her chart.

"Hello, Marie? How are you doing today?"

"*Comme si, comme ça.* And you?"

"I'm fine, thank you. Why don't you just hop up there and we'll see how you and your little friend are doing."

McPartland went to the sink and washed his hands, while Marie pulled herself up onto the examination table and lay down. They ought to have pictures on the ceiling, she thought. Like the Sistine Chapel. McPartland came over to her left side, separated her smock in the middle, and lay a hand on her abdomen.

"Cold?" he asked.

"No . . . well, a little chilly."

"Sorry." McPartland removed his hand and rubbed it against his other one. "Nothing worse than a gynecologist with poor circulation," he said, smiling. He put his hand back and gently palpitated her uterus through her abdominal wall. "Good. Now for the really cold stuff." He pressed a dab of K-Y Jelly out of a tube onto his finger tips.

"Are you going to be able to do something for Mrs.

Hollander?" Marie looked up at the doctor from the corner of her eyes.

McPartland rubbed the jelly onto Marie's belly. It was, indeed, very cold.

"Do you know her?" he asked.

"Not really. We just met out there. Poor woman."

"Yes." McPartland had walked over to the cabinet and removed an electronic fetal stethoscope from a drawer. "I'm afraid there's not too much I can do for her myself at the moment. But I was able to refer her to a specialist."

"I thought you were a specialist."

McPartland was standing over her again, the stethoscope dangling from his neck. "Not in postpartum psychosis, I'm afraid."

Marie raised her head. "She does have a baby, then."

"Hold still, please. Let's hear how we're doing in there."

McPartland popped the stethoscope into his ears and slid the receiver end across her belly. For a moment he held still, listening intently. He smiled. Then he held the receiver firmly on Marie's belly and handed her the other end. She put it into her ears and listened.

"It sounds like Grand Central Station in there," she said, grinning.

"Listen for a rapid beat in the background."

Marie concentrated. Somewhere behind the whooshes and squeaks, she heard a staccato beat, like a distant snare drum. The heartbeat of her child. Marie felt the blood rising in her cheeks. The heartbeat of her little baby. Oh, God. She felt tears gathering in her eyes. McPartland was reaching down for the stethoscope.

"She sounds strong, doesn't she?" he said.

"Yes."

McPartland wiped the jelly from her stomach with a tissue and then reached his hand down to hers and pulled her upright.

"Everything looks very good, Marie," he said. "Keep up the good work."

Marie slipped off of the examination table and padded in her bare feet over to the screen. She undid the smock, removed it, and started pulling on her blouse. Her face was still flushed with the thrill of hearing the baby's heartbeat. And she was again feeling the giddy urge to plant a big kiss on McPartland's cheek.

"Those magazine subscriptions are from me," she called over the screen. She laughed. "I'm lousy at keeping secrets."

"Beg your pardon?"

"The magazine subscriptions. *Soma* and *City Life*. They're from me. No big deal, really. I work there. Get them free. But I thought they'd look nice on your coffee table." Marie was slipping into her shoes.

"Oh, thank you, Marie."

Marie stepped out from behind the screen, smiling. "You don't know what I'm talking about, do you?"

McPartland smiled, almost shyly, it seemed. "Not really, I'm afraid. Miss Gold takes care of that sort of thing. But thank you."

"You're very welcome, Doctor." Marie brushed her hair away from her face with her hand. "By the way, whatever happened to your old partner? Our subscription department was trying to get him to pick up the subscriptions you took with you. But he didn't leave a forwarding address."

McPartland lifted Marie's chart from the top of a cabinet and studied it for a moment. Then he looked up and said, "I'm sorry. What was it?"

"Monroe, Dr. Richard Monroe. Do you know where he moved?"

McPartland looked at Marie almost sternly. "I'm sure if Dr. Monroe left no forwarding address it's because he doesn't want any junk mail following him," he said. "But what I'm concerned about right now is this hypertension, Marie. It's much too early in the game to be seeing that."

Marie stood quite still. She could feel her heart beating quickly in her chest. "I don't think it's anything to worry about. It was just a momentary elevation. You know, because of that business with the Hollander woman."

"Let's see." McPartland opened a drawer and pulled out a sphygmomanometer and stethoscope. "Roll up your left sleeve, please."

Marie took off her jacket and unbuttoned the cuff of her left sleeve. What was McPartland being so rigorous about? Hell, David's blood pressure rose twenty points every time he just walked into a doctor's office. She rolled up her sleeve.

McPartland wrapped the sphygmomanometer cuff around her arm and began pumping.

"I'm very sorry all of you had to see that little episode with Mrs. Hollander," he said, now fitting the stethoscope into his ears. "Her problem was that she wasn't really psychologically prepared for childbirth. Relax now, Marie."

He placed the bell of the stethoscope in the crook of her elbow, loosened the cuff valve and watched the mercury column. Marie watched it too. It took its first bounce at one hundred and fifty-eight. McPartland frowned, pumped again, and loosened the valve. One sixty. McPartland removed the cuff and slipped the stethoscope out of his ears and around his neck. He looked directly into Marie's eyes and grasped her arm firmly just above the wrist.

"Marie, I think you should consider tapering down your work load for a little while until this starts to look normal again. And try not to worry too much about things that don't really concern you. We have to consider your little friend in there."

Marie pulled a deep breath in through her nose. She felt drops of moisture forming on her neck and forehead. If McPartland was trying to calm her down, he certainly was going about it in a damned peculiar way.

"What could happen? I mean, if it doesn't go down? Or if it goes up? What could happen to the baby?"

McPartland patted Marie's arm. He smiled at her. "See what I mean? You look for things to worry about, Marie. Now what I'd prescribe is a nice warm bath with lots of bubbles and a good book. In fact, that's an order. Doctor's orders."

Marie rolled down her sleeve and buttoned the cuff. "Please. Just tell me. What could happen?"

"Nothing is going to happen," McPartland said. He slipped her chart into a manila folder. "The next time I see you, everything will be perfectly normal. Now don't forget to schedule your amniocentesis with Miss Gold on the way out. We should try for early next week, okay?" He walked to the door. "And don't forget my prescription either. Bath and book. Good-bye now, Marie."

Marie let the rain drum onto her bare head as she paced back and forth to the corner of Seventy-third Street and Park. There was a kerchief in her pocket, but she didn't want to put it on. The cold drops felt good on her scalp. Better than a warm bath she was sure. And certainly better than remaining in the waiting room until David picked her up. That room had seemed stifling when she came out into it and got her appointment card and pamphlet on amniocentesis from Miss Gold. Worse than stifling. Claustrophobic. Right now she wasn't too crazy about Raymond McPartland and his well-appointed office. It was a little too chic, like an art theater vestibule. Christ, if he had kept her in there any longer her blood pressure probably would have shot up to one eighty. She saw David walking up Park Avenue toward her. He, sensibly, was wearing his Borsalino. He kept it at the office.

"Hi. What are you trying to do, catch a cold?" David kissed Marie's wet cheek.

"His waiting room is overheated."

"Don't you have a kerchief or something?"

Marie stepped back from David. "I'm a big girl," she said, sharply.

"You certainly are." David took her arm and started down the street. "And I'm an old man who wants to get in out of the rain. Can I take you somewhere for a Shirley Temple before dinner?"

"Okay."

"What's the matter, hon?"

"Nothing."

They walked the rest of the block in silence. Then David flagged down a cab and they got in. David told the driver to take them to the Brasserie and then sat back in his seat and put an arm around Marie's shoulder.

"How was the checkup?"

Marie turned and looked at David.

"What's the cause of postpartum depression?"

David burst out laughing.

"So that's it. Jesus, honey, you are the all-time greatest long-range worrier I've ever met."

"This isn't funny," Marie said. She then told David about the incident with Franny and what McPartland had said about her. She finished just as they arrived at the Brasserie.

After they were inside and Marie had her milk and grenadine in front of her—she was in no mood for a phony cocktail named Shirley Temple—and David his gimlet, David said, "I don't know the details. But it certainly could be postpartum psychosis from what you've told me. I saw a few during my residency, but none since. There's a guy at Bellevue who specializes in it, and a lot of docs I know refer their cases to him. I'm not sure what he does with them. From what I remember, it usually blows over after a few months. I think Lithium helps. I could look it up, if you like."

"What causes it?"

"Like everything else, nobody's sure. The prevalent theory now is hormones. The sudden change. There's usually a hormone high right after giving birth. And then a few days later, a comedown. Most women feel a little depression then. And some really crash and don't come up for a long while."

"Can it be caused by anything else? Something psychological?"

David shrugged. "Yes, I think so. Some shrinks think there's a greater incidence among women who don't really want a baby. Not necessarily women who got knocked-up by accident, but women who have a submerged fear of babies. Their profile usually shows that during pregnancy they tended to deny what was happening. Sort of ignored it until the last minute."

"Oh." Marie sipped her milk. She wondered if she fitted into that category in any way. Her mother had certainly implied as much when she told her she was going to continue working. Unmaternal. And Franny had jumped fast when Marie mentioned her disapproving mother. Maybe they were two of a kind. Marie cupped her hand across her belly under the table. For a second, she thought she could feel that little heartbeat, although she knew that was impossible. She loved her baby. She knew that.

"You never told me how the checkup went?"

Marie looked up. "Fine," she said. "Perfect." No sense both of them worrying about her blood pressure. If he knew, David would probably drag out his old medical school sphygmomanometer and take hers every night before they went to bed. The way he had been about taking her temperature before she got pregnant. She would look up hypertension in pregnancy at the library tomorrow. And she wasn't going to worry about it until then.

Instead of going to Chinatown for dinner, as they had planned, they each had another drink and then ordered omelettes and salad at their table. David talked about a new patient he had seen that day, a stockbroker with insomnia, a middle-aged man obsessed with pork-barrel futures. When he finished the story he sighed and, as he had done once a month ever since Marie had met him, said that he should chuck it all and become a country doctor.

Later, while they were getting ready for bed, Marie remembered the other question she had wanted to ask David.

"What was that book you and Tom looked McPartland up in?"

"You mean the GYN Directory?"

"Yes. That's it. Do you have one at the office?"

"I think so. Why?"

"Could you do me a favor and look someone up for me? A Dr. Monroe. Richard Monroe."

David looked at Marie quizzically. "Honey, don't we have enough gynecologists?"

Marie laughed. "Oh, it's not for me. It's for someone at the office."

She felt her pulse quicken. Lying probably wasn't any good for her blood pressure either.

MARIE'S LITTLE daughter looked positively enchanting in the blue-and-white polka-dot pinafore she had bought for her at Saks. Strolling hand-in-hand down Fifth Avenue, the two of them caused quite a sensation and several people, including Ralph Lowenstein, stopped to comment on how beautiful the two of them looked together. And when the phone rang in the corner phone booth, Marie was sure that it was yet another admirer calling to tell them how lovely they looked.

"Jesus H. Christ. Who the hell can that be?"

Marie blinked her eyes open. David had turned on the lamp and was reaching for the ringing phone on the bed table.

"Hello," he said, gruffly.

Marie could hear a woman's voice on the other end. She sat up in the bed.

"Excuse me, but do you have any idea what time it is?"

"Who is it, David?"

"Who is this?" David said into the phone. He listened for a second, then covered the phone and said, "Franny Hollander. She says she's a friend of yours."

"I'll take it."

"What the hell kind of friend calls you at four-thirty in the morning?"

"Let me talk to her, David."

Marie took the phone and slid over to the side of the bed, her back to David.

"Hello, Franny. How are you?"

"Good. Sorry to call so late. Sometimes I forget that normal people don't have to get up for four o'clock feedings."

Franny's voice sounded quite normal to Marie. The way it had when they had first struck up their conversation in the waiting room.

"Is there anything wrong?" Marie asked.

"No. Well, yes and no. I've just been thinking about you. I felt—I don't know how to put this without sounding silly."

"Go ahead, Franny." Marie fitted her feet into her sheepskin slippers at the side of the bed.

"I don't know." She sounded almost shy. "Some kind of kinship thing between us. You know, neither of us are exactly the bootee-knitting type." Franny laughed.

"Yes, I know what you mean." Marie sucked in her breath. She didn't really like the comparison, considering Franny's performance that afternoon.

"And so I thought I'd better talk to you," Franny went on. "Before it's too late."

"Too late for what?" Marie felt her heart beating rapidly again. She sensed David listening behind her.

"Don't get him mad at you," Franny said. "He'll punish you if you're bad."

"Who? What are you talking about, Franny?"

"The power in his right hand."

"Franny, what are you talking about? What are you trying to tell me?" Marie was attempting to keep her voice low and calm so as not to upset David. Little chance. She could hear her own voice cracking.

"I knew you'd understand me," Franny was saying.

"But I don't."

David had moved over next to Marie. "What the hell is going on?" he said into her ear. Marie waved him away, but he didn't move.

"Of course you do. You do believe in miracles, don't—" Franny's voice broke off and Marie could hear a man talking to her in the background.

"What kind of miracles, Franny?"

The man on the other end was talking more loudly now, something about a pill, and a second later Marie heard a click and then the dial tone.

Marie held the phone to her ear for a moment longer, pretending that she was still listening. She knew that if she hung up the receiver right away, David would see that her hand was trembling. More than trembling. Shaking uncontrollably. Suddenly, David took the receiver from her hand and hung it up himself. Then he walked around the bed and crouched in front of Marie.

"All right. Now who was that, Marie? And what did she say to you?"

Marie's whole body was shaking now. And a sob was lodged somewhere in her chest, trying to get out. She couldn't talk.

"It was that woman in the waiting room, right? The psychotic."

Marie nodded her head. She couldn't look at David.

David stood up and walked to the closet to get his robe. He put it on and walked back in front of her. "Marie, what ever possessed you to give that woman your name and telephone number?"

"I didn't. She must have heard Miss Gold calling my name or something." Marie looked up at David. "What difference does it make? Since when do we keep our name and number a secret from people?" Marie felt a pulse of anger rising inside her and for the moment it displaced her fright.

David was shaking his head. "It's bad enough I have my cockamamie patients calling at all hours."

Marie pushed off her slippers and pulled herself back under the covers. "It's your cockamamie business. I thought you enjoyed it."

David sighed. "Marie, I just don't happen to think that phone calls from certified psychotics in the middle of the night are very good for your health."

"In my condition."

"Yes, in your condition, damn it."

"I'm going back to sleep, David."

"Just like that."

"Yes, just like that. I'm sorry she woke you."

David took off his robe and threw it on a chair. Then he crawled back into bed, turned off the lamp, and curled up away from Marie.

With the light out, Marie felt the fear returning. Her heart was racing. What was her blood pressure now? One ninety? Two hundred? She took long, deep breaths and let them out slowly. Try to think pretty thoughts. What was that dream she was having before? It had a very happy feel, whatever it was. Marie felt herself make a little sound in her throat. The pinafore. She remembered the pinafore in the dream. And the little girl that looked just like her. Try to hold that image. Polka-dotted pinafore. Marie was sweating. She could feel the drops running off her face onto her pillow. What miracles, Franny? What are you talking about?

In the dream that came several minutes later, there were no pinafores. A row of men wearing drab green uniforms were marching toward Marie. And they were beating drums. Snare drums. They didn't seem to notice Marie as they advanced closer. The drums were beating louder. And faster. Much faster. One beat seemed to begin before the other ended. And now they were marching right over her. Trampling her. Each boot planted squarely on her belly.

"What do you think, Marie?"

Marie jerked her head up and looked across the conference table at Murray Miller.

"I'm sorry," she said. "I was wool gathering for a minute there. What was the question, Murray?"

Miller, the new and rather young president of the periodicals division, smiled patronizingly at Marie.

"Wool gathering? Are you going to knit something for the baby?" He chuckled, looking around the table at the others for appreciation of his little witticism.

"What was the question, Murray?"

"We were discussing the expansion of the regional supplements. Putting some local gossipy stuff up against the restaurant guide. I gather from your memos that you have an opinion on the subject."

"Yes, I do, Murray. If those sample columns you circulated are an indication of what you're planning, I can't say I really like the idea."

Miller tilted his head back and stroked his chin. "Any particular reason why?"

"Yes." Marie was looking straight back at him. "I think it's tasteless."

"Really?" Now Miller leaned forward. "Does that mean you don't think it will appeal to our readers? Or is it—" He paused to smile at Michael Brooks, the regional editor of *City Life* who was sitting to Marie's right. "How can I put this delicately? Or is it your personal gut reaction?"

Marie felt her face flush. Of course the idea was tasteless. The man was tasteless.

"The idea is simply in bad taste, Murray. I'm not sure I'd know how to make that any clearer to you."

Miller sat back. He said he would discuss the idea further with Malcolm Hamilton and send out a memo on the results. For the rest of the meeting, he didn't address any of his remarks to Marie.

As soon as the meeting was over, Marie headed for the door. She could dispense with the *pro forma* post-meeting chatter today. It was a wonder she had gotten through the meeting itself, feeling the way she did. She had awoken a second time last night, this time with the sound of her pulse drumming in her ears and a sickening feeling in the pit of her stomach. She hadn't dared try to go back to sleep again, so she had showered and dressed and had her tea and cottage cheese in the living room, watching the sun come up over Central Park. Now, Marie headed for her office, stopping to tell her secretary to order in lunch for her from Healthworks. She went to her desk and dialed Franny Hollander's number. This was the second time she had tried. That morning, Marie had dialed half a dozen Hollanders before finding the right one and then she had been told rather abruptly by the woman who answered that Franny was out. The phone was ringing for the third time. The fourth. One more and she would hang up. It was foolish to be calling Franny anyhow. Probably bad for her health, just like David had said. And he didn't even know about her blood pressure. She wasn't even sure what she was going to say. Did she really expect a lucid conversation about anything? The woman was obviously out of her mind, poor thing. Why did so many crazy people quote the Bible? The phone was ringing for the sixth time. One more ring and she would hang up.

"Hollander residence."

"Oh. Hello. Mrs. Hollander, please."

"Didn't you call before?"

"Yes. This is Mrs. Preston."

"She's out."

Marie heard a whining sound in the background.

"When will she be back?"

"I can't say."

"Well, would you take a message for her, please?"

The whining sound had gotten louder. It was the cry of a baby. Marie felt an electric sensation shoot to the tips of her breasts.

"It wouldn't do any good. Mrs. Hollander won't be coming back."

"What do you mean?" Marie asked.

But the phone had already clicked off.

Marie rummaged in her top drawer for a cigarette. None there, of course. She walked to her secretary's desk, picked one from her pack of Parliaments, and lit it. The smoke caught in her throat and she immediately began to sputter it out. She pushed the cigarette out in her secretary's ash tray and walked back to her desk. Who the hell gave that nursemaid the right to be so unpleasant anyway? And so secretive? Maybe she should call back and be more aggressive this time. More insistent. Marie started to reach for her phone. Her hand was trembling. She pulled it back and held it tightly in her other hand. Get ahold of yourself, lady! Are you the same person who called Malcolm Hamilton at home last year and told him that if he continued to allow *About Town* to be turned into the *National Enquirer,* he could start looking for another vice-president in charge of development? And now we're afraid of nursemaids? Again, she reached for the phone and started to dial. She hung up before she had finished.

It wasn't the nursemaid she was afraid of.

She picked up the phone and dialed David's number.

"David Preston."

"Hello, David."

"Honey, I'm just starting a session."

"This will only take a second. I wanted to know if you'd looked up Richard Monroe for me yet."

"No. Not yet."

"Would you do it for me now?"

"Marie, can't this wait?"

"For crissake, David, it'll only take a second. Tell your patient that your wife's in labor and she wants you to look up the name of a good gynecologist quick."

Marie heard David sigh.

"Hold the line," he said.

Marie kept the phone pressed against her ear. Her secretary walked in and deposited Marie's lunch and change on her desk. Marie mouthed a "thank you" to her and she left.

"Three Monroes," David was saying. "One James Q.; one John N. and an Amelia. No Richards."

"Are you sure?"

"I've got the book open in front of me."

"What year was it published?"

"Last year. Marie, what the hell is going on?"

"Nothing, David. Thanks. Sorry to keep you."

"Marie?"

"Yes."

"Marie, I'm worried about you. You seem, I don't know, sort of jumpy . . . and closed, lately. Is anything wrong?"

"Of course not." Marie managed a light laugh. "Well, nothing serious. Maybe a little hormone imbalance. Don't worry about me, honey."

"Okay. See you later. Love you."

"Love you. Bye."

Marie stood up immediately. She felt a little dizzy and leaned for a second against her desk. Hormone imbalance, indeed. She picked the bag containing her lunch off of her desk, grabbed her coat and scarf from the hanger behind the door, and marched out of her office. As she passed in front of her secretary's desk, she waved the bag with her lunch in it and said, "Something's come up. I'll be back in a half hour."

She walked directly to the Forty-second Street Library, taking the long front steps two at a time. Inside, she rode the elevator to the third floor and strode rapidly down the hallway to Room 315, the medical section, her old haunt. The same bespectacled black woman was behind the desk and she smiled at Marie when she walked in.

"Hello," the woman said. "How are you today?" She was looking at Marie's belly. Did she remember the cartloads of books she used to drag out for Marie on infertility?

"Fine. And yourself?"

"Just fine. What can I do for you?"

"Do you have the GYN Directory?"

"Yes, we do. All physician directories are on the third shelf, top two rows."

"Thanks."

Marie walked over to the shelf and took the directory down. It was heavy. She cradled it in both arms and set it down on a reading table, then sat and pulled on the little lamp. A book full of gynecologists. Thousands of them. What had Marshall McLuhan called them—spinners of old wives tails? She pulled the book open to the M's. Ma. Mi. Mo. Monroe, Amelia, St. Louis. Monroe, James Q., Los Angeles. Monroe, John N., Toledo. No "R's." No Richards. And that was the name the computer had spit back, she was sure. She had double-checked with Kate that morning. Marie closed the book to the title page. It was current, this year's. She walked over to the reference desk.

"Do you keep those directories for past years?"

The black woman smiled. "We keep everything. It's just a question of finding them. How far back were you thinking of?"

"Well." Marie calculated quickly in her mind. "If it wouldn't be too much trouble, I'd like them all for the past seven years."

The woman raised her eyebrows. "I'd better take a cart for that," she said, rising. "This may take a little time." She disappeared out the door, pushing a book cart in front of her.

While she waited, Marie scoffed down her spinach and tuna salad with a carton of milk, then wandered over to the reference shelf and pulled out the Layman's Medical Encyclopedia. She carried it to her reading table and opened it to the index. "Hypertension in pregnancy: see Toxemia, p. 1337." She flipped through the pages. "Toxemia, a serious pregnancy disorder . . . Detected by rise in blood pressure and presence of albumin in urine . . . Can develop rapidly at any time and may be accompanied by headaches, blurred vision, sudden weight gain, puffiness of face and hands, dizziness . . . Evidence that anxiety or emotional upset may trigger its onset . . . If even one of the symptoms is present, salt intake must be reduced or eliminated . . . Drug treatment available before it causes permanent damage to mother and child."

Oh, dear God! Marie slammed the book closed and stood up. Permanent damage. Oh, God, please, no. She felt her knees shaking under her. And then the dizziness. Again, the dizziness! She sat down quickly and put her head on the table.

"Sorry I took so long. One of the boys had to help me lift them." The librarian had wheeled a cart full of GYN Directories next to Marie's table. "Madame? Are you feeling all right?"

Marie lifted her head.

"Yes. Fine." She looked at the cart. "Sorry to put you to so much trouble."

"That's what I'm here for," the woman said and returned to her desk.

Marie looked at the row of tomes next to her. What in God's name was she doing this for? McPartland was right, she was looking for things to worry about. Making things up. A nervous, middle-aged pregnant woman. She wasn't doing herself any good this way. Or the baby. Permanent damage, it said. What did that mean? Had they found albumin in her urine or hadn't they? Wouldn't they have called if they had? She had better call McPartland's office herself to make sure as soon as she got back to her desk. Marie started to pull on her coat. The librarian was staring at her perplexedly through her glasses. Christ, she couldn't make that woman lug all those books for her and then just leave. Marie pretended she was only fitting her coat over her shoulders and lifted the first directory off of the cart. She would just rummage through a few of them and then thank the woman profusely before going.

Without thinking, Marie opened the book to the M's. She ran her eyes down the page without really reading it. It was a page full of "Mc's." McAllister . . . McHenry . . . McPearson . . . Marie sat very still, focusing all her attention on the page in front of her . . . McNichol . . . McNulty . . . McNulty . . . McPadden . . . McPearson . . . She leaned forward, pushing the book closer to the light, and looked again. No McPartlands. Raymond McPartland wasn't listed.

She immediately flipped to the title page. It was from seven years ago. She had taken the last book first. She flipped back to the M's . . . Mo . . . "Monroe, Richard L., Springfield, Massachusetts, Harvard Medical School, Massachusetts General Hospital, general OB/GYN."

Now Marie stood and pulled the directory from six years ago off of the cart and turned to the M's. Monroe was listed, McPartland wasn't. She grabbed the directory from a year later. McPartland was listed, Monroe wasn't. Six years ago. The year Kate said McPartland had split up his partnership with Monroe.

Marie sat down in front of the table full of open books.

There had been no partnership.

McPartland had changed his name.

"COME ON, David. We aren't talking about Bernie Schwartz changing his name to Tony Curtis, for crissake. This man is a doctor, not a movie star. There's a special trust you expect with a doctor. You know that."

Tom Roundtree was pacing back and forth in front of the living room window in Marie and David's apartment. He and David had been going at it for almost an hour now and Tom's face was beginning to show the strain. Normally, Marie would have resented the men for dominating an argument, but this evening she was grateful to be able to sit on the sofa next to Bonnie and let them fight it out. She was afraid that if she started to talk, she would uncap the well of anxieties fomenting inside her. And she couldn't risk that. Her body couldn't risk it. Thank God for Tom. The angrier he got, the calmer she felt. And he was making every point she was thinking, rebutting every ridiculous apology David was making for McPartland with his good old midwestern moral outrage. At this particular moment, Marie would trade David's Harvard-bred even-mindedness for Tom's outrage without hesitation. Hell, she'd trade David for Tom altogether.

"Tom, let's be reasonable about this, shall we?" David was at the liquor table mixing himself a gimlet. "Can I get anything for anyone?" He smiled at Marie and Bonnie.

"No thanks," Bonnie said.

Marie looked away.

"People change their names all the time. That's a fact," David went on. "Look, I admit Tony Curtis was a silly example. It was a joke, really. But let me give you a serious example, okay? You're a big fan of Erik Erikson, right? We've talked about him. You put him right up there with White and Horney, correct? Well, hold onto your hat, Tom. When he came to this country, his name was Homburger."

"Oh, for godssake, I know that David. You don't have to go to Harvard to know that. But he changed his name in 1939. Isn't that reason enough? And anyway, now he makes no effort to hide it. And that's the point, damn it. McPartland does. He seems to have gone to great pains to hide the fact that he changed his name."

"Because he probably has his reasons, too, Tom! Just as Erikson did. Isn't the man entitled to that?"

"No!" Marie suddenly stood up. She couldn't hold it in any longer. "Not my doctor. Not while I'm pregnant. Not while Bonnie and I are under his care."

Tom walked in back of the couch and now rested his hands on Bonnie's shoulders.

"And that, David, is the real point," Tom said quietly. "Whatever McPartland's reasons are—a sloppy divorce, a crazy aunt, a glove compartment full of parking tickets—"

"Or worse," Marie said.

"Yes. Or worse," Tom continued. "Whatever his reasons are, we have to know what they are now. Before these two women get any more upset about it. It's either that or change doctors. And I, for one, would like to avoid that if possible."

David threw up his hands. "And the hell with the man's privacy?" he said.

"Yes, friend. The hell with his privacy," Tom said. "Look, I'll go see McPartland myself and ask him about it as discreetly as I can, okay? I won't even mention how I found out, Marie."

"It wouldn't bother me if you did," Marie said. It would. Right now she didn't know how she could ever see McPartland again.

"No," Tom said. "There's no use putting a strain on your relationship with him. I'll simply say it came to my attention, and I'd like to know why. Look, I'm the one who put you onto this doctor. I think it's my responsibility."

"Bravo," Marie said. She walked over to Tom and squeezed his arm. "You're a good man, Tom Roundtree. I can't tell you how much I appreciate this."

David set his drink down and walked toward the two of them, his head slightly bowed. "I guess I appreciate it too, Tom. Whatever I said. I mean, the whole thing still strikes me as a bit of an overreaction." He looked at Marie and smiled tentatively. "But then again, I'm not the one who's pregnant."

Marie didn't even pretend to hide her sneer. "And empathy never was your strong suit."

"Hey, come on, you two." Tom put an arm around Marie's shoulders and reached for David with his other hand. "We aren't leaving until you guys kiss and make up."

Marie slipped out from under Tom's arm. "I guess I'd better change the sheets in the guest room. You're going to be here a long time."

Bonnie stood up, smiling. "Let's go home, Tom." She turned to Marie. "He's impossible. A psychiatrist who can't stand to see people mad at each other."

"What's so strange about that?" Tom said, grinning.

At the door, Marie put her arms around Tom and hugged him tightly. "Thanks for everything, Tom. I feel better already."

"Good."

As soon as the Roundtrees had left, Marie walked

directly to the bathroom and closed the door behind her without saying a word to David.

Smug, that's what he was. And insensitive. Even if he were right and McPartland's reasons for changing his name were strictly personal, she wasn't ready to label her response to the whole business as an overreaction. That was just another of David's control-words. Like, "inappropriate." He could never just say that he didn't like what she was doing, that it embarrassed him or something. He had to say that it was inappropriate. As if it were a symptom of some kind of character disorder. Marie had taken off all of her clothes and now turned sideways to look at her profile in the full-length mirror behind the door. It wasn't just her breasts and belly that were changing. Her whole body looked different. Fuller. Pinker. More maternal. She put both her hands on her abdomen and stroked it with a circular motion.

"Watch out for your father, Doodles. He loves to be right."

Marie froze. The phone was ringing. Franny. She was sure it was Franny. She pulled on her robe and opened the door. The ringing had stopped. David must have picked it up. She strode across the bedroom and into the living room. David was speaking softly into the phone.

"Who is it, David?"

David said, "Thank you," into the phone and hung it up. He looked at Marie. "Gracie Square. I've got a patient there."

Marie stared at him, her mouth slightly open.

"You ought to put something else on, hon. You look cold."

Marie looked down at her hands. They were trembling. "David. Who was that on the phone?"

David stood up, frowning. "I just told you, honey. Gracie Square Hospital." He started walking toward her.

"Are you sure you're feeling all right, Marie? You don't look too good."

Marie took a step backward. "I feel fine, David."

David stopped walking. He looked into Marie's eyes for a moment before he spoke. "Babes, I think we'd better talk."

Marie said nothing.

"Really, Marie, I don't like the way we've been for the last few days and I think—"

The phone rang again. Neither of them moved. A second ring.

"Maybe you ought to take it," David said.

Marie looked at him. The phone was ringing a third time. She walked quickly to it and lifted the receiver. "Hello."

"Hello," a man's voice said. "Is Dr. Preston there, please?"

"Who—" Marie had to stop a second to clear her throat. "Who should I say is calling?"

"This is Dr. Grumbacher. At Gracie Square Hospital. I'm sorry to have to disturb him again so soon. This won't take a moment."

Instinctively, Marie covered the phone so that the caller could not hear the sob which was breaking from her throat, but her hands were shaking so violently that the phone dropped to the floor. David rushed over and put his arms around her, holding the back of her head gently in one hand.

"It's all right, baby. Everything's going to be all right."

"Oh, God . . . I'm sorry, David . . . Forgive me."

"Shhh . . . Don't talk now." David stroked her hair.

"But . . . but I'm sorry, David. I didn't believe you . . ."

"It's all right. Shh." David rocked her back and forth, like a child.

Marie suddenly pulled herself away from David, smiling embarrassedly. "The phone," she said. "Dr. Grumbacher."

David grinned at her, he leaned over and picked the phone up from the floor.

"Aaron? Are you still there? Sorry to keep you. What's the trouble?"

He listened for a second and then said, "Let's stick with the Thorazine for now, okay?"

Marie had gone to the couch and sat hugging her knees, rocking herself. David hung up the phone and turned to look at her. He smiled. "Hey, what do you say I make a pot of tea and some English muffins? We never did eat."

Marie smiled back at her husband. "That," she said, "is the best idea I've heard all night."

She followed David into the kitchen and silently watched him while he put up the water and separated the muffins. The crying had helped her immeasurably. She was feeling better than she had in a week.

Back in the living room, neither of them said anything until each had eaten two muffins apiece along with most of a tin of smoked oysters. Then Marie poured them both a second cup of tea and looked at David seriously. "David, I hope you can forgive me for before. I . . . I was sure that was someone else calling."

"Franny Hollander?"

"Yes."

David set his cup down. "I guess I ought to apologize too," he said. "About the line I took on this name-changing business. Mostly, I just didn't want you to get any more upset than you were already." He reached across the coffee table and took her hand in his. "I've been worried about you, babes."

Marie felt tears again gather in her eyes. "Oh, shit, here we go again," she said, trying to smile.

"What's the matter, honey?"

Marie swallowed hard, holding back the new tears, and she told him. She told him about her encounter with Lowenstein at Saks, about her sympathy for Franny and her concern for her after that horrible conversation with the nursemaid, and finally, although she was hoping she could leave it out, she told David about her blood pressure and what she had read about toxemia in the library.

David sat quietly while she talked, nodding almost imperceptibly as one story ran into another. When she finished, he stood and walked to the window and looked down onto the park for a moment, then turned and looked at her warmly.

"Honey, first I want to tell you that I really love you very, very much."

"I love you, too, David." Marie smiled up at him. "I'm almost afraid to ask what's second."

David laughed.

"Second," he said. "I'm really sorry that I'm a psychiatrist. But I can't help it." He shrugged. "I mean, my daddy spent all that money on me and here I am."

Marie tried to hold her smile, but it had already begun to feel stiff and awkward. "Go ahead," she said.

Again, David looked out of the window for a moment and then turned back, his lips pressed tightly together.

"Sometimes, a particular emotional set latches on to a special combination of circumstances and certain symptoms are elicited that normally wouldn't—"

"Oh, David, no double-talk tonight. Please." Marie sat back in the sofa. "Just give it to me straight, whatever it is. I'm sure I can take it."

David smiled. He sat down across from her. "Let me try again," he said, leaning toward her. "All I'm trying to say is that you've been through a lot these past few years. The whole infertility business. The operation. All the changes going on in your system every day now. Any one of those things could make the strongest person a little shaky."

Marie closed her eyes for a second. She didn't really want to hear anymore. "And?"

"And." David sighed. "And I think it's made you susceptible to things that normally wouldn't get to you."

"Like?"

"Like Franny Hollander, Marie. She's obviously suffering from some kind of persecution delusions and—"

"And you think I'm catching it from her. Like a cold." Marie had pulled her legs up in front of her and wrapped her arms around them.

"Something like that, yes."

Marie rested her head against her knees and again closed her eyes. He was right, of course. She'd been feeling a little persecuted by everybody lately, even Murray Miller, for godssake. And it had begun with Franny.

"I'm going to ask our service to screen our calls for a while," David was saying. "I mean, if that's all right with you, hon. Right now, I don't think talking with Franny is a particularly good idea for you. Or for her either, for that matter."

David walked around the coffee table and sat down beside Marie, putting his arm around her shoulders.

"And I'll bet you've got nothing to worry about with your blood pressure either. Dr. McPartland would have called if he'd found any signs of toxemia in your urine."

Marie kept her eyes closed as David brushed his lips against her cheek. If it were possible, she would spend the six months until the baby came curled up like this with David's arms around her. No sounds. No worries. Nothing.

"Our own family," David murmured. "Our own happy little family."

PAUL PLACED slide O-671-KA into the jar of trypsin and pulled the arm of the timer to two minutes.

Ochre light was glazing the laboratory window. He walked over and looked up the East River to where the Triboro Bridge glistened in the early morning light, golden. New York looked its best from heights, from distances. Geometric. Sculptural. A stone garden.

In the jar, the trypsin was eating the protein from the chromosomes on the slide, digesting the husks which encapsuled each strand of DNA. A microscopic etching.

The timer rang and Paul walked back to his bench, lifted the slide out with his forefinger and thumb, shook it twice, and then immersed it in a jar of distilled water. He let go of the slide for a moment. No hurry. He had been at it for over ten straight hours now. Alone. Methodical. Trying not to think the obvious thoughts until he was absolutely finished. No conclusions until all fifty cells were Q-Banded and tallied. He pulled the slide from the water, shook it again, then immersed it in the quinacrine fluorescent stain. The sunlight streaming in the window made the jar of quinacrine glow under his hands. Once, he had brought his father over to the Elmwood Labs to show him what he did for a living. He had taken him through every step of the process, the culturing, harvest, hypotonization, fixation, dropping and finally, the band staining of the chromosomes. His father had walked beside him, clasping and unclasping his hands behind his back, not saying a word until just before they left and then the big man had taken Paul by the shoulders and said quite solemnly, "You don't see such wonderful colors in the mines, that's for sure."

Now Paul removed the slide from the quinacrine, rinsed it in the phosphate buffer and, holding it by its edges, directed the blower across its surface. Once, twice. A third sweep for luck. What kind of luck did he want? Proof positive? What kind of work was it anyhow where success was measured in anomalies, where you shouted, Eureka, when you discovered a disease?

He slipped his clipboard under his arm and walked to the far end of the laboratory. There, he opened the door to a room no bigger than a closet—it had, in fact, been a supply closet only three years ago—and sat down in front of the fluorescence microscope. He clipped the slide under the lens, snapped on the ultraviolet light and pushed the door closed behind him with his elbow. Wonderful colors. Such wonderful colors. He placed his eyes against the eyepieces, focused, looked at the circle of glowing lavender light. It was a good spread. No chromosomes were overlapped. All paired, like inchworms at a square dance. He scanned them quickly for the largest, number one. Counted the bands, examined the structure. Good, of course. Number two, the same. No hurry. No jumping ahead. Methodical. Methodical. Number three, number four, number five. All normal.

Number six.

And it was there again. That pinpoint of light shining through like a star in a microscopic sky. Beautiful. Wonderful. And wrong.

Paul turned on the overhead light and snapped off the microscope. Next to slide O-671-KA on the Karyotype Tally in his clipboard, he wrote "band fifteen" under "Location," "excellent" under "Quality of Cell," "Six" under "Number of Abnormal Chromosome." He paused a second when he came to the column labeled, "Description of Abnormalities." For the forty-nine cells above it, he had written, "possible breakage." Now he wrote those words again, paused another second, and added, "Radiation damage?"

He removed the slide from the microscope, turned off the light, and walked back across the laboratory to his desk. There, he placed slide O-671-KA into a case, closed it, fastened the latches. Then he removed the tally sheet from his clipboard and placed it in the folder labeled "Fetus, Margo Whiting."

In the hallway outside his laboratory, the others were arriving now, carrying their styrofoam cups of coffee and little sacks of hard rolls and donuts. The genetic troops gathered from all over the world—Rumania, Italy, Pakistan, Sweden. Good morning, good morning, good morning.

Paul placed the Whiting file in the corner of his desk, on top of the Roundtree file, and opened his top drawer. He removed two "Parental Genetic Analysis Request" forms and quickly filled them out. Then he ripped a memo sheet from the pad next to him. On it, he wrote, "Attention: Fine, Bernstein, Persson, et al. Urgent. Blood samples for genetic analysis of the Whiting and Roundtree parents should be scheduled immediately. Both show identical anomalies on number 15 band of chromosome number 6. Repeat: the anomalies are identical. N.B.: both patients are under the care of the same doctor, Raymond McPartland, M.D., OB/GYN."

He clipped the memo to the top of the request forms, folded them length-wise and slipped them into the pocket of his coat. He stood. Fine wouldn't be in for another half hour. Time enough for breakfast.

17

"LOOK, MARIE. She's waving at you."

Marie squinted at the ultrasound screen above her head. Hard as she tried, she still could not make sense out of what she saw there, could not isolate the image the others said they saw. It reminded her of when her father used to take her and her sister for Sunday walks and he would point up at a cloud and say, "Look, two buffalos carrying an umbrella," or some such. Her sister would immediately see it too, or at least she'd say she did. But Marie never once saw the buffalos or the tigers or the unicorns. Too literal minded, she supposed. No imagination.

She smiled to herself. Oh, she had imagination, all right. Too much, in fact. How many fantastic reasons for McPartland's name change had she conjured up before Tom came back with the all too prosaic truth: that the doctor had a bitter ex-wife with a penchant for taking out extravagant loans in his name. McPartland had told Tom how sorry he was to have caused him any worry and how much he appreciated his coming to him right away. He had even told Tom that he had originally considered advising his patients of his name change so that no one would have to be unduly concerned if it simply turned up, as it had with Tom. But, McPartland had told him, that had seemed as if it would just create confusion.

When Tom had reported his conversation with McPartland to David and Marie, she had felt perfectly ridiculous and told them so. "Hormones," she kept telling them, giggling nervously. "Blame it on my hormones." David had been good about it. No I-told-you-sos. He had even said that he was a bit relieved to hear what the name change was all about, although it was more or less what he had guessed.

Facing McPartland again was another thing. Marie was certain that McPartland knew where Tom had come up with his information and she had been debating with herself all weekend whether to say anything to him about it. But how do you apologize for having bad thoughts about someone?

When Marie and David had been ushered into the ultrasound room at Hebron this morning, she had felt herself blush when she first saw McPartland. Yet, if anything, the doctor had seemed warmer than usual. Friendlier. "Hello, Marie," he had said, taking her hand. "You're looking very well today." He had immediately taken her blood pressure and when the mercury had bounced at one thirty, he had smiled broadly and said, "Very good. I see you're taking my advice." Their eyes had met then and Marie was positive that he knew, that he didn't hold it against her, that everything was just fine. She had smiled back at him. Thank you, Doctor. Thank you very much indeed.

McPartland was now running his finger across Marie's greased abdomen, eyeing the ultrasound screen, seeking a window where he could insert the needle for the amniotic tap. And Marie was still studying the screen, desperately trying to decipher the squirming shadows before they turned off the machine and began the tap.

And then it clicked. Like one of those pictures where two profiles suddenly become a vase, the image snapped into place in Marie's optic cortex. She saw the flailing arms and legs, the spine, the bulbous head, and wide-set eyes. The fluttering heart.

"Oh, my God! Doodles! It's Doodles!"

Tears flooded Marie's eyes. She reached her hand out blindly and David took it in both of his, pressing it tightly.

"Our baby, David. Our baby."

With her free hand, Marie quickly wiped the tears from her eyes. She stared, spellbound, at the picture of the child living inside of her.

"She's a beauty, all right," McPartland was saying above her. "Let's get a Polaroid of her, Miss Bailey. You can have your first baby picture, Marie."

"Oh, God. I love her already, David," Marie said.

"I know. I do too," David said, quietly.

A minute later, McPartland had inserted the long needle in through her abdominal wall and uterus into her amniotic sac and begun to withdraw the clear, champagne-colored fluid which contained sluffed-off cells of the unborn infant. Each cell with a complete genetic message. Each cell telling the entire genetic biography, from birth to death, of that person-to-be.

Marie had closed her eyes when she first saw the needle go in. She wanted to hold the image from the screen in her mind's eye. The little hands with budding fingers. The tiny mouth. The heart. Her baby. Her baby.

When the tap was finished and the nurse had scrubbed her belly clean and Marie was up, off the table, buttoning her skirt, McPartland handed her the Polaroid photo taken from the ultrasound image. Marie immediately placed it in her handbag without looking at it. She wanted to save it for later, for when David and she were alone. She thanked McPartland and she and David left the room, their arms around one another's waists. They walked to the elevator without saying a word. Never had Marie loved David so much. Family. They were really a family now.

The elevator doors opened and a tall, tossel-haired man in a white medical coat stepped out. He smiled awkwardly at Marie and David before walking away down the corridor. He looked like an unhappy man to Marie, and at this moment she wished that everyone could be as happy as she was.

But, at this moment, Paul Kingsmill had very little to be happy about.

PART 3

CULTURING PROCEEDED on schedule. After the fetal cells were separated out of the amniotic fluid in the centrifuge, they were dropped with a pipette into a flat-sided flask along with a medium of glutamine and fetal calf serum. A day later, they were again fed the medium. And a day after that, they received their first bubbles of carbondioxide. By the fourth day, the pellets had attached themselves to the bottom of the flask. By the fifth, mitosis had begun. And six days after the amniotic fluid had been withdrawn from Marie Preston's womb, the first fetal cell reproduced itself in culture. A perfect clone.

"WHAT IN the name of God do you mean this McPartland man refuses? Don't you have any say in this? Don't his patients, for godssake?"

Paul paced back and forth in front of Samuel Fine's desk, rubbing the side of his face.

"Paul, would you sit down, please? I want to explain this to you so you understand it properly." Fine's tone was patient in the extreme, almost fatherly. He gestured to the chair across from him.

Paul took the seat reluctantly. An explanation, of course. At this point in his life, he should be an expert on administrative explanations. Heaven knows, he had seven years of them from Sir Edmund. And yet, Paul knew even before Fine took his pipe from his lips that he wouldn't understand a word the department head would say, that Fine's explanation would seem like just so much smoke.

Fine tapped his pipe in a cork-lined ash tray. "Here at Hebron," he began, "here at Hebron, we serve two distinct functions, a clinical function and a research function. And it's important, as much as possible, to keep these two functions separate and discreet. Now—"

Smoke. Fine came from the same school of administrative jabberwocky as Sir Edmund. No doubt, that's how both these distinguished white-haired gentlemen became

the heads of prestigious departments—they knew the dialec-
tics of smoke. With it, they chaired conferences, determined
which papers were published in the most influential journals
and, most importantly, garnered the grants which kept their
departments affluent. Fine probably hadn't spent more than
ten consecutive minutes in front of one of his well-endowed
laboratory benches in the past twenty years.

"Now, the genetic analyses we do on the amnios someone like Dr. McPartland sends up here are strictly clinical,
Paul. It's a clinical service we perform as part of this hospital. And in that capacity, we have no more discretion of
what to do with them than if he sent his amnios out to some
commercial lab in Brooklyn." Fine sucked on his pipe for a
moment, undoubtedly musing on how far he had come from
Brooklyn himself. He leaned across his desk and looked at
Paul, raising one eyebrow. "Paul, we can't expect a private
Park Avenue gynecologist to subsidize our research."

"Sam, this isn't research—we've got two live fetuses
with identical chromosomal anomalies coming from the
same doctor. If that isn't a clinical problem, I don't know
what in the name of God is."

Fine opened his mouth, emitting a large cloud of blue
smoke. "Now listen, Paul," he said. "I think the key word
here is anomaly. What you insist on calling an anomaly only
looks to us like an unusual marker, an unusually bright
marker. Not breakage. As you yourself pointed out, there's
nothing that looks quite like it in the literature. So, what
we've really got here is just some kind of hunch about radiation or whatever. And as a good, imaginative scientist, you'd
like to follow up your hunch with some research, right?"

The smoke had found its way into Paul's brain and for
the moment he was having trouble trying to figure out what
Fine was getting at.

"Sam, you know as well as I do that there's a very simple clinical procedure to find out whether this is an anomaly
or just some quirky family thing. We take blood samples

from the parents, these Whiting and Roundtree people, and we do a genetic work-up on them. See if these markers run in their families. Simple as that. That's all I'm asking for. Not a research grant. Just a standard clinical procedure."

Fine smiled, shrugging his shoulders. "Paul, I think you've been away from the wards too long. You're not thinking about this from the human side. Dr. McPartland doesn't want to alarm his patients because of some hunch you have. Think about that a moment."

"Alarm his patients?" Paul was on his feet before he could think about it. "For godssake, you'd think this McPartland would be begging us to check this out before he has a nursery-full of birth defects to answer for. Good Lord, isn't he at least worried about getting saddled with one of your famous American malpractice suits?"

Fine laughed softly. "And I thought you English were all stiff upper lip." He smiled at Paul. "Actually, I've heard you were a little on the excitable side. Do sit down, Paul. You're making me nervous."

Paul sat down. The bad boy again, the forty-two-year-old bad boy. Fine had probably heard a story or two about him from Sir Edmund. Not to mention what he'd heard from the critics Paul was steadily collecting right here at Hebron. Bouchard had surely dropped a few disparaging words on his behalf. Miss Saint Ambrosio too. Five months in the United States and he was already the bad boy.

"Now listen, Paul," Fine said. "I know Raymond McPartland. He's a well-respected doctor. And he's a reasonable man. If I could bring him a report and point at it and say, look, we've got a clear case of chromosomal breakage on our hands, he'd be more than willing to help us follow through. But until that time, I can't blame him for wanting to protect his patients."

Paul's jaw went slack. There it was again, the Sailor's Knot. His father had told him about it when he was just a boy: You can't join the merchant marines without seaman's papers, and you can't get seaman's papers without experience in the merchant marines. The Sailor's Knot right up here in the Ivory Tower. Paul slowly rose to his feet. He couldn't go around another time with Fine. He was too tired. His brain too full of smoke. He nodded to Fine and started for the door.

"By the way, Paul, how's the project coming along?"

Paul turned and looked at Fine. The project, of course. The research papers, the grants. Maybe a prize in the department.

"Super," Paul said. "Just super."

He let himself out of Fine's office and started down the corridor. His throat felt tight and sore. He needed some air, some cold New York air.

"Well, well, if it isn't St. Sebastian the Martyr?" Bernstein had lifted his head from the corridor water fountain and was smiling at Paul. "Or is it St. Paul the Naïve?"

Paul stared at Bernstein a moment and then continued walking.

"You still don't get it, do you?" Bernstein called.

Paul stopped and turned slowly. Bernstein was grinning at him, shaking his head back and forth.

"Paul, when these East Side ladies fuck around, nobody tells on them. Especially not their Park Avenue docs." Bernstein laughed.

Paul felt his face flush. So that's what it was all about. That's what Fine and McPartland were afraid of. That the identical markers meant Mrs. Whiting and Mrs. Roundtree had the same lover and a work-up of their husbands would give them away. A fate worse than . . . what? Birth defects?

Paul turned away quickly, Bernstein's laughter still echoing on the tile walls behind him. He'd just get his coat and go outside. He needed to be alone. To think. To breathe. He opened the door to his laboratory.

"No luck, huh?"

Paul looked up. Eva was seated on the edge of his desk and she was looking up at him sympathetically.

"No."

Eva walked over to him and put her arms around his neck.

"What do you say to a long soothing lunch at your place?" she said.

20

"COME ON, Ham, I'm no Polly Rudert."

Malcolm Hamilton set his teacup down on the coffee table in his deskless penthouse office and gave Marie a bemused grin. "And who, may I ask, is Polly Rudert?"

"She was in sixth grade with me. She always sat in the back of the class and never said a word. We all felt sorry for her until we discovered that every day after school she gave the teacher a detailed report on who'd been passing notes and who'd been whispering and who had comics behind their books."

Hamilton laughed. "I wonder where Polly is today? Highly placed somewhere in Washington, no doubt." He leaned forward and filled both their cups from the Limoges teapot. "Listen, Marie, far be it from me to ask for any scuttlebutt on Miller. But you could give me a little perspective on the man, couldn't you? I'm afraid I'm sometimes a bit out of touch up here."

Marie took a sip of tea. What a lovely opportunity this was, really. In a less contented mood, she might have given Hamilton a succinct acerbic analysis of Murray Miller that would have left the man's character in tatters. But just now it seemed out of keeping with the day, with the generous view from the top of the Hamilton Building.

"Dear me, aren't we the soul of discretion. I can't say

that's a virtue Mr. Miller shares with you." Hamilton gave
Marie a sly, eyebrow-arching smile. "He's more of the Polly
Rudert school."

Marie smiled back. So that was the game. Miller had
been bad-mouthing her to Hamilton and now good old Ham
was giving her equal rebuttal time. How far we'd all come
from sixth grade.

"Let me put it this way, Marie," Hamilton went on. "Is
there any one thing you can think of that might prevent
Miller from performing his job adequately?"

"Yes. Just one," Marie said, setting down her cup.
"Considering that our magazines have an eighty percent female readership, it does seem a little inappropriate to have
them managed by a man who doesn't like women."

Hamilton put his hand to his mouth as he chortled, as
if he were covering a yawn. "That's the old Marie I remember. Who says you've gotten all soft and reticent with
maternity?"

"Who, indeed?"

On the way back down to the twentieth floor in Hamilton's private elevator, Marie commended herself for not
stooping to ask what Miller had said about her. Not that it
was hard to imagine. That she was distracted. Emotional.
Uncritical. And worst of all, obviously much too happy
about being pregnant. She smiled to herself as she got off
the elevator and started down the hallway for her office.

"There's a woman who's been holding five minutes on
line two," Marie's secretary said as Marie walked past her
desk. "She says she's an old friend of yours. Wouldn't give
me her name."

"Thanks, Nance. I'll take it inside."

Marie sat down at her desk and popped a mint drop
into her mouth. Heartburn. Doodles was doing cartwheels
against her stomach again. She punched the second button
on her phone and lifted the receiver.

"Hello," Marie said.

"Hi. Is that you Marie?"

Marie bit down hard on the mint. Jesus, she hadn't expected this.

"Franny?"

"Yes. How are you, Marie? I've been thinking about you. Gee, you must be in your fourth month by now."

Franny's voice sounded calm, almost girlish. And chummy. Marie sat straight up in her chair. There was no need to get upset. That was all behind her. But there was no need to be unfriendly either.

"I'm great, Franny. We're both terrific. The baby and me, I mean. How are you? You sound good."

"Oh, I'm great too. Never felt better." Franny laughed. "Although you'll never get them to believe it."

Marie swallowed the mint. Don't rise to the bait, girl. Don't ask questions. Just let it pass you by.

"I'm glad to hear that, Franny," Marie said. "Glad that you're feeling so well."

"I'm a prisoner," Franny said in a flat voice.

Marie held the receiver away from her ear. She was feeling remarkably calm. And why not? Everything was fine. Completely in control. She could very easily hang up the phone right now. Hang it up and forget all about this crazy woman. It wasn't a question of being heartless or not. That didn't apply. Not in the case of crazy people. Not in the case of crazy people who were virtual strangers. Not when you had your baby to think about. Not when everything had been going smoothly for weeks. Marie brought the phone back to her ear.

"Franny, I'm going to have to ask you not to call here again. I'm sorry, but I'm very busy. And there's really nothing I can do for you. All right? Do you understand?"

"Oh, I understand," Franny said.

Marie could hear the hurt in Franny's voice. She bit her lower lip.

"But I'm not sure that you do," Franny went on, her

voice now quite strong-sounding. "It's too easy to dismiss me as just some postpartum crazy lady, Marie. Much too easy. And you know it. Look, I'm shaky. Damned shaky. And even I know that I have lapses. Times when I'm too upset to think clearly. Or talk clearly. But you would, too, Marie. I mean, that's really the whole point, isn't it? It could happen to you."

Marie closed her eyes. Now was the time to hang up, of course. Right now. Just put the phone down. Quickly hit the button and put the phone down.

"I'm afraid I have to go now," Marie said. "I've got people waiting. Take care of yourself, Franny, okay?"

"I'm going to die in here, Marie," Franny said in a monotone.

"Where? Where are you Franny? What are you talking about?" The words came out without her thinking. Her voice was high, squeaky, barely her own.

Franny didn't answer.

"Franny?"

Marie heard another voice, indistinct, distant. She pressed the phone against her ear. The other voice was saying, "What are you doing here, Franny? You know you shouldn't be here."

Then Marie heard Franny again. Her voice sounded childlike, frightened. Whining.

"My sister," Franny was saying. "I had to talk to my sister. Please. I want to see my sister."

"Hello?" It was the other voice on the phone now. A cool, professional woman's voice.

Marie cleared her throat.

"Hello," Marie said. "This is Marie Preston." She paused a moment. "Mrs. Hollander's sister."

"Hello, Mrs. Preston," the woman said. "I'm sorry, but your sister shouldn't be using the phone now. This is her activities period."

"I know," Marie said. Her voice was back to normal

now. More than normal. She sounded sensible, almost matronly to herself. "It's really my fault. I . . . I've been away. And I haven't been able to see Franny. I really feel terrible about it. Can you tell me when visiting hours are?"

"Twelve to two. And six to eight. All day Sundays," the woman said automatically.

"And let me get the exact address there. I've mislaid my—"

"One hundred Liberty Avenue," the woman said. She was sounding impatient.

"In White Plains," Marie said, trying to sound matter-of-fact.

"Riverdale," the woman said coldly.

"Of course, Riverdale. Thank you."

But the woman had already hung up.

Marie set the phone down in its cradle, turned in her chair, and looked through her side window down onto Fifth Avenue. The end of April and it still looked like winter out there. Not even winter. Gray, seasonless. The baby was due in October. Spring, summer, fall and there we are. Marie closed her eyes. Nothing was shaking. No racing heartbeat. Nothing. It was as if it had been a wrong number. A crossed wire. It didn't really have anything to do with her. She pressed the button on her inter-com.

"Nance," she said to her secretary. "Any calls? I've been tied up."

"No," her secretary said.

"Uh, when's that Hepperman meeting?"

"Three."

"Right."

"Are you eating in? I'm going to the deli. I could bring you something."

Marie looked down again onto the Avenue. Some sunlight was glinting on the mica in the sidewalks.

"Thanks. I might go out," she said.

Marie released the inter-com button, then picked a pile

of letters from her "In" box and set them in front of her. An invitation to a women executives' conference in Des Moines. She could pass that up, although it might be fun to tell Murray Miller stories to some colleagues. Malcolm's favorite reader's-letter-of-the-week: a lady from Saddle Brook, New Jersey, who thinks *About Town*'s cover story on ethnic foods was a calculated slight on Armenian-Americans. An inquiry from the Harvard-Radcliffe Career Placement Office. An outfit with a new back-issue storage system.

Marie pushed the letters to the back of her desk. She sat quite still for a moment, then suddenly stood, took her coat and scarf from the back of her door, and walked out of her office. Ten minutes later she was sitting in a taxi on the Henry Hudson Parkway on her way to One hundred Liberty Avenue in Riverdale.

"Hi, sis."

Marie's jaw dropped. She had been standing in the Visitor's Room of the mental illness wing of Tower Hospital for almost five minutes surveying the faces of the men and women in various-colored robes and paper, hospital-issue slippers. She had been astonished to see how young most of the patients were; all but a very few were younger than she. Yet none of them looked truly mad, not in the classical wild-eyed, twitching sense.

Except for Franny.

Franny was right in front of her now.

"It's me, sis," she said. She winked.

There was no way Marie could have picked Franny out of that room on her own. All that was left of the woman Marie had met a month ago in McPartland's office were the eyes. Black eyes. Now sunk into her emaciated head like coals. Her cheekbones stuck out in sharp ridges, brittle-looking, like chicken bones. And beneath them her gray cheeks caved inward, hollow gray holes. Even her lips were gray, bluish gray. And her hair, her real hair which Marie had only glimpsed for a moment when Franny's wig had tilted as she kissed McPartland's hand, now stuck out from her head in two-inch lengths, coarse, black and white, punklike.

"It's a great place for losing weight," Franny was saying, her smile stretching her skin so thinly across her cheeks that it looked like it could tear. "Lots cheaper than those California health spas."

Marie tried to smile back, but it was impossible. She felt dizzy.

"Can we sit down somewhere?"

Franny slipped her stalklike arm inside Marie's, and Marie couldn't help from shuddering. The woman looked like death. Her arm felt like death. She didn't want that arm near her baby. She took a step sideways, letting Franny's arm drop from hers. Immediately she felt guilty. She forced herself to smile at Franny.

"Why don't we go to your room so we can talk?" Marie said.

"Not allowed," Franny said. "We do everything in groups here. Togetherness. I already got one bad conduct mark today for sneaking off from jigsaw-puzzle hour to call you. There's a free couch over by that window. Great view of the terminal cancer wing."

They walked side-by-side to the green, vinyl couch and for a second, Marie imagined what the two of them looked like together: one four-months pregnant, pink, full-bodied, glowing; the other drained of all life. A study in contrasts. They sat down. It was right that she had come, Marie thought. It was the least that she could do for this poor woman. She looked warmly at Franny and Franny smiled back.

"It's really just a question of how badly you want a baby, isn't it?" Franny said, abruptly, still smiling.

Marie sat perfectly still. Her eyelids suddenly felt terribly heavy. That question. The same question Lowenstein had asked over three years ago. No, she shouldn't have

come here. A perverted impulse brought her. Self-destructive.

"I mean, how much you're willing to give up to have a
baby," Franny went on. Her tone was intense yet impersonal, like a college sophomore discussing some abstract
ethical puzzle.

Marie gazed at the mad, emaciated woman next to her.
What did she want with Marie? To drag her down into the
pit with her? Company in the abyss?

"I guess you made a mistake," Marie said, keeping her
voice even. "Not everyone should have babies."

Franny's laugh burst out of her like shattered glass.
Marie looked up. No one had even turned his head to see
where the manic laughter came from. Then, as suddenly as
it had come, the laughter stopped and Franny's expression
turned serious, mournful. She stared into Marie's eyes.

"I wanted that baby more than anything in the world,"
Franny said. "More than anything. For ten barren years
there was nothing else I wanted. Nothing else *we* wanted."

Marie had not taken her eyes away from Franny's. Mad
or not, the woman was speaking the truth.

"I took a vow that I'd give up anything for a baby,"
Franny said. Then her expression again changed instan-
taneously and she was grinning. "But I never thought I'd
have to give up this."

She was pointing her forefinger at her temple and making a little circular motion, a child's jeering sign of madness.

"I'm very sorry, Franny," Marie said. "I mean that."
She did. Postpartum psychosis must be Nature's cruelest
twist.

Franny's face brightened.

"What do you suppose they'd do with the Virgin Mary
in a place like this?" she said. Her black eyes glittered.

Marie put her hand to her forehead. She felt dizzy
again, weak. As soon as her head was clear she would excuse herself and leave. Maybe ask if there were anything

Franny needed—a book, some fruit—but she would leave. She had to. She had a meeting at three.

"Dr. McPartland told us to make love exactly ten days after the culdoscopy," Franny was now saying. The glitter had vanished from her eyes. She was deadly serious again. "I told Syd not to chance it. The McCullum account wasn't going to go anywhere. It would still be there in ten days, two weeks. You don't lose accounts you've had for twenty years by delaying a trip to Chicago for two weeks."

Marie wanted to get up now, to leave. Enough was enough.

She couldn't move.

"Syd said there was plenty of time. He'd be back in plenty of time. A two-day margin. He said he'd get off the plane with his pants off so we wouldn't lose a minute." Franny made a weak smile that creased her cheeks like a folded piece of paper. "He hadn't counted on the accident. It could have just as well happened in New York, I suppose. But it didn't. It happened in Chicago. The afternoon he was supposed to return. A crazy accident, really. Right in the hotel. In the shower. Third-degree burns. He was in Cook County Hospital for a month."

Marie looked over Franny's shoulder at a young man reading a book. She tried to concentrate on making out the title. Anything but listen to this crazy prattle.

"Syd was so happy," Franny went on. "He was so happy that he never once asked me how I got pregnant."

Marie suddenly looked at Franny and smiled. She felt wonderfully relieved. So that is what this confession was all about. An infidelity. A very timely infidelity. No wonder Franny had gone over the edge. What a terrible secret. But part of Marie couldn't blame her. Not completely. To lose your first chance in ten years because of some freak bathtub accident in Chicago. Women had been unfaithful for less pressing reasons than that. That was for sure. No, she couldn't completely blame Franny. Hadn't Marie, herself, once had fleeting fantasies of spending the night with some anonymous lover? Some anonymous lover with a high sperm count? Thank God those fantasies were only fleeting. Look what it did to you. Franny's eyes now looked glazed, vacant. Dead. Marie wondered if she had ever told her secret to anyone else.

"Don't be so hard on yourself, Franny," Marie said, reaching her hand out to touch Franny's arm. "Don't blame yourself so much. Your husband . . . your husband seems to understand."

Franny's mouth opened wide, as if to scream, but again the brittle, piercing laugh came.

"Understand what?" Franny leaned her face directly in front of Marie's. "What is there to understand?"

Marie pulled back instinctively. She reached for her pocketbook. Now was the time to go.

"I never slept with another man in my life. Not then. Not ever." Franny had raised her open right hand to alongside her head. "I swear to God."

Marie was on her feet.

"I have to leave now, Franny. I've stayed too long already. Is there anything I can get you?"

Franny stood up beside her, her hand still raised.

"I swear to God," she said.

"Yes. Yes, of course," Marie said. She couldn't make herself tell Franny that she believed her. Couldn't lie. That wouldn't be good for either of them. She started walking toward the door of the Visiting Room. Franny followed beside her, step for step.

"It's really a question of how badly you want a baby, isn't it?" Franny said.

Two young men in seersucker robes were standing in the doorway talking to one another intently.

"Pardon me, please," Marie said.

One of the young men smiled at her. Then he shoved his hand out in front of her.

"Tollgate," the young man said, grinning.

"Please let me by," Marie said. Her whole body was trembling.

Franny pantomimed pulling a coin from her robe pocket and deposited it in the young man's palm.

"Thanks, Franny," he said, stepping aside.

Franny winked at Marie. But Marie was looking up and down the hallway, trying to remember where the elevator was. She remembered and started striding quickly to her left, hoping that she would leave Franny behind her. She had to get out of here immediately. Before the dizziness started again. Before the blood pressure thing began again. She should have never come. It wasn't fair to the baby. To David. To herself.

Franny was right beside her.

"I mean, if you want a baby badly enough, you'll do anything. Deny anything. You won't even ask any questions."

Marie pressed the down button of the elevator. She wasn't even pretending to look at Franny anymore.

"Sydney never asked me any questions. And I never asked McPartland," Franny said. "Not until afterward."

Where the hell was the elevator?

Franny put her hand on Marie's arm.

"But the minute the baby is born, you can't deny anything anymore. The minute you see him, live and warm on your belly—"

The elevator door slid slowly open. Inside, a tall black man in a white medical coat stood beside a rolling stretcher that contained a gray-bearded old man. The old man looked dead. The black man held his hand out in a stop gesture.

"Next car," he said.

The door slid closed.

Marie pressed the down button again. Then, at the end of the hallway, she saw the fire stairway. She started for it immediately.

"I have to go now, Franny," she said. "I have to go right now."

"McPartland told me not to ask crazy questions," Franny called after Marie. "He told me he won't let me out of here until I stop asking crazy questions. I'm going to die in here!"

Marie put her hand on the knob of the stairway door and pulled. It was incredibly heavy.

"Do you think they'd put the Virgin Mary in a booby hatch?" Franny was coming up behind Marie. She was laughing again.

Marie tugged the door with both hands and it slowly swung open.

"But it's not McPartland you have to be afraid of, Marie," Franny said. "It's Monroe. Monroe's the one who gets you in the end."

Marie froze. She was leaning her whole body against the open door. She couldn't move. Monroe! She hadn't even thought of that name in a month. "He gives you the bad babies," Franny said. "Monroe gives you the bad, ugly babies."

Marie's head was spinning. She could feel her mind slipping and tumbling into the pit Franny was digging around her.

"You don't know what you're talking about, Franny," Marie said. "You're making things worse for yourself by imagining these things. They're the same. Monroe and McPartland are the same person."

"Why, of course they are." This time Franny's laugh was soft, throaty, sarcastic. "Let me guess which story he told you. The one about the ex-wife, right? Never mind that he's never been married. You don't have to be a genius to figure that out. You don't even have to have all your marbles."

Franny's manic grin swam in front of Marie's face. The dizziness was overtaking Marie. She was afraid that if she

moved she would topple over, bang her way down the flight
of stairs. She closed her eyes.

"Ask him again and he'll tell you you worry too much.
He'll tell you you have high blood pressure." Franny had
moved her face right next to Marie's and she whispered
directly into her ear. "Ask him a third time and he'll tell you
you're ungrateful." Again, the laugh. "That's when he puts
you in here."

Marie suddenly opened her eyes, ran to the stairway
and started down. One more minute and she would never
be able to leave here. She held tightly to the railing as she
raced down the concrete steps. At the turn, she swung herself around and continued on without a pause. Finally,
above her she heard the heavy door swing shut with a thud
and, at the next landing, she stopped a moment to catch her
breath.

And at that moment she heard Franny's wail echoing
off the tile walls.

"The question is," Franny screamed, "how badly do
you want a baby?"

As soon as they reached the Saw Mill River Parkway,
Marie rolled down the cab window and let the cold damp
air splash onto her face and whip her hair against her
cheeks. She saw the driver scowl in the rearview mirror and
then slide closed the glass partition which separated the
front of the cab from the rear. Never mind, the winter air
felt good, sobering. It was as if she were awakening from a
drugged sleep. From a nightmare which clung to her brain
with talons. That is all it was, a nightmare. The warped fantasies of a sad, sick mind.

Monroe's the one who gets you in the end.

Marie shook her head, trying to dislodge Franny's
voice. She gazed out of the taxi window. Above her, the
George Washington Bridge stretched gracefully west across

the Hudson River like a gigantic fan. She could make out two workmen in a suspended scaffold painting the cables a silver gray. When they finished the entire length of the bridge it would be time for them to start all over again at the far end. A Sisyphean labor. Did the repetition have a calming rhythm, like a mantra? Or one day high above the murky waters would the futility of it finally get to them?

Ask him again and he'll put you in here.

Marie sat forward in her seat, her mouth near to the thin slits in the partition.

"Driver, let's get off at the next exit, okay? I think I will go to that Park Avenue address."

The taxi driver yanked the wheel to the left and cut across two lanes of traffic to the Riverside Drive exit, slamming Marie back in her seat. She could feel her stomach lurch inside of her. Or was it her womb? Her baby? What had she put that poor baby through already today. She considered asking the driver to drive more slowly, but she knew his patience with her was already running low. She had changed her destination twice already.

The cab moved south along the Drive, past Presbyterian Hospital, Riverside Church, Grant's Tomb. She could change her mind again without losing any time. She could still make the Hepperman meeting easily. Again, she leaned forward in her seat.

Which story did he tell you? The one about his ex-wife?

Which story, indeed? How carefully had Tom questioned McPartland? Not very, she was sure. Who could presume to doubt the word of the good doctor? Marie sat back. Could she really put this off? If she ignored it, would it go away?

If you want a baby badly enough, you'll deny anything. You won't even ask any questions.

Which was worse for her health? For the baby? No

questions asked? If she just left it, wouldn't it gnaw away at her inside? Wasn't it better to know?

They were in the park now, circling under the bare-limbed plane trees which lined the drive.

To know what? Answers to questions raised by a scrambled mind? David would say that she was letting herself be sucked into Franny's delusionary system. That she was susceptible in her condition. But Franny did know something. Crazy or not, Franny knew something which Marie did not. Something about McPartland . . . Monroe . . . her baby.

"That's fifteen bucks even, lady."

Marie paid the driver and let herself out of the cab directly in front of McPartland's office. For a second, she remained motionless on the sidewalk, as if she were trying to remember where she was. Then she went to the door, opened it, and marched across the waiting room to Miss Gold's desk.

"Mrs. Preston. I didn't know we were expecting you today."

Miss Gold was staring up at her with an expression of cold, patronizing concern. And behind her, Marie heard the waiting room chatter diminish to a whisper. The way it had when Franny made her scene in here. Instinctively, Marie put her hand to her hair. It was sticking out from her head. Wild. Crazy looking.

"I . . . I . . ." Marie heard herself giggle nervously. "I left the window open and the wind—"

She could feel every woman in the waiting room staring at her. She patted her hair against her head.

"Are you feeling all right, Mrs. Preston? Perhaps you should sit down for a moment."

"No. No, I'm fine." Marie could feel the blood draining from her face. She did feel a little dizzy. She rested one hand on the corner of Miss Gold's desk.

"Well, what can we do for you, then?" Miss Gold asked, intoning the question as if she were addressing a child.

Marie gazed at Miss Gold, feeling very much as if she were indeed a child. What was she doing here? What in the name of God was she going to ask McPartland anyway? Had he been married? Did he have any proof? My God, her mind really was slipping.

"I . . . uh, I was just wondering if the results of my amniocentesis had come back," Marie said.

"Oh." Miss Gold smiled. "I don't believe so. Let me just look." She took a folder from the corner of her desk and thumbed through it. "I don't see it here. Would you like me to check with the doctor?"

"Uh, that won't be necessary. I just—"

"Let me just ask him." Miss Gold rose from her chair. "And maybe, if he has a spare moment, it would be a good idea if he saw you."

Miss Gold disappeared through the door behind her. In back of Marie, the chatter had resumed. She could hear the inevitable discussion about diapers. Another about breast feeding. A third about twins. She thought that perhaps she should sit down, joining one of these groups. And then when it was her turn to see McPartland she would explain to him that waiting for the results of her amniocentesis had been making her anxious. Maybe that was it, after all. Maybe that was what had made her so susceptible to Franny's paranoic blatherings. Marie started to turn around. And then, jutting out from under a pile of envelopes in Miss Gold's "Out" box, Marie saw the corner of a white business envelope. Above McPartland's return address was typed the name, Dr. R. Monroe.

Marie didn't move for a moment. From behind the door which led into the examination rooms, she could hear voices. And footsteps. She took one step sideways so that her back obscured the box from the others in the waiting

room. Then, quickly, deftly, she put her fingers on the envelope and slid it out from under the pile. It was addressed to
The Almquist School, Whitfield, Massachusetts.

Miss Gold pushed open the door and stepped back into
the waiting room where Marie was standing, the envelope
under her fingers. Marie froze. Then she suddenly spun
around, her sleeve knocking the box to the floor, and raced
to the street door and out.

Marie ran three full blocks before she stopped and
hailed a cab.

Monroe's the one who gets you in the end.

HAVE YOU HUGGED YOUR CHILD TODAY?

"No! Have you hugged your husband? How about your doorman?"

Marie eased her car into the left lane and began to overtake the Volvo with the nosy bumper sticker. As she pulled alongside of it, she turned and looked at the driver, a frizzy-haired woman wearing tinted aviator glasses.

"How about your hairdresser? Have you hugged him lately?" Marie said out loud. "How about your gynecologist?"

She pressed down on the accelerator and passed the Volvo, the speedometer on her Rabbit registering seventy. It was almost four o'clock now, an hour since she had picked up her car at the garage. Not much more than that since she had run out of McPartland's office. Tripped out, was more like it. Marie laughed. What a comedy that had been. Letters all over the place, Miss Gold's little mouth open in a perfect, comic strip "O," all those Sassoon-coifed East Side pregnant ladies atwitter. And the mad woman with the windswept hair tripping out the door.

HONK IF YOU LOVE JESUS!

Marie pressed her horn as she sped alongside a Comet station wagon. Again, she glanced sideways to see the occupants, a bearded young man and his long-haired companion. A crucifix dangled from their rearview mirror. They were smiling at her, knowing, beatific smiles.

"Not me," Marie mouthed. "I'm honking for a friend."

Between bumper stickers and lettered T-shirts, there was no need for talk anymore. The whole world could be struck dumb and communication would continue apace— HAVE A HAPPY DAY: KISS ME, I'M ITALIAN—*en passant*, behind glass windows. She cruised by the Jesus-loving pair doing seventy-five. Ahead of her, a sign announced that Danbury was only ten miles east. She pulled back into the right-hand lane and, peering in her rearview mirror, caught sight of her face. It looked bright, vibrant, happy. She winked to herself. Ever since emerging from Manhattan, she had been in an unaccountably good mood. Alone, hurtling through the tree-lined parkway, panic had given way to giddiness.

"Well, Doodles, it's been a long time since you and I have had a good old heart-to-womb talk. First, no matter what the neighbors say, I want you to know that your mom is not crazy. I repeat, not crazy. Maybe a little flaky, but that's an altogether different thing." Marie laughed softly. "Now second, where, you may ask, are we going to now? An excellent question, Doodles. Bright girl. Right to the point. We're going on a little field trip, tiny friend. Some solo research. Straight to the source. No more hearsay for us, Doodles. We want some facts so we can be done with this whole business and settle back to being normal human beings again. That'll be better for both of us. Better for our health. You see, every time your mom gets upset, she shoots a little of her upset-juice into you. You could come out of there a nervous wreck if your old mom doesn't settle down."

The road was narrowing from four lanes to two and Marie slowed down, allowing a sports car to pull ahead of her. In a matter of minutes, the surroundings had changed from impersonal highway to small town New England. She rolled past the Heidi Motel, the Red Rooster Ice Cream

Parlor, Teddy's Dew Drop Inn. Familiar terrain. David and she had spent many a weekend up here in the good old days. Making love in gingham-curtained country inn rooms. Popovers for breakfast.

Two teen-age hitchhikers in jeans and tweed sports jackets were standing near the turn-off to Sharon. Prep-schoolers, no doubt. She could pick them up and ask them what they knew about the Almquist School. A little preparatory research. Marie grinned at her unintentional pun and passed them by.

"So that leaves just one question, right, little friend? Why the hell are we doing all this on a Wednesday afternoon with Sol Hepperman waiting for us in our office with the new budget?"

An excellent question indeed. Panic had sent her bounding out of McPartland's office—she could work on her excuses and apologies for that later. But now the panic was long gone, and she still hadn't done anything about her meeting, her job. No doubt this was just the kind of absent-minded, irrational behavior Murray Miller had been hinting at. And it was sure to get back to Ham. Hepperman always went straight to the top with his little peccadilloes.

Marie slowed to a crawl as she entered Salisbury, then pulled off the road in front of Graham's Pharmacy. Inside, she got change for two dollars, went to the wall phone, and dialed.

"Sol Hepperman's office. Good afternoon."

"Hello, Sylvia. This is Marie Preston. Could I speak with Sol, please?"

"He's not in his office. I thought he was with you, Mrs. Preston."

"Uh, no. I'm afraid I wasn't able to make our meeting, Sylvia. I . . . I had a little accident at lunch and—"

"I hope it's nothing serious."

"No, no," Marie said. "Not at all. A little fall. It just shook me up a little."

"Oh, that's not good. I mean, with the baby. Have you seen a doctor?"

"Yes, Sylvia. That's why I couldn't call earlier. Please tell Mr. Hepperman I'm sorry I couldn't get to him earlier."

"I'm sure he'll understand, Mrs. Preston. I'll tell him as soon as I see him."

"Maybe we can reschedule for tomorrow. Is he free at eleven?"

"Yes. I think that's fine."

"Great. Thanks, Sylvia. Bye."

"Bye now. Take care."

Marie hung up the phone, grimacing to herself. What a talented liar she was turning into. She sighed, lifted the receiver, dropped in more coins, and dialed again.

"Marie Preston's office. Can I help you?"

"Nance? It's me."

"Hi. Where are you? We've been worried. Are you all right?"

"Fine, Nance. Just a little shook up. I fell off a curb. Twisted something, I'm afraid." She would have to remember to do a little limping in the office tomorrow.

"I'm sorry. Are you sure you're okay?"

"Yes, fine, Nance. Look, I already called Hepperman's office and made my apologies. Would you clear the rest of the afternoon for me?"

"Sure. Uh, Marie?"

"Yes?"

"I'm afraid when you didn't show up for your meeting I got a little panicky. I . . . . I called your husband at his office to see if he knew where you were."

Marie stared across a rack of greeting cards to the front window of the pharmacy. There were only three people in the street and they were all together, a mother and her two children wheeling groceries from the market to their car.

"Yes," Marie said.

"He told me to have you call him if I heard from you,"

her secretary went on. "I think he was a little upset. He said your doctor had called him too. Dr. McDonald."

"McPartland," Marie said automatically.

The little family had gotten into their car and was backing out into the street. If Marie wanted to, she could stay in this town. Find a little room somewhere over an antique shop. Get a job in the library. Raise her little girl in the country.

"I hope that wasn't the wrong thing to do," Nancy was saying.

"No," Marie said. "Not at all. Thanks for your concern, Nance. See you tomorrow."

"Okay. Take care of yourself."

Marie hung up the phone, her eyes still on the street in front of the store. It was completely empty now. Still, like a calendar picture. So McPartland had called David. Of course. Checking up on his loony wife. Man to Man. Doctor to Doctor. She looked down on the little shelf below the phone. Only thirty-five cents left. She would have to get more change to phone David. She pulled a dollar from her wallet and walked over to the boy behind the lunch counter.

"Yes, ma'am?"

Marie was looking at herself in the mirror behind the boy. The color in her face was gone. And her eyes had lost the luster she had glimpsed only minutes ago in her rearview mirror. Now they looked dull and tired.

"Ma'am?"

"Could I have a coffee? And maybe a sandwich? Do you have a cheese and tomato sandwich?"

"I've got cheese and I've got tomatoes," the boy said, grinning. "I guess I could make a cheese and tomato sandwich. Is that for here or to travel."

She looked up at the wall clock. Four-fifteen.

"To travel," Marie said, patting her hair. "Do you know how far I am from Whitfield, Massachusetts?"

"Not far. About twenty minutes straight up forty-four. Just over the border from Canaan."

"Thank you."

Back in her car, Marie ate her sandwich and gulped down her coffee while the motor warmed up. She realized that she hadn't eaten since breakfast. Now, she slipped the car into gear and pulled back onto the road.

"Okay, Doodles. Let's get it over with," she said. And the hell with David.

Fifteen minutes later, she crossed the Massachusetts border, entering Whitfield. If Salisbury had been a calendar picture town, Whitfield was straight out of Currier and Ives. All that must have changed in the past hundred years was the addition of a macadam top to the one road that snaked through the valley past Whitfield's gray-and-white clapboard houses, smoke puffing picturesquely out of their chimneys from wood-burning stoves. Marie cruised past the white, tall-spired church, the long, one-story abandoned mill, the Whitfield Grange. Ahead, she saw the general store and post office and was about to stop to ask directions when she noticed a neat, black-on-white wood sign indicating that The Almquist School was a quarter of a mile farther up the road. She crossed a low metal bridge and was there.

The moment Marie saw the Almquist campus she felt totally ridiculous. The stately Georgian main buildings and colonial dormitories reminded her immediately of her own alma mater, Abbot Academy. It was a wonder she had not heard of Almquist before; it was clearly in the same league. Abbot probably faced off against them every spring in field hockey. She didn't really know what she had expected. Like so many other things today, she hadn't thought it out. But now, seeing the long, elm-lined paths and warmly lit, shuttered windows, it all became terribly, embarrassingly clear to her: McPartland sent his son or daughter to Almquist and paid the bills under his former name, the same name his child bore, Monroe.

She had brought her car to a halt in front of what looked to be the administration building, but her motor was still running. If she continued along the crescent, she could be back at the Whitfield General Store in a minute and call David to tell him that she was fine, that she would be home in a few hours and explain everything. Maybe she would even treat herself to a hearty country inn dinner on the way back. Over coffee, she could work out the details of the explanation she would give David. Make it sound more reasonable than it really was.

A group of young students in duffel coats and ski jackets was walking toward her, their long scarves slung smartly over their shoulders. A tall, bare-headed teacher was strolling beside them. Nothing changes, Marie thought. Not even the angle of their scarves. She wondered if she would be able to pick out McPartland's child if she saw him. Would he have the doctor's long jaw and warm, wide-set eyes?

"My God!"

Marie suddenly grasped her belly with both her hands, as if by holding it she could protect her womb from the shock which had shot directly to it.

The students had come to within a few yards of Marie's car. And none of them looked like McPartland. Or anyone else she knew. Their large, moon faces, their bulbous-lipped open mouths, their flat, wide-nostriled noses, their fleshy-lidded, vacant eyes were not the features of normal children. They were mongoloid children.

Monroe gives you the bad babies. The ugly babies.

Marie continued to hold her pregnant belly, rocking herself back and forth in her seat. Then she abruptly snapped off the ignition, opened the door, and jumped out of the car. In a moment, she had caught up with the group of children and was beside the teacher who was accompanying them.

"Pardon me," she said. "I'm sorry to bother you. But I'm looking for the Monroe child."

The teacher stopped and looked down at Marie questioningly.

"Monroe?"

The children immediately gathered in a circle around Marie, their faces suddenly animated. Every one of them was smiling happily up at her.

"Hello, Missus," one of them, a girl of about twelve, said in the unmistakable thick-tongued voice of a retarded child.

Then they all chorused, "Hello, Hello. Hello, Missus," some of them hopping up and down on the balls of their feet.

"Hello," Marie said. She looked from one happy face to another. She wished that she could apologize to them for the shock she had felt at first seeing them, a sensation that still lingered inside her. "Hello. My name is Marie."

The little girl suddenly reached out her hand, touching Marie's coat over her belly.

"Going to have a baby, Marie?" the little girl asked.

Instinctively, Marie stepped backward and covered her abdomen with both her hands. The children were laughing now, chanting, "Baby, Baby." The teacher took a step toward Marie, the children remaining behind him. He was smiling at her.

"My students often notice things that I don't," he said. "It can be disconcerting."

"I didn't mean to jump like that," Marie said.

The teacher looked directly into Marie's eyes, his brows arched in criticism—not, she guessed, for her jumping back, but for apologizing for it.

"No harm done, I'm sure," he said, evenly. Then, "You asked me about a child named Monroe. There's no one with that name here. Are you sure you have the right name?"

"No," Marie said without thinking. "I mean—"

"The administration building is right there," the teacher said abruptly, gesturing with his head and turning back to his charges.

Marie watched the group continue down the path in the twilight. From the rear, they looked again like a normal gang of school children sauntering back to their dorm. She wanted to think that there wasn't any real difference, not ultimately. They were cheerful children. They were innocent, good. But in her womb, the sensation still had not gone away.

"Please, God," she murmured. "Not my one and only child."

She turned and strode directly into the administration building. Inside, a gilt-lettered sign directed her up one flight of stairs to the Headmaster's office. She raced up the steps and arrived in front of a mannish secretary in Franklin glasses behind an oak-topped desk.

"Good afternoon," Marie said. "I'd like to speak with the headmaster, if I could."

"Do you have an appointment?"

"No, I'm afraid I haven't. But I've just driven up from New York and—"

"You are aware of our visiting policies, I hope, Mrs.—?"

"Preston," Marie said. "Look, I'm afraid you don't understand. I don't have a child at Almquist—"

The secretary removed her glasses and frowned up at Marie questioningly.

"Not yet," Marie blurted out. She hadn't planned that lie. She hated it the moment she said it.

The secretary's expression softened.

"Of course," she said. "I do hope you're staying over. You'll want to see our classrooms. Almquist looks so beautiful during the day."

"Yes." Marie started to turn.

"But I'm sure Mr. Reilly will see you now," the secretary continued, smiling. "After such a long drive. I think he's in Dr. Anderson's office. Why don't you wait in his office, and I'll go see if I can pull him away."

The secretary had risen and was walking toward the open oak door behind her. Marie hesitated just a second and then followed her. A moment later, she was seated in a ladder-back chair, alone in the headmaster's office of a school for retarded children one hundred and ten miles away from home.

She looked around the office. It could have been the office of the headmistress at Abbot. There was the obligatory oil portrait of the founder—one surprisingly, cheery-looking old man named Thomas Almquist—over the mantel; the diplomas and accreditation certificates lacquered on wood on the wall behind the headmaster's desk; a floor-to-ceiling bookshelf. One row of books, at desk level, looked well-used. Marie stood and walked to the shelf to read their titles.

"Learning Patterns in the Mentally Retarded" . . . "The Socialization of the Special Child" . . . "The Guilty Gene: Parents and the Mongoloid Child."

In the corner of the room, next to the bookshelf, Marie saw a maple file cabinet. Student records. She shot a glance at the door. No one there. The secretary must still be getting Mr. Reilly. In three steps, Marie was in front of the cabinet. She crouched down, her back to the open office door. The top drawer was labeled "A–K," the bottom, "L–Z." She pulled on the bottom drawer. Nothing. She pulled harder. No give. Locked. Then, in back of her, she heard a muffled thump. She froze, her pulse thudding in her ears. A second passed. Two. Three. Slowly, she craned her neck around. No one there. But her handbag was lying on the floor where it had slipped from the arm of her chair.

Suddenly, Marie remembered how these old cabinets worked. She turned back and pulled the top drawer. It slid open easily. She pulled the bottom drawer. Open. She pushed the top drawer closed and ran her fingers across the file tabs of the open drawer.

Lefflar, George . . . Lomansky, Jennifer . . . Mallory . . . Maple . . . McHenry . . . Monroe.

Dr. Richard Monroe.

Marie yanked the file out and opened it.

Empty. Nothing. Another dead end. She stuffed the file back into the cabinet.

She snapped back her hand. Something had scratched her palm. A paper clip. A three-by-five card was clipped to the back of the file. She pulled it.

"Monroe, Dr. Richard. See Guilford, Janet."

She dropped the card into the file and pushed the drawer. It banged shut. Marie snapped her head around. Still no one there. But how much time did she have left? A minute? Two?

Her legs ached from stooping so she slid onto her knees. She pulled the top drawer open. Spotted the Guilford file immediately. Yanked it. Opened it.

"Guilford, Janet . . . age, six . . . standard trisomy mental retardation . . . I.Q., 60 . . . associated congenital heart defect . . ."

Marie heard faint footsteps on the stairs. Without turning, she flipped through the file . . . medical report . . . performance tests . . . evaluations . . . tuition schedule . . . She pulled it.

"Payment, quarterly . . . $5,000 . . . Tuition paid by (check all appropriate) . . . State, no . . . Parents, no . . . Other, yes . . . Dr. Richard Monroe, 300 Park Avenue, New York, New York."

The footsteps had reached the landing.

Marie jammed the file down and rocked herself back onto her feet. She turned to the door. Two shadows stretched toward the doorway. She took three long strides, scooped up her handbag, and sat down stiffly in the ladder-back chair, her heart thumping in her chest.

"Sorry to keep you. Mrs. Preston, isn't it?"

"Yes, Marie Preston." Marie rose slowly and turned as the headmaster entered the office.

"Please don't get up." Reilly, an open-faced, ruddy-complected man in his early thirties, passed alongside Marie, touching her elbow with his hand, and then took a seat behind his desk. "I understand you've driven up from the city today."

"Yes, this afternoon," Marie's voice surprised her—it was calm, perfectly natural. She was getting better at this.

"So, Mrs. Preston, what can we do for you?"

"Well, I guess I'd like to hear a little about the school. Your facilities, programs."

"Of course," Reilly said. He leaned down and pulled open the middle drawer of his desk. "I have a brochure here, somewhere. I think it tells the Almquist story better than I can."

Reilly pulled a thick, glossy booklet from the drawer and started to hand it across the desk when he suddenly frowned. He was looking at the corner of his office. The bottom drawer of his wooden file cabinet was open.

Marie abruptly took the booklet from Reilly's outstretched hand and hid her face behind it. She heard Reilly rise from his chair and walk to the corner of his office, then the soft thump of the file cabinet drawer closing.

"How old is your child, Mrs. Preston?"

"Nine," Marie said, without looking up. On the page in front of her was a photograph of the Almquist swimming pool.

"Living at home?" Reilly had seated himself behind his desk again.

"No," Marie said quickly, setting the booklet down on the desk in front of her. This wasn't going well. She should be asking the questions.

Reilly leaned across his desk and looked at Marie sincerely.

"I think I could be of more help to you, Mrs. Preston, if you were able to tell me a little bit more about your child."

Marie looked away from Reilly. She couldn't go on with this lie. It was too ugly.

"I know it's sometimes hard," Reilly was saying. "But you have to understand, I spend my whole life with special children."

Marie put her hands on the arms of the chair. She could say that she was tired. She could say that she would come around tomorrow and they could talk then.

Reilly was smiling at her.

"Why don't we start with something simple," he said softly. "Who recommended the Almquist School to you?"

Now!

"Dr. Richard Monroe," Marie said quickly.

Reilly slowly rose from his seat, his palms planted on his desktop as he leaned toward her.

"I'm not sure who you are talking about," he said. His already ruddy face had turned crimson and his eyes were stone cold.

"Dr. Richard Monroe," Marie said distinctly. She was looking directly into Reilly's eyes. "You know, Janet Guilford's doctor."

Reilly snapped erect. In two rapid strides he was around his desk and standing over Marie.

"I don't know who the hell you are, Mrs. Preston. But I think you'd better leave here right now. Do you understand me?"

Marie didn't move.

"But I don't understand," she said evenly. "Dr. Monroe is Janet's doctor, isn't he?"

Reilly leaned his florid face directly in front of Marie's.

"You're making a terrible mistake, lady," he said in a low voice. "That whole case is closed. You'd be very unwise to pry into it now."

Marie held her head stiffly, determined not to flinch or look away. "What case are you talking about, Mr. Reilly?"

The headmaster's face hovered in front of her's, his upper lip lifted in a menacing smile. "Very unwise," he said. "Especially in your condition."

Marie abruptly pushed herself up from the chair almost bumping her head against Reilly's and marched to the door. In the vestibule, the secretary peered at her over her glasses as Marie flashed by to the top of the stairway and started racing down the well-worn wooden steps. A moment later, Marie was out the administration building's door, alone in the now-black night. She walked quickly down the brick path to her car, trying not to think. Not yet. Not until she was far away from here.

Suddenly, a hand shot out from behind her car waving something metallic in her face. Marie froze.

"You know, this could be hazardous," a man's voice said. "Not so much for you, but the children."

Marie's heart was beating almost audibly.

"Like any other children, they're sorely tempted when they see keys in an empty car."

Marie let her breath out slowly. It was the teacher she had spoken to earlier. And he was holding her car keys out to her. She took them from him and leaned against her car, trying to make out his face in the darkness.

"I'm sorry. Did I frighten you?" the teacher said.

"Yes. Yes, you did. But . . . but thank you for the keys."

The teacher opened the door of Marie's car and the interior light shone out on them. Marie could see the look of concern on the teacher's face as she got into her car. He leaned down to her over the open door.

"It's no business of mine," the man said, "but whatever they tell you, it's never worth it. It's too painful. I'm sure I couldn't take it myself if they were mine."

Marie stared at the teacher blankly. His face looked ghostly in the dim, yellow light.

"You'd be surprised how many women like you come here once they know. Trying to make up their minds. Trying to decide what's the right thing to do."

Marie closed her eyes.

"But anything's better than this. It's always better to abort and try again."

PULLING ON the old socks. The ritual pulling on of the old socks. After the screams and scratches, the tumbles and thrashes, there are still the old socks to pull on. Theresa used to call it the moment of truth.

Paul paused on the edge of his bed, one sock on, the other in hand, and surveyed the long, milk-white body dozing belly-down beside him. Her bum alone—two monumental scoops of vanilla ice cream—was enough to offer a man a lifetime of happiness. Not to mention the delicious curve in the small of her back. What a lovely consolation that was. Paul pulled on his other sock. Ah, there's the rub, eh, Theresa? What need has this just-laid, almost-young man for consolation?

Paul stood and began slipping into a cotton turtleneck sweater.

"Good God, Paul, what's become of your head?"

Paul laughed from inside the half-on sweater, his head completely covered.

"Nothing serious," he said. "Just a bit of surgery. A radical turtle-necktomy. It's the latest thing. Does wonders for relieving tensions."

In fact, there was something comforting about being buried inside the sweater. The ostrich effect. Theresa always said he needed a womb of his own.

Eva was giggling. He heard her crawl toward him on the bed.

"Why, you're a modern woman's dream, Paul. Headless and half-naked."

"Hello. What's this?"

Her fingers were opening the fly of his shorts, lifting out his penis. Her mouth closed around it.

For one second, Paul saw the two of them in his mind's eye: he, in socks and shorts, still headless in his half-on sweater; she, naked, incredibly beautiful, sprawled on all fours in front of him, his cock in her mouth. A comic image, really. It needed a caption.

But now the warmth of her mouth was spreading to every point of his body, his penis already hard, swelling between her lips. And there were no more images. No thoughts. Just sensation. Pure and delicious. Building in intensity as she rocked gently forward and back, her lips tightening around the head of his cock, her tongue flicking the tip. Building, tightening, tugging. Paul reached his arms out blindly and cupped the back of Eva's head, her corn-silk hair cool under his palms, and he pulled her toward him just as he came, ravished to the tips of his stockinged feet.

A moment later, he pulled his sweater down over his head and smiled down at Eva.

"Good grief! It's you!" Eva said and burst into laughter.

"Indeed it is. And feeling quite marvelous just now, thank you."

"My pleasure." Eva tucked her hand under his sweater and ran her finger tips across his back. "Maybe now you'll take off that silly-looking outfit and come back into bed with your friend. Where were you going anyway? Out for a late night jog?"

"Actually, I've got a date," Paul said. He paused, deadpan, then added, "With a centrifuge."

"Oh, one of those girls with hundreds of legs. I hear they're positively gripping in bed."

Paul chuckled. "I thought I'd told you I left something spinning at the lab. I won't be an hour." He reached to the chair for his slacks. "I really am sorry to run off like this, Eva."

"Hate to be eaten and run, eh?"

"Ugh." Paul made a mock grimace. "You do have a way with the English language, my *svenska flicka*." He leaned over and kissed the top of her head. "Don't go away, will you? I'll bring you back something delectable, like an anchovy pizza."

Eva lay back in the bed.

"Make it an oyster," she said, grinning.

At ten o'clock at night, Madison Avenue had an almost small city look. Like Oxford at midday. Scattered, quiet-talking couples walking slowly, arm-in-arm. Here and there, a solitary dog-walker. A distinguished old fellow carrying a violin case. Even, yes, a jogger in luminous-striped pants and headband. At ten o'clock, the place looked quite livable indeed.

Paul cut across the avenue at the corner and started up-town at a brisk pace. The night air felt good on his face, invigorating. In fact, he felt altogether quite nice. This—he hesitated to use the word, "affair"—this liaison he had with Eva was, if nothing else, a great tonic for his disposition. When he didn't dwell on the "if nothing else," of course. And that was becoming easier. He probably wasn't capable of anything much more intense these days in any event. Certainly not a Theresa-style, deep-probing relationship.

At Ninetieth Street, he turned left and continued to-ward Fifth Avenue. Perhaps he should treat his whole life in the same way, as recreation. Not just his lovelife, but his work as well. The game-theory of living. Very American and up-to-date. Paul smiled to himself. About the only way he could deal with his world more playfully—with his Sir Edmunds and Bouchards and Fines—would be with a sweater over his head. With a turtle-necktomy.

Paul pushed himself through the revolving front door of Hebron Hospital, signed himself in at the reception desk, saluted Collins, the West Indian security guard, and walked through the main hallway to the elevators. One was waiting, open and empty. He entered it and punched the button for the sixth floor. The only time he looked forward to coming to the lab anymore was at night, alone. Without Fine creeping around peering over his shoulder, fogging the eyepiece of Paul's microscope with his omnipresent smoke. Paul was feeling more and more like a graduate student and less like an esteemed research fellow with every day since he had brought the Roundtree and Whiting anomalies to Fine's attention. What had Fine's latest memo said? "Pending a complete review of procedures, all clinical amniotic cultures selected for research analysis must be approved by the department head." A paradigm of smoke. But it's meaning was clear to Paul: leave the McPartland amnios alone.

But there wasn't a chance Paul could do that, Dr. Fine. Not a chance. Not with his head still on. And, as luck would have it, the laboratory supervisor was a particular friend of Paul's: Eva had promised to set aside a few cells from the next McPartland patient's amniotic culture harvested for Paul's personal—nocturnal—analysis. That culture could be ready any day now.

The elevator doors slid open and Paul stepped out into the dimly lit corridor. As always, a sense of security settled over him. Home. One of Theresa's parting shots had hit it right: "Your idea of the hearth is a Bunsen burner." He turned left at the end of the corridor.

Paul stopped short. A shadow was moving in front of Gen Lab 2. Lurking silently by the door. The janitor? No, Paul knew that he never arrived at the sixth floor until three or four in the morning. Bernstein? Fine? He hadn't seen either name on the sign-in sheet. The figure turned in front of

the door, swirled. Better to go back downstairs. To get
Collins. Paul took one step backward. The figure turned
again.

"Hello?" A woman's voice.

Paul stood still, not answering.

"Can you help me, please?"

"Who are you? What do you want?"

The woman was walking toward him.

"I . . . I have to talk to someone about my baby," she
said.

She was in front of Paul now, a tall woman with a fine,
intelligent face and frightened eyes.

"My name is Marie Preston."

"And mine is Paul Kingsmill. I work here." He searched
her eyes for a moment as if he might find something familiar there. Then he walked around her to the laboratory
door, unlocked it and snapped on the light.

"Why don't we talk in here? I'm sure neither of us will
look quite so frightening in the light."

Marie hesitated.

"As a matter of fact," Paul went on, "I was just going to
look in on your culture, Mrs. Preston. Your amniotic culture."

Marie walked slowly into the laboratory. "I have come
to the right place then."

"Yes, I think you have. And probably at the best time
of day, too," Paul said quietly. Then he smiled and Marie
realized that she had seen this rumpled Englishman once
before: getting off the hospital elevator as she and David
had gotten on. She had found his face sympathetic then,
too. "Although heaven knows how you managed to sneak up
here."

"Quickly," Marie said. "Very quickly."

They both laughed. And then they both fell silent. Paul
could hear the whir of the centrifuge in the other room. It
would have to wait. Marie was looking beyond him at the

beakers and vials of bright-colored liquids on the laboratory bench.

"Can you tell me if my baby is all right?"

"No. Not just yet, Mrs. Preston. But I should be able to soon. In a few days, I'd hope."

"A few days," Marie repeated. After three hours of driving from Whitfield, Massachusetts, directly to the hospital, the full weight of her fatigue was finally descending on her. She could very easily imagine crawling under the bench and going to sleep there. "I'm sorry to have troubled you so late at night like this," she said, turning back to the door.

"You're a patient of Dr. McPartland's, aren't you?"

Marie stood perfectly still, facing the door. "Yes. Yes, I am. Do you know him?"

"No. Although I'd be very curious to meet him."

"Why?"

Marie turned back and Paul studied her face. It looked tired and painfully fragile. No, he couldn't press her for information about McPartland now. Not tonight. He tried to make his shrug appear casual. "Just professional curiosity. McPartland seems to have a great deal of influence at this hospital."

Marie looked steadily into Paul's eyes for a long moment. And then, her voice quavering, she said to this virtual stranger what she knew she could tell no one else, "I'm scared to death he's done something to my baby."

She had no sooner said it when a sob broke from her throat, a sob she had been holding back for most of the day. Paul stepped toward her and put his hands on her shoulders. "It's going to be all right. I promise you it will be all right." He took her arm and guided her across the laboratory to his desk chair. Then, he pulled a stool from his laboratory bench and sat across from her. "I want you to know that whatever you tell me I promise to hold in the strictest of confidence."

"I . . . I don't know what there is to tell . . . I mean, I don't know if any of it means anything or—"

Paul reached behind him for some lens tissues and handed them to Marie who wiped her nose with them.

"Just tell me why you're worried. What's made you frightened. Even if none of it makes sense."

Marie again took a long deliberate look into Paul's eyes. She saw no judgment there, no professional indulgence. Whoever this man was, he honestly wanted to know what had brought her to his laboratory at ten o'clock at night. And now she told him. Everything. About her discovery of McPartland's name change. Her encounters with Franny. The Almquist School. It took better than an hour of stops and starts, cutting back here to tell about the explanation McPartland had given Tom, jumping ahead there as she remembered the name of the student Monroe supported, all the while Paul nodding encouragingly, his eyes fixed on hers. It was a few minutes past eleven when she finally came to a halt, then smiled almost shyly and said, "I suppose you think I'm just another hysterical pregnant lady, don't you?"

"No. Not at all." Perhaps if he had known nothing else, Marie's rambling story might have struck Paul as the product of hysteria. None of it really fit together. All of it allowed for some perfectly reasonable explanation. But from the moment she began, he had felt a growing, horribly confirming sense of foreboding. If her story were bizarre, it was because something bizarre was going on. "To tell you the truth, Marie, I wish you were crazy."

"You do think there's something wrong with my baby, don't you?"

"I really don't know. Maybe not. Maybe none of this has anything to do with you." Paul stood and walked to the window and stared out across the river. Then he turned back to Marie and said, "I don't want you to be alarmed. Not anymore than you are already. But I have to tell you this—I've been concerned about McPartland's patients too. About his procedures."

Marie shut her eyes. Did she really want to hear this? "Why?"

"Just something that's turned up here in the lab." Paul walked back to Marie. "On the amnios of two of his patients. A possible anomaly."

"What?" Marie swallowed hard. How much more was there? "Tell me! Please, tell me what's wrong with them."

Paul crouched down so his eyes were level with Marie's. "I honestly don't know," he said, keeping his voice even. "It could be nothing. But there's no way I can know for sure without taking samples of the parents' blood. Without doing a genetic work-up of the parents. And McPartland has forbidden me to do that." He paused, looking at Marie's mouth. Her lips were trembling. "It could be nothing, Marie."

Marie's whole body began to shake and, when she opened her mouth, her words came out in a bitter cry.

"Damn it! What's wrong with those babies? Why the hell aren't you telling me everything?"

Paul reached out and grabbed Marie's shoulders tightly.

"Listen to me, Marie. I am telling you everything I know," he said. "But I don't know very much yet. Nothing conclusive. I can tell you my guesses. But that's all they are." Marie's body had stopped shaking and he let his hands drop. "I don't know what good it would do to hear them, Marie."

Marie groped in her pocketbook for a Kleenex. "Give me a second, would you?"

She slowly lifted herself out of the chair, leaned for a second against the desk, and then began to walk across the laboratory. She paused when she came to the end of Paul's bench and looked along the top of it at the beakers and burners, the rows of test tubes in their racks, the pipettes and syringes and opaque plastic jars. It must be calming to work up here among all this precisely shaped paraphernalia. Everything in order. A purpose for every movement. Alone. She turned and looked at Paul. "Sorry about that outburst," she said. "There's been an awful lot to take in one day."

"I know."

Marie walked slowly back to the chair and sat down.

"I have to know your guesses, Paul. Whatever they are."

Paul rubbed his hand across his cheek and chin, then abruptly dropped his hand to his side.

"All I have to go on is an unusual marker I came up with on one of the chromosomes. An illumination. Something I've never come across before. There is a chance it could be some sort of genetic damage. Perhaps something caused by radiation. That's my most unhappy guess, Marie. And it may very well not be true at all. What I saw may just be a rare marker. Some perfectly normal characteristic that runs in a family."

"I thought you said there were two of them. Two babies with it."

"Yes. Yes, I did. But it still could be that. Perhaps the babies' families are related. Or perhaps . . . perhaps these women were impregnated by the same man. And no one knows that but them. That's the prevailing theory in this department right now."

Marie stood up directly in front of Paul.

"When can you check mine? My amnio?"

Paul cupped Marie's elbow and led her to the near wall of the laboratory. Set in the wall was a large, heavy wooden door with a small, double-glass window at its center.

"Here's where they incubate," Paul said. "The warm room." He flipped a switch on the wall and a light went on inside the room.

Marie looked in through the window. It was no bigger

than a small closet. At the rear, a small metal tank with a pressure gauge at its top sat on rollers, and on each side wall were shelves the length of the room. On the shelves were rows of cafeterialike plastic trays and on each tray were a half-dozen glass flasks lying on their sides, each containing a quarter inch of a pale pink fluid.

"I'll just be a second," Paul said, gently moving Marie aside. He unlatched the door and left it open while he walked into the room, leaned over one of the trays, selected a flask and brought it out with him. Then he pushed the door closed with his foot.

Marie shivered. The sound the door made when it slammed shut had jogged something inside her. An echo of something she could not quite remember. But before she could begin to retrieve it, she saw Paul gesturing to her from his bench. He was examining the flask under his microscope.

"We're close," he said. "There are some excellent cells here. We're maybe two days away from harvest. Three at the most."

Paul slowly turned the knob on the platform which supported the flask, moving it across the circle of light that shone up through the bottom of the microscope. There were some very good cells indeed. Clear. Little overlap so far. But before harvest, before fixation and staining, there was nothing more he could tell.

"Paul."

Paul lifted his head from the eyepiece. Marie was standing next to him. The fright he had seen before in her eyes was now completely gone and replacing it was an expression of aching sadness.

"Paul, I don't know what I'll do if you find out there is something wrong with my baby. I . . . we waited almost three years before I conceived. I'm thirty-eight years old now. If . . . if there is anything wrong, I . . ." Marie stopped. She couldn't finish that sentence. She didn't even know what the end of it was.

Paul nodded.

"I hope to God there is nothing wrong, Marie."

He slowly stepped off of his stool, then carried the flask back to the warm room, opened the door, deposited the flask on the tray and came out again, closing the door softly behind him. Marie was still standing next to the microscope.

"Marie, I have to ask you one thing. The work I do on your amnio is going to have to be done in secret after the clinical people have done their routine analysis. I'll work at night. Here. Alone." He took a step toward her. "And if I do discover something out of the ordinary, I'll need to do a genetic work-up of your blood"—Paul paused a fraction of a second—"and the child's father."

"My husband," Marie said quietly. "I can assure you it's my husband."

"But that is something we will have to do in secret too. We cannot let McPartland know about that either."

Marie nodded. She felt immensely tired. She could not think about any of this anymore. Not until she'd slept.

"Let me put you into a cab now," Paul said.

"I have my car here."

"I'll drive you home," Paul said. "Just give me a moment. I have to turn off something in the other room."

Paul left Marie leaning against the side of his desk, her eyes half closed, and walked to the rear of the laboratory through an open door to the small centrifuge and counter room his lab shared with Bernstein's. He snapped on the light, went to the spinning centrifuge and turned it off. Then he unfastened the cover of the cannister inside the spinner and began to lift out a vial of fetal calf serum. He stopped, his hand in mid-air. He had seen a shadow move on the other side of Bernstein's door.

"Mel? Is that you?"

No answer.

He went to the door to Bernstein's lab and pushed it open.

"Mel?"

He flipped on the light.

"Mel?"

"Did you call me?"

Paul spun around. Marie was staring at him perplexedly.

"Is something wrong?"

"No," Paul said. He turned off the light in Bernstein's lab and smiled reassuringly at Marie. "It's just an old lab ghost. He sometimes visits me late at night up here. I'm ready. Let's go now."

Paul led Marie by the arm out through the laboratory into the hallway. He fitted his key into the lock and began to turn it. What was it his father used to say? "Only idiots believe in ghosts, but it takes a damn fool to ignore one." Paul turned the key back.

"I'm sorry. I'll just be one more minute," he said to Marie.

He let himself back into the laboratory, leaving Marie alone in the corridor, dozing on her feet. A moment later he was back, leading her to the elevator.

Paul drove Marie directly to the entrance of her apartment building. Other than instructions on which garage to leave her car in and an exchange of phone numbers, they did not speak until Marie opened the car door. Then she turned to Paul and said, "Paul, before I said I didn't know what I'd do if you . . . if you find something wrong with my baby."

"You don't have to think about that now," Paul said. "Let's hope you won't have to think about it at all."

"Yes. But if you do, Paul, if you do find something, I want to know. I want to know everything, Paul. There are too many things I don't know already."

Paul reached out across the seat and took Marie's hand in his. "I promise you that," he said. "We're going to have to count on each other for many things. For a while, at least."

"Yes."

"Get some good rest now." Paul squeezed her hand tightly and then let it go. He smiled. "And do try to think optimistic thoughts for the next few days."

Marie smiled back. "I'll try."

When Paul let himself back into his apartment, it was a few minutes past one, more than three hours since he had left Eva. He took off his shoes at the door and walked on the balls of his feet into his bedroom. The bed lamp was on and his bed was empty. There was a torn piece of brown paper lying on his pillow. He picked it up and read the note Eva had left for him:

"You owe me one."

He took off his clothes and lay back on the bed. He slept with the light on.

PART

4

AND, BEHOLD, the angel of the Lord appeared in a dream saying, Arise and take thy young child and flee, for Herod will seek the child . . .

Franny sat upright in her bed, sweat streaming from her face onto her nightshirt. Someone was crying. Someone was always crying.

She swung her feet over the side of the bed and listened. Who was it? Who was it who always waked her with that awful wail? She slipped off the bed and walked barefoot between the rows of curtained-off beds. Hide and seek. Seek the crybaby.

At the last bed, the one next to the door, she stopped. There. He was hiding there behind the curtain. He didn't think she could hear him, but she could. The pathetic little sniffles and sobs. She grasped the edge of the curtain and held it, counting silently. One. Two. Three. She yanked it open.

Nothing.

The bed was empty. He was gone.

Take thy young child and flee . . .

Franny stuck her head out into the hallway and looked both ways. There was no one there. Quiet. Sleepy time. She grinned. Sleepy time in the loony bin.

She tiptoed out into the corridor and turned to her

right, running her fingernails along the tile wall as she walked. She would never get out now, he had told her. Not now. She hadn't listened to him. If she didn't listen, how was she ever going to get better? And he couldn't let her out until she was better.

At the end of the corridor, she turned left and started for the door. The floor here was concrete, like a sidewalk. Step on a crack, break your mother's back. Franny hopped across a crack and landed in front of the elevator. A red light was flashing above it. She froze. Someone coming. The elevator doors slid open, throwing a shaft of yellow light into the corridor. No one got off. The doors slapped closed, like jaws.

Franny ran to the stairwell door and slammed her palms against it. It opened a fraction of an inch and then swung closed against her. She turned her back to the door and pressed against it with her rump, curling her toes to grip the concrete floor. The door slowly opened. She jumped to the side and the door slammed closed behind her. She was alone in the stairwell.

They'd given her exactly what she wanted, hadn't they? Her heart's desire. And she was so ungrateful. She spoiled everything. And now she wanted to spoil it for everyone else.

At the second landing the firedoor was propped open. Franny craned her head around the opening and peered in. Two men in green smocks and shower caps and canvas slippers were walking away from her. She stepped into the corridor. Much nicer floor here. Shiny tile, like glass under her naked feet.

And then she heard it again. The crying. The baby wail. He was down here. He had been down here all the time.

Franny walked quickly down the corridor, the bottom of her nightshirt flapping against her knees. She was nearer now. The wail was getting louder, sharper, like a knife

keening against slate. She would find him this time. She
would set him free.

He told her she asked too many questions. If she had
faith in him, she wouldn't have to ask questions. If she had
faith, she wouldn't spoil everything. He told her now she
would never see her baby again.

Franny stopped short. The two men in the green
smocks and canvas slippers were now coming toward her.
She turned, opened the door next to her, and stepped in before they saw her.

It was dark inside. Dark and safe. Only a thin stripe of
light glowed under the door, glinting like stars on the shiny
steel tools hanging from the walls. The silverware. The silverware closet. Franny stood quietly while she heard the
two men pad by the door.

And then there it was again. That sorrowful wail.
Shrill. Clammering. Begging. It was in here. In the closet.
Franny cocked her head, listening. Trying to trace the
sound. Her eyes scanning the shelves. Where was it coming
from?

And then she knew.

She put her hands to her belly and held it, feeling the
vibrations of the tiny voice bawling inside her womb. She
reached to the wall and grasped the cold shaft of steel.

"Still, baby. Mama's here now."

*Arise and take thy child and flee, for Herod will seek
the child to destroy him.*

MARIE OPENED her eyelids a crack and swiveled her eyes to the right, crocodilelike. The pillow was empty. She raised herself slowly up onto her elbows, scanning the bedroom, peering through the open bathroom door. Not there.

"David?"

She waited a few seconds and then called again, more loudly this time.

"David?"

No answer.

She sat fully upright in her bed and sighed, relieved that David was already gone. After last night, she needed a full day on her own before she could confront him again. Tonight she would give him the complete story in a calm, orderly fashion. And she would tell him about Paul Kingsmill.

Marie got out of bed, pulled on her robe, and walked into the bathroom. She turned on the water in the shower. Maybe she should ask Paul to join them this evening. The three of them could have dinner together and talk. She could tell David everything then. She reached her hand into the shower and felt the water. Too hot. She turned the cold water spigot, then slipped out of her robe and pulled her nightgown off over her head. That was the cowardly way, wasn't it? Having Paul there for support. Corroboration. To insure that David took her seriously, that he didn't treat her like a case.

Marie stepped into the shower, turning her back to the warm spray. No, she would talk to David alone first and then, if he wanted her to, she would call Paul. She wasn't a coward. If she had learned nothing else yesterday, she had learned that.

The water felt delicious on her back and buttocks. Soothing. Strengthening. Last night, she had fallen asleep the moment she had closed her eyes and she hadn't moved a limb the entire night. Had David still been talking to her when she closed her eyes? Still quizzing her in his modulated professional voice as though if he raised it she would shatter? Marie arched her head back under the water. David's attitude had in fact calmed her, although certainly not in the way he had intended it to. The more he had treated her as if she were in some precariously balanced mental state, the easier it had been for her to evade his questions. As a "case," she was relieved of that responsibility. For the night, at least. And last night she couldn't possibly have told David where she had been, what she had seen. She hadn't had the strength. So she had told him that she had gone for a ride in the country, that she had needed a day alone. To think.

Marie turned off the water and stepped out of the shower shivering. Today there would be no thinking. Not today or tomorrow or possibly even the next day. Not until there was something definite to think about. Not until Paul told her the results of her amniocentesis. Until then, she would carry on, take care of business, be a normal human being. Even think optimistic thoughts, as Paul had said. She wrapped the bath towel around her trunk, tucking in the end at her bosom so that it hung loosely around her waist. She wouldn't think about the baby today. Not at all. She would pretend she wasn't even pregnant.

She went to the sink and picked her toothbrush out of

the rack. Jesus, her eyes looked peculiar. She leaned closer to the mirror. The lower lids were rimmed with red as if she had been crying. She brushed her teeth quickly, her head bent over the sink, and then returned to her bedroom.

Had she promised David she would stay home today and rest? Probably. She had nodded her head obediently to everything he said until she had crawled into bed and closed her eyes. What else had she promised? Marie sat down on the edge of her bed. David had said it was time they had another three-cornered chat with McPartland, a mid-pregnancy consultation. "You know, a half-time conference," he had said, winking, patting her hand. And she had nodded. Yes, David. Of course. Whatever's best. But now I have to sleep.

Marie stood up. She pulled off the towel and dressed rapidly, choosing a loose-fitting wool dress that all but camouflaged her pregnancy. Out of sight, out of mind. Five minutes later, she was stepping out of the elevator into her apartment building vestibule, her attaché case under her arm, the New York *Times* in her hand, looking for all the world like the competent, if slightly overweight, executive that she was. That she had to be. She strode rapidly to the door.

"Good morning, Mrs. Preston. I thought you were staying in today."

Marie gave Raoul, the doorman, a frozen smile. "Did my husband say that?"

"Yes, Dr. Preston told me you weren't to be disturbed. That's why I didn't bring this up. I signed for it myself." Raoul handed Marie a small parcel.

"Dr. Preston must have been talking about his other wife," Marie said, deadpan. She slipped the parcel into her attaché case. Another token from Mother, no doubt. Last year it had been little Zen fertility statues. This year it was nursing bras. She hailed a taxi and climbed in, determined to read every word on the front page of the *Times* before she reached her office.

"Hi. How's the leg?"

"Oh, fine." Marie had forgotten about yesterday's alibi. She affected a slight limp as she continued past Nancy's desk into her office. "Could you get me a tea and something gooky? Maybe one of those chocolate-covered things filled with day-old lemon pudding."

"Sure. You've got Mr. Hepperman in ten minutes."

"Yup. Send him right in when he gets here."

"Oh, and your husband called. Twice. He wanted you to call as soon as you got in. Should I get him for you?"

"No." Marie sat down behind her desk. "Not just yet."

Yesterday's mail was still lying on her desk where she had left it less than twenty-four hours ago. For an instant, the little pile of envelopes looked surreal to her, the way the objects in her room at her parents' house used to look when she returned home for vacations after months away at college. Relics from another time warp. Good. It made things easier. She plunked her attaché case down in front of her and looked at her watch. Still a few minutes before Hepperman. Time for one quick call. And it wouldn't be to David. She picked up the phone and dialed three digits.

"Research. Ms. Hendricks."

"Hello. This is Marie Preston."

"Oh, hello, Mrs. Preston. How are you? I heard you're pregnant."

"Yes, I'm fine. Listen, is Paula handy?"

"Let me look. Hold on, okay?"

"Sure." Marie absently unzipped her attaché case and pulled out the folder containing last year's budget.

"Marie?"

"Hello, Paula. How have you been?"

"Not bad. And yourself? How's the little image coming?"

"Fine. Look, Paula, can you dig something up for me? It's for a personal project. For mine eyes only sort of thing."

"Shoot."

"I need some background on a man named Monroe. Richard Monroe. He's a gynecologist obstetrician."

"Let me jot this down. Is that Monroe as in Marilyn?"

"Yes." A button lit up on her phone. Now it blinked on to hold.

"Okay. Go on," Paula said.

"He's from Springfield, Massachusetts. Or at least he practiced there until about six years ago. He was involved in some kind of case then, I think. It had something to do with a child named Janet Guilford."

"How do you spell that?"

"G-U-I-L-F-O-R-D."

"Okay. Anything else?"

Nance stuck her head in the door. She mouthed the word, "David" and pointed to the phone.

"Marie? Are you still there? Is there anything else?"

"No. No, that's it, Paula. Thanks."

"No trouble. I have a friend from journalism school who works for the *Springfield Union.* Maybe I can have something for you today."

"Yes, thanks, Paula."

"Any time."

Marie hesitated a second, then hit the button flashing on her phone.

"Hello, David."

"Marie? I tried to reach you at home. What in God's name are you doing there?"

"I have an important meeting this morning. I forgot to tell you."

"Marie, for crissake, I can't keep up with you. Last night you were—"

"David, please, I'm fine today. Terrific. And I'm very busy. Couldn't we talk later?"

"No! There's something we have to talk about right now."

Marie looked down at her hands. She was twisting the corners of her budget sheets. The top one had started to tear. She put her hand into her attaché case and pulled out the parcel the doorman had given her. "What?"

"Marie, I think we ought to have that conference with Dr. McPartland as soon as possible. Today, if he'll see us."

"I can't make it today, David." Marie had ripped the flaps of the parcel with her fingernails. It was from Saks. When had her mother been down to Saks? "Look, let's talk about it tonight, okay?"

She lifted the top off of the box.

"I'm going to make an appointment for tomorrow, Marie."

Marie was staring at the box, her lips parted. Neatly folded inside it was the blue-and-white polka-dotted pinafore she had fallen in love with. The one she had dreamed about.

"Marie? Are you listening to me?"

"All right, David. Anything. Anything you say."

"Marie? Are you all right? Marie, what's wrong?"

"I . . . have to go now, David."

Marie set down the phone, still staring at the pinafore. She slowly lifted it out of the box and held it in front of her. A card fluttered to the floor. She leaned over and picked it up. The writing was in block letters.

It said: DON'T SPOIL IT NOW.

"Isn't that a pretty little thing." Sol Hepperman banged into Marie's office, a paper bag in one hand, a sheaf of folders in the other. "But how do you know if you're going to have a girl?"

Marie's hands were trembling. She folded the pinafore over them so that Hepperman wouldn't notice. "Good . . . good morning, Sol. I, uh, I'm sorry about yesterday."

"Couldn't be helped, I'm sure." Hepperman plopped his

corpulent body down into the chair on the other side of
Marie's desk. "Say, I bet I know. You had one of those am-
bionesus things that tells you what sex it's going to be.
Amazing, isn't it? Sophie tells me if she had one, she
wouldn't want to know. The sex, that is. She says it takes
away half the fun."

"Yes."

DON'T SPOIL IT NOW.

Spoil what? Damn it, what? Who sent this? What do
they want?

Marie's mind raced. Whom had she told about that pinafore? Bonnie, of course, she was there. Her mother. Kate
. . . David.

"Well, shall we?" Hepperman set his folders down on
Marie's desk. "Oh, your secretary gave me this." He handed
Marie the paper bag. "Breakfast."

Marie opened the bottom drawer of her desk, threw in
the pinafore and slammed it shut. Then she picked the card
off of her desk, tore it into small pieces, and dropped the
pieces into her wastepaper basket.

"I'll tell you what worries me, Sol," she said, leaning toward him. "These projected mill-time increases. Where did
you get these figures from?"

All business. No thinking now. Not now, for godssake.

"From Kemp. They're just estimates, Marie."

"Well, we were off by almost twelve percent last year.
Maybe we should be a little less conservative this time
around." Take care of business. Be a normal human being.
"Why don't we start from scratch, Sol, and see what we
come up with?"

Marie rolled her chair around her desk next to Hepperman and leaned over the budget sheets in front of them.
And she worked. Quickly. Efficiently. Picking out loosely
calculated estimates. Jotting down new developmental
costs. For over an hour she didn't lift her head and when, at
twelve-thirty, Hepperman suggested that they break for

lunch, Marie asked him if he could hold out until one. She told him she would take him out for three courses at Mama Leone's then.

At a quarter to one, Nancy buzzed her.

"There's a Miss Gold on line one."

Marie swallowed hard. David had already made an appointment with McPartland. To find out what could be done about his wife's out-of-kilter hormones.

"Tell her I'm tied up, will you, Nance? I'll call back after lunch."

"Okay."

Marie sat back down and bent her head over her desk. "Where were we, Sol?"

The phone buzzed again.

"What is it, Nance?"

"She says it's important. She says she has to talk to you right now. What should I tell her?"

"I'll take it." She turned to Hepperman. "Excuse me just a second, will you?" She walked around the desk and sat on its edge facing the window, her back to Hepperman. She pressed the first button on her phone, paused a second and said, "Marie Preston."

"Mrs. Preston, this is Miss Gold in Dr. McPartland's office. He wants me to schedule a second amniotic tap for you as soon as possible. Could you make it for Thursday afternoon at two?"

Marie stared out the window. A man in the neighboring building was watering his plants.

"Mrs. Preston? Can I put you down for that time?"

"I already had an amniotic tap two weeks ago, Miss Gold. I believe you should have the results in a day or two." Marie spoke in a monotone.

"Yes, we're sorry, but this sometimes happens, Mrs. Preston. It would have been ready tomorrow, but there's been a bit of an accident. We were only notified by the hospital a few minutes ago. It's been contaminated. Your amniotic culture died."

"JESUS CHRIST, Kingsmill, do you have any idea what this could do to the department? Do you have any idea?"

Fine's pipe was nowhere in evidence. For once he appeared to want to be absolutely clear.

"I'm not just talking about the clinical work we'll lose. We've already lost. Bouchard tells me he's already had two cancellations today. I'm talking about funding. I'm talking about NIH and Rockefeller. They'll hear about this. You can be sure of that. We've got a total of seven applications for grants out with them alone. This could dry us up. This could kill us."

Paul sat quietly across from Fine who was pacing behind his desk. Not once had Fine mentioned the twelve expectant mothers whose amniotic cultures had been virally contaminated the night before. For five of those women, it was too late for a second tap. They were in their twenty-second week of pregnancy. Preemies had been known to survive at twenty-five weeks.

"I've spoken with Dr. Miller and Dr. Henderson. I didn't want to take any action until I had consulted with them." Fine sat down and looked across his desk, his eyes seeming to focus somewhere above Paul's eyebrows. "Paul, until we've completed a thorough investigation, we have no choice but to suspend you from all activity in the laboratory."

Paul nodded and began to rise from his chair. He supposed he should look devastated. Or at least shocked. But the fact was his status at Hebron Hospital was the least of his worries just now. It would make his investigation of the McPartland babies that much harder, of course. But he had been thrown out of better places.

"Paul, I considered it a great honor to have you join us. Despite what I'd"—Fine interrupted himself to open the top drawer of his desk and ferret out his pipe. He lit it. "Despite some of the things that have been said about you."

"I appreciate that, Sam." Paul was on his feet. "I'll just get a few of my things from the lab and be on my way."

"Paul, there's going to be a thorough inquiry into this business. Miller's getting up a committee now. There may be some law suits involved. Dr. McPartland has lodged an official complaint with the board. I'm hoping that if I approach him personally I can get him to drop it."

Paul smiled sardonically. "I'm sure you'll do your best, Sam." He started for the door.

"Paul, I have no choice in this. You were the only one who was here last night. The only one who signed in, the only one the guard saw."

Paul put his hand on the door knob.

Fine stood up. "Paul, why the hell couldn't you leave those McPartland amnios alone?"

Paul turned back slowly and looked at Sam Fine. A cloud of smoke enveloped the distinguished old man's head. "Sam, just between you and me, you've got the wrong man." He let himself out of the door.

On his way to the laboratory, Paul encountered Miss Saint Ambrosio, the genetics counselor. She looked at him as if she were about to say something, then shook her head and passed him by. The pariah. The contaminator. He wondered how long it would take before the news of his latest fiasco reached London. A day. Two at the most. Theresa would know of it by the end of the week. She would certainly make it an occasion for one of her better *bon mots*. "Well, at last he has an international reputation." Something like that. It didn't matter, really. Only one thing mattered now.

Paul entered his laboratory and went directly to his desk. He scanned the room a moment, then quickly unlocked the top drawer and removed three lab notebooks and a large, string-tied cardboard envelope. He pushed the drawer closed, leaving it unlocked. Save them the trouble of breaking it open. He lifted his briefcase onto his desk and opened it.

"Damn it, Paul!"

Paul spun around. Eva was standing just inside the door. Her face looked puffy, her eyelids red and swollen. By God, she had been crying. He had underestimated her. Maybe something decent would come of this whole business after all.

"Damn it, why couldn't you have stayed with me last night? None of this would have happened." She walked slowly toward him.

"Perhaps not."

Eva reached her arms around his neck and pressed her cheek against his. Her cheek was damp. He kissed it.

"You're a darling," he said.

"Thanks." She kissed his neck, then pulled her head back and looked into his eyes. "Shit, Paul, couldn't you have waited? I was going to get those cells for you. No one would have known."

Paul stiffened. He dropped his arms from around Eva's waist. "Eva, I didn't contaminate those amnios. I never opened a flask. They were killed by a virus."

Eva let her arms drop too and looked away. She said

nothing. So she didn't believe him either. Paul sighed. That made her sympathy all the more touching, he supposed. Those were tears of loyalty on her cheeks. He turned back to his desk and quickly stuffed the notebooks and envelope into his briefcase. He zipped it shut.

"I'd better be going," he said. "Before the royal guard ushers me out."

He started to walk around Eva, but she took a step to the side, blocking his way.

"What does this mean about us?" she asked.

"I don't know." Paul studied her face. Her luminous blue eyes had a soft, plaintive expression he had never seen there before. A sign of what had been missing, what he had been hoping to find in her all these months. And now he wasn't sure what to do with it. "Nothing, I suppose. I'll call you, Eva. Soon." He leaned toward her and kissed her cheek.

"Paul."

"Yes."

"I didn't report that a flask was missing."

Paul felt his face redden. He looked down.

"And I won't," Eva said. "I won't tell a soul."

"I'll call you," Paul said, and he walked out into the corridor. He went to the elevator, pressed the button, and waited. Were there other good-byes he should make? Not really. He remembered regretting making the rounds the day he left Elmwood, shaking hands, kissing cheeks, accepting pitying well-wishes. Afterward, he had gone to The Three Feathers and gotten steaming drunk with a pub-load of other unemployeds. Unemployables.

"I'm glad I caught you." Bernstein loped toward him from around the corner. "There's been a frantic lady calling you for the past hour. I thought you were still with Fine."

"Is she on the line now?"

"No. She said she was coming here. She wouldn't leave her name."

The elevator door slid open and Paul reached his hand back to hold it.

"Well, Mel, I'm sure we'll see each other again."

"Of course." Bernstein stepped closer to Paul, putting his big head directly in front of his. "Paul, you didn't . . . you didn't mess around with those amnios, did you?"

Paul stepped backward into the open elevator. "No, Mel." The door started to close. "Did you?"

Marie was coming through the front door of the hospital just as Paul got off of the elevator. He saw her immediately and rushed to her. Her face was ashen and she had been crying. She was still crying.

"Marie."

"Oh, God, Paul. I couldn't get through to you. What's going on? They called me at work. McPartland's office called and—"

"Marie, your amnio is all right. At least enough of it is to find out what we have to."

"What? What do you mean? They called me, Paul. They—"

"Your amnio is fine, Marie. Believe me." Paul clasped her arm in his hand. "But we can't talk here," he said quietly. He guided her back to the entrance and out onto the street. They crossed Fifth Avenue and entered the park before he spoke again.

"Do you remember last night when I left you for a moment in the hall just before we left the hospital?"

"Yes." Marie's legs felt shaky. She hadn't been able to find a free cab until Seventy-second Street. She had run most of the way there. "I think I have to sit down."

They walked a few feet up the park path to a green wooden bench and sat down. An elderly man was reading a Greek newspaper at the other end of the bench.

"I don't actually believe in ghosts," Paul said. "There was somebody else in the lab last night."

"While we were there?"

"Yes. And afterward. Whoever it was contaminated most of the cultures in my warm room after we left."

Marie put her hand to her forehead. She was thinking of the pinafore. The note.

"While you waited in the hall," Paul went on, "I took one of your flasks out of the warm room—we usually keep five of them going in case one doesn't take. I put it in a chemical storage closet. It's the same temperature. And this morning I came in at around three and brought it upstairs to the warm room of a colleague, Hopkins. It's up there now, safe and sound."

Marie leaned back in the bench. She could feel the cold wooden slats through her coat.

"I've been sacked from the hospital. They think I'm responsible for the contaminations. I'll be using Hopkins' lab from now on. On the q.t., of course. I'm going to be spending a lot of time climbing back stairs for a while." Paul lifted his briefcase onto his lap, unzipped it, and pulled out the large cardboard envelope. "I've already had a bit of practice this morning. I've been doing a little detective work."

Marie was gazing blankly up the path. Three teenagers in satin jackets were flipping a miniature football back and forth as they walked. She knew that she should feel relieved that her amniotic culture was still alive, but she felt nothing. Numb.

"Marie, do tell me if—" Paul paused, fingering the envelope. "I mean, I wouldn't blame you if you didn't want to be a part of this anymore."

Marie turned her head back and looked at Paul. She smiled ruefully. "Paul, I am part of this," she said quietly.

Paul reached out and touched Marie's hand lightly. "Yes. I guess you are."

They were both silent for a moment. Then Marie smiled and said, "You were going to show me something, weren't you?"

"Yes." Paul withdrew his hand and unclasped the envelope in his lap. He pulled out a sheaf of Xeroxed forms. Marie could smell the chemical odor of the freshly made copies. "These are the birth records of the McPartland babies for the past five years."

Marie sat up straight. McPartland babies. She remembered the nurse using those words when she had visited the nursery with David.

"I stole them this morning and Xeroxed them. I didn't get them back any too soon, I can tell you." He smiled.

"Paul! Are they normal?"

"Yes, they are," he said. "More than that, Marie. They're all perfectly normal. Look." He pulled off the top sheet and handed it to Marie, pointing to a box in its corner. "The minute a baby is born it's given a rating. An Apgar Score it's called. It's based on a series of vital signs and functions: respiration, movement, reaction to light, mental alertness. Most newborns get a score of nine out of ten. Maybe ten or fifteen percent get less than that. And maybe seven or eight out of every hundred babies get all ten points."

Marie looked at the sheet in front of her. It was for a baby boy born to a Frank and Marilyn Brandt three years ago. The Apgar Score was ten.

"They're all tens, Marie." Paul flipped through the pile of forms. "Every damned one of them."

"Thank God!" Marie hugged the Brandt birth record to her bosom. "Thank God!"

For a moment Paul was perplexed. To him, McPartland's Apgar record was one more anomaly in an expanding series of anomalies. He looked up at Marie and forced himself to smile. "I suppose it is good news of sorts, isn't it?"

"Good news? It's fantastic news, Paul. It's the best news I've heard in months." Marie jumped up and virtually danced in front of him.

Paul hesitated. Then he said, "But it's not normal, Marie. Statistically, it's considerably abnormal."

Marie stared at Paul, her face beaming. "Who gives a damn?" She pressed a hand against her belly. "I'm not a statistic, Paul. I . . . I'm going to be a mother."

Paul looked down at the pile of sheets in his lap. Indeed, who did give a damn? If not Marie, then who? Theresa, finally, was right: He invariably ended up victimizing the people he was trying to protect. He lifted the pile of papers and began to insert them back into his briefcase.

"You still think something's wrong, don't you?" Marie sat down beside him. She hadn't wanted to ask the question.

"I don't know. Maybe." Paul reached out for the birth record Marie still held in her hands.

"What?" Marie held onto the sheet. "What do you think is wrong, Paul?"

Paul shrugged. "Just another statistic."

Marie felt a chill pass through her. Her moment of euphoria was gone. For an instant, she hated Paul Kingsmill for taking it away from her. "Tell me," she said. "Everything."

Paul slowly set the birth records back onto his lap. A small breeze began to lift them at their corners. The topmost one flapped against his hands.

"When they take the sonogram—the ultrasound picture of the fetus just before the amnio tap—it's fairly routine to take a measurement of the baby's head, the cranial width. The technician usually does it. And she can calculate the age of the fetus from that measurement fairly precisely. Within days. It's the most reliable way of projecting the baby's due date. Based on it, the obstetrician sometimes has to revise the original projected due date, the one every mother calculates from her date of conception."

Marie nodded. "Go on."

"They're all about a week early," Paul said. "Every one of the McPartland due dates had to be revised. Every McPartland fetus was a week or ten days older than the mothers thought."

"What does that mean, Paul?"

Again, Paul shrugged. "I wish I knew." He shook his head, turning over the sheets one by one. "I wish I knew what any of this meant."

"Adam!"

Marie shot her hand out and grabbed one of the birth records.

"That's Adam. Adam Roundtree."

"You know this child?"

"Yes, I know him. He's a wonderful boy. He's—" Marie hesitated. "He's half the reason I went to Dr. McPartland in the first place."

"His mother is pregnant again, I believe."

"I know that. Bonnie's a very good friend of mine." Marie stared at Paul. He was biting down on his lip. "What is it, Paul? What about Bonnie?"

"The baby she's carrying. I analyzed its amnio. It's one of the anomalies, Marie."

26

A BLACK woman wearing a short wool coat over her white uniform was pushing a baby carriage toward the corner opposite the phone booth. If everything is all right, I'll quit my job, Marie thought. If the baby is all right, I'll take care of it myself. That's a promise. I swear to God it is.

She dropped a dime into the phone and dialed, just as the baby was wheeled past her. Pink. A girl. A sweet little baby girl.

"Hello?"

"Bonnie. It's me."

"Marie. How are you? We were worried about you. David called twice last night wondering if I'd heard from you."

"I'm fine, Bonnie. Terrific. David and I just got our signals crossed. A little breakdown in family communications."

Bonnie laughed. "Oh, I'm glad to hear that's all it was. I was going to call you later."

Marie pressed her forehead against the booth's cold glass. This was the easy part. The hard part came later.

"Bonnie, I wondered if we could get together. I'd like to talk." Nothing personal. I'm just doing a little research. I just want to know who you've been sleeping with. Who the father of your babies is.

"That'll be nice. It's been too long, hasn't it? How

about lunch tomorrow? Wait'll you see me. I'm big as a house. I put on eight pounds in three weeks. Dr. McPartland is going to kill me. Is tomorrow good, Marie?"

"Not really, Bonnie. How about today? Do you have any free time this afternoon?"

"Golly, I don't think so. We—a few of the mothers in my building—we're taking the kids to the museum. The Museum of Natural History. Adam is crazy about dinosaurs. He knows all their names."

"When are you leaving?"

"Let me see . . . gee, I'm late already, Marie. I should be leaving now. They'll be waiting in the lobby."

"Could you get away for a few minutes, Bonnie? I'll meet you at the museum. We can take a walk."

"Is something wrong, Marie?"

"I don't know, Bonnie. Maybe. I'll tell you everything when I see you. I'll meet you at the front entrance in fifteen minutes, okay?"

"Oh God, something is wrong, isn't it?" Bonnie's voice cracked. Marie shut her eyes. How the hell was she going to do this?

"Fifteen minutes, okay, Bonnie?"

Marie heard the phone click.

"Bonnie?"

The phone clicked again and the dial tone came on. Marie hung the phone up and stepped outside the booth. Although the temperature was just above freezing, it was a clear day and the sun was warm on her face. She could walk through the park and be at the museum in ample time if she set out now. She could rehearse her interview with Bonnie. Plan a strategy.

"You using the phone, lady?"

Marie turned. A long-haired young man in an aviator's jacket was standing next to her.

"Yes," she said. "I'll only be a minute."

She stepped back into the booth, opened her handbag,

and withdrew two coins from her change purse. One more call. One more piece of business. She dropped the coins into the phone and dialed.

"Mrs. Preston's office. Can I help you?"

"Nance. It's me, Marie."

"Marie! Are you all right?"

That seemed to be everybody's greetings these days.

"Yes, Nance. I'm fine. Look, I may be a little late this afternoon. Fourish. Something like that." She changed the phone to her other ear. "Listen, uh, did Hepperman recover from my little outburst without any side effects?" Marie affected a small chuckle.

Nancy did not laugh.

"He's fine now, I think," she said. "He's just not used to these things."

"No."

"My sister had a terrible first pregnancy," Nancy went on. "Just terrible. She was always bursting into tears and throwing—"

"Nance, were there any calls?"

Marie heard her secretary hesitate a second.

"Yes, your husband. And . . . Mr. Hamilton called. He said he wanted you to come up to his office as soon as you came in."

For a little discussion about hysteria, no doubt. Sol Hepperman would probably be there. And Murray Miller. Perhaps they could call David in as a consultant.

"Anybody else?"

"Uh, yes, Paula Taylor called from research. She said she has some kind of report you wanted."

"Oh. Listen, Nance, I'm at a pay phone. Can you switch me down to Paula?"

"Sure. I'll see you at four then."

"Right. Thanks."

Marie braced the phone against her ear with her shoulder while Nancy clicked the switchboard operator. A small circle of the glass had been fogged over from her breath. Marie absently traced her initials in it.

"Paula Taylor, research."

"Hi, Paula. Marie Preston."

"Hello, Marie. Are you okay?"

"Terrific, despite rumors to the contrary. I'm in a phone booth, Paula. What did you come up with?"

"Some interesting stuff. I'm surprised *Soma* never picked up on this. Although it's kind of old news now."

"Let's have it." Marie erased her initials.

"Are you going to take this down? Should I go slowly?"

"No, not now. You can send it all up to me later. What do you have?"

"Well, it was a case, all right. A malpractice suit up in Springfield. This Dr. Monroe took quite a beating."

Marie leaned back in the corner of the phone booth. "Go on."

"It was one of the first of its kind," Paula said. "They called it a 'wrongful life' suit. You know, kind of a switch on 'wrongful death.'"

"Yes."

"It seems this Dr. Monroe had a normal GYN practice up there. In the better part of town. A good rep. He's a Harvard man. Nothing out of the ordinary."

Marie let her back slide slowly down against the booth's glass wall.

"And then one of his patients, a Mrs. Arnold Guilford from Agawam—that's a little suburb nearby—got pregnant. It was her first pregnancy. She was thirty-eight at the time. And when she had the baby it was a Down's Syndrome child. You know, a mongoloid . . . You still there, Marie?"

Marie was crouched, fetallike, in the booth. Her eyes were closed.

"Yes. Go on, Paula."

"Well, somehow the ACLU got involved and they sued

Monroe for failing to warn Mrs. Guilford that she was what they call 'at risk' for having a Down's. You know, because of her age it's more likely. Their argument was that Monroe should have given her an amniocentesis. He should have tested her baby for that while she was still pregnant. Apparently Monroe hadn't even told her about that test."

Marie swallowed hard. Her mouth was dry. She couldn't say anything.

"Marie, you had an amniocentesis, didn't you? I mean, you've got nothing to worry about, do you?"

"Yes. Is that all you have?"

"No. This is the most interesting part, I think, at least. The court decided that Monroe had to pay for the support and special care of Mrs. Guilford's baby for the rest of its life. You know, doctors, special schools, things like that. But that's not the part I meant. It was Monroe's reaction to the whole thing that I found fascinating. I can't help admiring the guy a little. He issued a statement—"

"I'm sorry, your first three minutes are up. Please deposit ten cents more for your next—" A rasping, New York accented monotone totally eclipsed Paula's voice. Marie stood up. She only had quarters in her purse. She dropped one in.

"I'm still here," Marie said.

"Aren't those things a nuisance?"

"His statement, Paula. You said his statement was interesting."

"Yes. Let me read this to you . . . I've got it right here. He said, 'For centuries, physicians have been criticized for playing God. This decision now makes us culpable for failing to play God.' . . . I think he has a point, don't you?"

"I don't know, Paula."

"Well, that's pretty much it. He closed up his practice in Springfield right after the case. I suppose he moved somewhere else. Alaska or someplace. I wonder what he's doing today, don't you? Maybe *Soma* could do a follow up on him. Do you want me to look into that?"

"No, Paula. Not just now. Look, I have to go. Thanks."

"I'll send everything I've got up to your office, okay?"

"Fine. Thanks again, Paula. Bye."

"No trouble. I found it all perfectly fascinating, to tell you the truth. Bye."

Marie hung up the phone. My God, what would Paul make of all of this? Outside the booth, a cab was just leaving the light. She went to the curb and hailed it.

"Museum of Natural History, please."

The cabbie pulled down the meter flag and Marie sat back in her seat. Bonnie would be waiting and she wasn't at all prepared. Not that she could be even if she had hours. Paul was asking too much really. It wasn't right to put all of this on Bonnie. To frighten her too. The way Franny had frightened her. Marie jammed her hands into her pockets. None of it was right. None of it.

The cab cut through the park at Eighty-sixth Street. One thing was certain, there was no way Marie could ask Bonnie to give Paul a blood sample. On the q.t., as he said. And to ask her to ask Tom for one too? No way. No way at all. She didn't even know how she was going to ask David for one. Or if she would. The light was red where the park drive intersected Central Park West.

"I'll get out here," she said. She handed the driver two dollars and let herself out of the door.

Maybe she wouldn't have to tell Bonnie anything. Maybe it wasn't necessary. Paul had said that if he could take blood samples from both Bonnie and Tom, she wouldn't have to pry into Bonnie's sex life. With blood specimens, he could tell if Tom were the baby's father without asking. Marie crossed the street at Eighty-fifth. She heard another pedestrian dashing behind her just as the light changed.

She could say that she had a friend who was doing research. And you know how secretive all these research people are. Always afraid someone else would publish first. He was doing blood research and he needed specimens. Of couples.

Marie suddenly stopped. Someone was behind her. Whoever had raced across the street in back of her was still behind her. And had stayed just behind her for three blocks now. She slowly turned around. A pair of fur-coated matrons were strolling toward her. No one else. Paranoia, no doubt. Born of the lies she was fabricating in her head. The matrons smiled at Marie and she smiled back before turning and crossing the street.

Bonnie might believe the blood research story. Maybe. But not Tom. For all his Midwestern innocence, Tom had a certain wily skepticism too. Hadn't he been the one whose curiosity was piqued the most by McPartland's name change? But then again, Tom had bought McPartland's version of that completely, without a flicker of suspicion. Maybe he would believe the research story after all.

Marie was in front of the museum. She glanced at her watch. Five after three. Only five minutes late. She looked up the long stone stairway to the entrance. Scores of schoolchildren were milling in and out, some with name tags flapping from their coats. Marie started up the stairs. Bonnie was probably waiting in the lobby. She hoped she hadn't given up on her. She looked through the glass partition next to the door. Adam was there, peering out, his hands shading his eyes like a bird watcher. What a fantastic-looking child. Among all those children's faces, his shone like a beacon. Bright. Incredibly beautiful. She raised her hand to wave at him.

And then it grabbed her. A hand in back of her. It closed around her arm and spun her around so fast that her right foot twisted around and both of her knees popped from under her. For an instant, she was balanced on her knees, facing down the granite steps. And then she catapulted forward, her arms wrapped around her belly, and rolled, thudding down three steps before she flung out a hand, hooked it around the railing post and twirled to a halt.

27

PAUL LAUGHED.

Greek. It would be Greek. French he could have at least muddled through, picking out the key words. And German, if memory didn't fail, would have presented no problem. But Greek?

Yet then again, if the paper had been written by a Frenchman or a German—or even a Swede, for that matter— it would have been listed in the bibliographies. The *Lancet* would have noted it. It would be common knowledge for the English-speaking world of geneticists. But in Greek or Chinese or Hungarian or even often Russian, a discovery could remain hidden from the rest of the scientific world for years, possibly forever. Babble's brake on progress. Only last year, an astute and polyglot California professor had unearthed a short article written by an unknown Soviet-Armenian mathematics student that was now causing an unprecedented revolution in computer programming. The article had been written three years earlier.

Paul again leaned over the black-and-white plate and studied it through his pocket magnifier. The reproduction was poor, perhaps out of focus to begin with. And only God —and the Greeks—knew if it were truly relevant. But that pinpoint of illumination, fuzzy as it was at the edges, was too similar to dismiss out of hand. And the placement on the chromosome was clearly identical. Still, it was a long shot. But that's all he had to go on now. Long shots. And hunches.

Paul picked the journal up off the table and walked to the librarian's desk.

"Pardon me, you wouldn't have a Greek to English dictionary, would you?"

The librarian looked up languidly from the book he was reading, a novel, judging from its back cover, about sex and violence in the fashion industry. This fellow had not been too happy about helping Paul in the first place, insisting on inspecting Paul's credentials as a Fellow at Hebron—too recently canceled for him to know—before admitting him to the Columbia Medical School Library's august stacks.

"Greek?"

"Yes. Greek."

"I don't think so, Doctor. Would Latin do?"

"No. Nor would Turkish."

The librarian scowled at Paul and returned to his book.

"We've got one somewhere here." A woman's voice from behind a metal bookcase. "Yes. I'm afraid it's rather out of date, though." A tall, white-haired woman in a medical jacket appeared from behind the bookcase carrying a heavy, red-covered tome.

"That's all right. So is my Greek." Paul took the book from her and smiled. "I cannot thank you enough."

He carried the dictionary back to the table and set it and the journal down. Best to begin with the title, he supposed:

"Ἐμβρυο-Μητρικὴ συνταυτζσις: Ὁ κρισιμος γόνος."

"Ἐμβρυο." Paul opened the dictionary to the Es. The pages were brittle, like autumn leaves. He turned them slowly, then stopped and ran his thumb along the inside margin. "Ἐμβολή, Embolism." "Ἐμβολι, Graft, Inoculate."

"Ἔμβολον, Ram, Sting." "Ἔμβρυο, Embryo, Foetus." An aus-
picious start.

"Μητρική." Paul turned to the Ms. The first two pages
were torn. He pressed the jagged edges of the torn pieces
together, trying to align the letters.

"Μητρική, Womb."

Fifteen minutes passed before he finished translating
the title: "Embryo-Womb Compatibility: The Critical
Gene."

Paul sat back in the wooden chair and rubbed his chin.
On the mark. His hunch was paying off. In spades, as the
Americans would say. He leaned over the open journal.
Where to go next? At this rate of progress, it would take
him several weeks to translate the entire paper. He could
look for a Greek, he supposed. There were several working
at Hebron. But he couldn't even risk the time for that. Because Paul had another hunch, one that hung over him like
an admonishing angel: He didn't have many days left to
figure all of this out.

He turned again to the black-and-white plate, the single illustration. It had a caption.

"Ἔκτον χρωμοσωμα, δεκάτη πέμητη θεσις: γενικός Εμβρυο-δοτης."

An hour later, Paul slammed the dictionary closed.
There were beads of sweat gathered on his forehead. He
had to get to Marie immediately. He had to speak to her re-
markable friend in the insane asylum.

MARIE CREPT along the wall, terrified. Suddenly, she jumped in front of the door and slammed the bolt closed. She stood perfectly still, stark naked and shivering. She listened. Footsteps were treading toward her in the hallway. Her eyes darted around her living room. The wrought iron trivet on the coffee table. She started to back toward it. The footsteps grew louder. She picked up the trivet and raised it over her head. She heard the jingling of keys and then a door opening. Her neighbor had entered the apartment across the hall.

Marie sank down onto the sofa. Her whole body was trembling. She let the trivet drop to the floor with a thud. The nap of the sofa cover stung her buttocks, a patchwork of cuts and bruises. There were tears in her eyes.

"God help me," she murmured.

She leaned back against the sofa, trying to calm herself. And then she felt the baby moving inside her again.

She sat bolt upright, her right hand darting to her vagina. She slipped her middle finger inside it. Wet. She withdrew her hand and held it in front of her eyes. No blood. Nothing. Thank God.

She stood up slowly and started back to her bed. Her pelvis ached with every step. She should see a doctor. Any doctor. She could call Ralph Lowenstein. He would see her in an emergency, maybe even come to the apartment. She could trust him, for godssake. Couldn't she? She stared at the phone on the bed stand. She hadn't even called David. How the hell was she going to call Lowenstein?

She lay down on her side on the bed. Why didn't she call the police? She had been attacked. Deliberately, ruthlessly thrown down a flight of granite steps. There was not a single doubt in her mind about that, despite the story about slipping on an icy step she had told Bonnie and the first-aid nurse at the museum. They had believed her, of course. No one saw her attacker. She hadn't either. What could she tell the police? That someone had tripped her on the steps of the Museum of Natural History? Someone who had sent her a pinafore and an anonymous note? Would David even believe that?

Again she felt the baby curling inside her. She cupped her hand around her belly. She was crying.

He hadn't wanted to kill Marie. He wanted to kill her baby.

The phone rang.

Marie shuddered. If she answered, he would know she was at home. And then he would come. He would get the baby this time. He would rip it out of her.

The phone rang again.

And again.

What if it were Bonnie? The only way Marie had gotten her to leave after she had taken her home was by promising to call her in an hour. She looked at the clock-radio on the bed stand. It was almost an hour and a half since Bonnie had left. If she didn't answer, Bonnie would surely call David. If she hadn't already. Marie rolled on the bed, her skin smarting against the sheets. She reached out her hand and brought the phone to her ear. She said nothing.

"Hello? Marie?"

Paul.

Marie let out her breath.

"Hello." She swallowed hard. "Hello, Paul."

"Marie? Is something wrong?"

"No."

"Are you sure? You don't sound quite right."

"I . . . I had to run to the phone."

"Oh. I tried you first at your office. I thought I'd try you at home. How did it go with Mrs. Roundtree?"

Marie's laughter rose in her so suddenly, so uncontrollably, that she dropped the receiver on the bed. She shook with the laughter, gasping for air. How, indeed, had it gone with Mrs. Roundtree? Trippingly. Yes, trippingly. A full minute passed before she could again pick up the phone.

"I'm sorry, Paul."

"Is someone there? Should I call later?"

"No. No one's here." The laughter was completely gone. "Paul, can you come over right now? I'll tell you everything when you come over."

"Of course." Paul hesitated. "I was going to ask you if you were free for a while. I, uh, I'd like to visit your friend in the hospital. Franny. I thought we might go together."

Marie closed her eyes.

"Does it . . . does it have to be today, Paul?"

"No."

"I'll go," she said abruptly. "Come right away. Come right up to my door, will you, Paul? Fourteen C."

"My God, you should have told me all this before we left. You should still be in bed."

"I'll be all right. Really." Marie leaned her elbow on the armrest, easing some of the weight off of her throbbing buttocks. "I feel better just being out of the apartment. With somebody."

"I should have at least examined you."

Marie looked at Paul. "I didn't know you were an M.D. too."

"Yes." Paul looked in the rearview mirror and cut the car into the right lane. Marie had not told him anything until they were on the Sawmill River Parkway. "I think I'd better turn around and take us back."

"Please, don't."

"Are you sure there's no bleeding? No spotting at all?"

"None, Paul. The nurse examined me. I've checked myself a hundred times." She looked out of the window. "We're almost there. It's the next exit. Woodridge Avenue."

Paul slowed the car. He was silent for a moment and then he said, "I think we'd better go to the police, don't you?"

Marie shook her head.

"Why not?"

"Because we don't know enough," Marie said. "Not yet." But she did not want to know any more either. She just wanted to keep driving. Far away. Never stop.

Paul took the turn at Woodridge Avenue.

"Why do you want to see Franny?"

Paul shrugged, keeping his eyes on the road. He wasn't going to tell Marie his hunches. Not now. They were too farfetched. Maybe he wouldn't have to at all.

"I just want to ask her a few questions about McPartland," he said.

"She's crazy, Paul. I told you that." Marie raised her voice without intending to.

"I know. You don't have to see her, Marie. I don't think you should."

Marie said nothing. She saw the brick rear wing of Tower Hospital looming in front of them. "Over there," she said. "I think you can park in the back."

Paul turned and entered the parking lot. He stopped the car and looked at Marie. "I'll leave you here," he said.

"No."

"You can lock the doors."

"I'm coming with you, Paul."

Paul got out, walked around the car and then opened the door for Marie, taking her arm as they walked to the hospital's entrance. He paused at the reception desk, but Marie tugged him past it toward the elevator. She didn't want to answer any questions.

"She'll be in the visiting room," Marie said. "I know the way."

The elevator doors slid open. Paul took Marie's arm and started to step in, but Marie held back. There were three men in the elevator, all wearing tweed coats. She studied their faces. How would she recognize him? Them? She gripped Paul's arm and stepped in. They turned and faced the door. Just as the doors closed, she saw a bald-headed man in a black trench coat rushing toward them, waving his arms. One of the men in tweed coats reached a finger toward the "Open" button. Marie pushed his hand away. She was sure she had recognized the bald-headed man.

"I beg your pardon," the man whose hand Marie had pushed said indignantly.

Marie said nothing. She pressed the button for the third floor. Paul touched her shoulder.

"Did you know that man?" he whispered.

"I don't know. I think so." She was trembling again. "But I don't know from where."

Paul put his arm around her waist. "We'll make this fast," he whispered.

"Good."

The doors opened at the third floor and they stepped out. All three men in tweed coats remained on. Marie led Paul down the tiled corridor to the visiting room. Maybe this wasn't so terrible a place for Franny to be. Maybe it was safe. If any place was safe.

The two young men in seersucker robes were standing in the waiting room doorway exactly where she had last seen them yesterday. My God, was it only yesterday? The young man on the left shoved his up-turned palm in front of her. "Toll bridge."

Marie jumped. Then, her hand shaking, she deliberately mimed withdrawing a coin from her coat pocket and depositing it in the man's hand. He bowed, grinning, and let them pass. She surveyed the room, still gripping Paul's arm. It seemed quieter than yesterday. More subdued. The faces looked more tortured than she remembered them. She searched for Franny's gray, bony face and wild, glittering eyes.

"You're Mrs. Preston, aren't you?"

Marie stiffened. A middle-aged nurse, her hair pulled back in a severe bun, had appeared in front of them. Marie nodded.

"Mrs. Hollander's sister, I believe." The nurse eyed Paul. "Mr. Preston?"

"Yes," Paul said quickly. "We want to see Franny."

"Follow me," the nurse said and immediately turned to the door.

Marie didn't move. "Where is she?"

The nurse continued walking without answering. Paul took Marie's arm and followed behind the nurse. At the door, the man in the seersucker robe again stuck out his hand. The nurse shoved it aside. At the elevator, she turned left. "The stairs will be faster," she mumbled. She opened the heavy door leading to the stairway without any apparent effort. Paul and Marie stepped in behind her. As the door swung shut behind them, Marie shuddered.

"What happened to Franny?" Marie said.

The nurse started down the stairs. "We don't know," she said.

Marie tightened her grip on Paul's arm. What had they done with Franny? Was she straitjacketed in a padded cell? Under sedation? Franny had said they would never let her out.

At the first landing, the nurse led them out through the

open door and down a green-tiled hallway. Then she abruptly turned to her left and opened a large, opaque-glass door.

"Well, here we are," she said.

"Jesus God!" The blood drained from Paul's face.

Marie stared at him.

"It's the morgue," he said.

Paul caught Marie around the waist just as her knees buckled under her. He dragged her to a chair and slid it beneath her, holding onto her shoulders. Immediately, the morgue attendant, a tall, bespectacled black man in a blood-spotted white coat, pulled an ammonia ampule from his pocket, crouched in front of Marie, and broke it under her nose. The entire maneuver was fluid. Well practiced. He watched as her respiration deepened.

Consciousness returned to Marie like a flash of blinding light. Without opening her eyes, she pushed the attendant's hand away from her face.

And then she remembered.

"Oh God, no. No!" Tears flooded her eyes. "No!"

Paul held her quaking shoulders.

"I'm sorry, Marie. I'm very sorry," he said quietly.

Marie opened her eyes. The nurse was gone. She stared at the attendant through her tears.

"What did you do to her?" she wailed. "What did you do to her?"

The attendant walked slowly back to his desk and sat behind it.

"Whom did you wish to see?" he said calmly, looking at Paul.

"Franny Hollander," Marie said sharply. "Mrs. Franny Hollander."

The attendant opened a card file, flipped through it, then stopped at a card and read it. "Number forty-one," he said, standing. "Right through here."

He started for a second glass door on the far side of the vestibule.

"I don't think we have to see her," Paul said.

Marie suddenly sprang to her feet.

"Yes we do," she said.

"I don't think that's a good idea, Marie."

"I have to."

Paul nodded. He put his arm around Marie's waist and they followed the attendant through the door into the biting cold room. The walls were scrubbed white tiles, like a butcher shop. Marie's legs wobbled under her. She leaned against Paul.

The attendant pulled a ring of keys from his pocket, inserted one in the lock of a wide, file-like drawer in a huge metal locker at the rear of the room.

"I don't want you to look," Paul said quietly. "Not right away."

Marie nodded. The smell of formaldehyde pierced her nose. Her stomach churned.

The attendant pulled on the drawer's handle. It slid toward him soundlessly as he backed away its entire length. The body was covered with a sheet.

"Can you stand alone all right?" Paul said.

"Yes."

Paul released his arm from Marie's waist and stepped alongside the open drawer. He lifted the sheet. His eyes went immediately to the body's arms, the wrists. No cuts. Her neck. No bruises. Nothing. His eyes ran down along the emaciated torso. He closed his eyes, pulling in his breath.

"Marie. Please go into the other room."

Marie was trembling.

"Why?"

"Now, Marie!"

Marie turned and rushed to the door, her footsteps echoing loudly on the ceramic walls. She pushed through the door and went straight to the attendant's desk and opened his card file. She pulled Franny's card, her hand shaking wildly.

"Hollander, Frances Weiss. Age: 40.

Cause of Death: Self-inflicted wounds, genitalia and uterus."

Marie made a whimpering sound deep in her throat.

Suddenly the outer door swung open. The bald man in the black overcoat stood there, his face twisted in a grotesque grimace. Marie backed against the wall, terrified, her arms hugging herself. She opened her mouth, but no sound came out. She knew who he was.

"You," Sydney Hollander growled. "You killed her."

DAY BY day, Marie's fetus gained in definition. The hermaphroditic bud sprouting between its legs separated into two symmetrical mounds, the fleshy clues to its gender. Arched above the eyes, lying obliquely along its upper lip, and whorling from the crown of its head, hair follicles appeared containing the first molecules of pigment. On the pads of its fingers and toes, ridges elevated from the dermis leaving a unique pattern of identifying swirls. And in its inner ear, the tympanic membrane, malleus and incus were now completely formed, receiving the sounds of the splashes and gurgles in the adult stomach just above its head, the cries and murmurs of the voices in the outside world.

"'ISN'T IT romantic?' Da-da-da-da, da-da, da-da." Marie sang as she lit the slender Danish tapers on the dining room table.

"I think I may be underdressed for this occasion," David said, clasping his hand to his chest. He was wearing his faded Harvard sweatshirt. He grinned. "Perhaps I should change into my smoker and foulard."

"No, it's a come-as-you-are." Marie folded the napkins into elaborate fans and placed them on the two plates. She looked at David and smiled. "I'm coming as the Buddha." She patted her belly.

"Charming." David crossed in back of her to the bar. "Can I get you something? How about a gimlet without gin?"

"A gimlet without gin? Why that's like St. Moritz without snow . . . Mahler without horns . . . April without love." Marie giggled.

"Ho, ho." David measured the lime juice into the mixing cup. "How about some unadulterated grade-A, then?"

"Sounds yummy." Marie lifted her chin and sniffed. "Oooops, I think my chateau is brianding."

She turned and walked briskly into the kitchen. She opened the oven door, slid the shelf toward her, and examined the tight roll of filet on the roasting pan. A fine charcoal crust had formed over it. Perfect. She took a carving fork from the hook above the stove and lifted the meat onto a grooved steak platter. Then she put on a pair of quilted mittens and hoisted the pan, dripping the juices over the meat. Using the fork, she turned the meat in its gravy. Very slippery. Just right. She removed the mittens and reached to the knife rack. Her hand trembled in front of her. She brought her arm in back of her and leaned on it against the counter, counting to herself silently. One. Two. Three.

"David? Could you give me a hand? This meat keeps getting away from me. I think it wants to go back to Oklahoma."

She reached to the rack and drew out the Sabatier.

"Maybe we should give it a sporting chance." David entered the kitchen and set his drink down on the counter. "We could turn our backs and give it a head start."

Marie forced a smile. "Here," she said, handing him the fork.

"Let me." David reached for the knife.

"No," Marie said abruptly. Again, she forced a smile. "This . . . this is my party."

"Sor-ry." David dug the fork into the chateaubriand. He looked at Marie. "You know, hon, you're being absolutely terrific about all of this. I mean it."

He was talking about the second amniotic tap. McPartland had scheduled it for tomorrow morning. It was all David knew about. Thought he knew about.

"Thanks." Marie brought the knife down, slicing a thick slab of meat from the far end.

"I know none of this has been easy for you. But it's going to be worth it, babes. I promise you." David braced his hip against the counter, holding the fork upright.

Marie turned the platter.

The meat skidded.

Now.

She jabbed David's thumb with the tip of the blade.

"Ow! Jesus!"

"Oh God, David! I'm sorry!"

In a flash, Marie reached into her apron pocket and pulled out the tissue. David's thumb was in his mouth. She yanked at his wrist, covering the oozing wound with the tissue.

"Let me look."

There were tears in Marie's eyes. She brushed them away with her shoulder, then peeled away the tissue and looked at David's thumb. Thank God, the cut was only superficial.

"Jesus, you are lethal with that thing." David was trying to smile through his grimace.

Marie turned the cold water on in the sink. "Put it under there. I'll get a Band-Aid."

She raced out of the kitchen, through the living room and bedroom into the bathroom. She closed the door behind her. The blood-soaked tissue was still in her hand. She reached again into her apron pocket and withdrew the test tube half-filled with clear fluid. She removed the stopper and stuffed the tissue in with her middle finger. Immediately, the fluid turned a luminous pink. She fitted the stopper tightly back into the tube, then pulled the envelope from her pocket, inserted the tube, licked the flap and pressed it closed. She put the envelope back into her pocket. Then she opened the bathroom door, went to the medicine cabinet, opened it and slammed it shut.

"We're out," she yelled. "I'll try Mrs. Finklestein."

She rushed back through the living room to the apartment door.

"I can use a handkerchief," David called to her.

Marie opened the door. "I'll just be a minute. Keep it under the water."

In the hall, Marie pressed Mrs. Finklestein's doorbell,

then ran to the elevator and slammed her palm against the "Down" button.

"Hello?"

Mrs. Finklestein had opened her door a crack, the chain still on.

"Do you have a Band-Aid, Mrs. Finklestein? It's me. Marie Preston."

"I'll be right back," Mrs. Finklestein said.

The elevator's pulleys finally started to rumble. Marie closed her eyes. It's not worth it, David. None of it.

The elevator thudded to a halt and the doors slid open.

"There's a man in front of the building, Franco. Give him this." Marie handed the envelope to the elevator operator. "And be careful with it. It's breakable."

"Sure thing, Mrs. Preston." Franco smiled and the doors slid closed.

"Are you still there, Marie?" Mrs. Finklestein.

"Yes." Marie walked slowly back to her neighbor's half-open door. A hand jutted out containing a single bandage. "Thanks, Mrs. Finklestein."

"I hope it's nothing serious," the neighbor said.

When Marie reentered the kitchen, David was still standing dutifully by the sink, his thumb under the running water. A sweet, trusting man.

"I love you, David."

Tears were silently slipping down Marie's cheeks.

"AND WHAT are you doing after dinner, my dear?"

Paul rolled a leaf of lettuce into a scroll and slid it through an opening in the mesh wall of the hamster's cage. Paul ripped another leaf off of the head of lettuce and stuffed it in his own mouth.

"I knew a sister of yours in London. Died a horrible death, I'm sorry to say. Kidney failure. She was a drinker."

The hamster stared at Paul with her beady eyes. Her whiskers were fluttering.

"Just kidding, old girl. She lived a long and prosperous life."

A timer rang on the bench in back of him. Paul lifted the top of the cage and dropped the rest of the lettuce inside. "Have a ball."

He walked to the rear of Hopkins' laboratory and punched the "Off" button on the centrifuge. It slowed to a halt, a carrousel at the end of the ride. He snapped the lock on its cover and tilted it back against the hinge. Then he lifted out the vial nearest to him and held it to the light. The label had an "M" on it. M for Marie, dear, sweet soul. He examined the fluid inside the vial. Perfect separation. He carried the vial to the Bio-gard hood and set it in a rack under the lavender light. Then he pulled a pipette from the stack above the hood, ripped off its sanitary paper wrapper, and placed one end just above the Ficoll-Hypaque layer in Marie's vial. The white blood cells. The lymphocytes. He placed the other end of the pipette in his mouth and gently aspirated. An inch, then an inch and a half of the cells suspended in buffer solution entered the pipette. He withdrew it from his mouth, immediately covering the open end with his index finger, then held it over a test tube containing the rabbit complement and released five drops. He swirled the tube, flicking the side with his nail, then set it down in a rack.

On his way back to the centrifuge, Paul paused in front of the hamster's cage. The little beast was lolling on its side with one eye open.

"Don't wait up for me, Theresa," Paul said.

At the centrifuge, he withdrew the second vial. "D" for David. The vampire victim. Paul grimaced as he examined it for separation. A psychiatrist. Harvard educated. Marie had told him nothing more than that. Nice looking, no doubt, in the clear-eyed American manner. And earnestly skeptical, like the grave Rhodes Scholars he had so often dined with at Oxford. He carried the vial back to the Biogard and began to repeat the cytotoxicity test prep. He could not help envying David, whoever he was. Whatever her deceptions, blood-letting and all, Marie was loyally bound to him. Paul was sure the histocompatibility typing would prove that at the very least.

Paul peered into the cage. The hamster was sleeping.

"And now for our mystery guest," Paul whispered and walked back to the centrifuge. The last vial. "F" for fetus. He held it to the light, then returned with the vial to the hood and began to aspirate the cells.

It was a girl. Paul knew that from the karyotyping he had completed earlier that night. Marie wanted a girl. She had said so when she had told him about the pinafore incident. The threat.

The karyotype had shown something else too. On the

fifteenth position of the fetus's sixth chromosome, the violet lamp of Hopkins' microscope had beamed through like a searchlight. The same illumination as on the Roundtree karyotype. And on the Whiting karyotype. And on the chromosome in the Greek Journal.

The Typ-Jul trays, two-by-four plastic cases looking like children's toys with their rows of tiny semihemispherical wells, were prepared and waiting under the hood, a specific HL-A antigen in each well. Using a Tersaki dispenser, Paul released a lambda of Marie's cell solution into each of one tray's wells simultaneously. He clicked the tray cover shut and set it on the bench next to him. Then he prepared David's tray. Then the fetus's.

Paul pulled the lever on the timer to ten minutes and walked to the window. Hopkins' laboratory gave off on the same vista that Paul's had, only from a higher perspective. He could see automobiles crossing the Triboro Bridge, tinier to his eyes than the trays on the bench. Paul sat down on a stool. It would all be over in a matter of minutes.

And then what?

Confrontations? Allegations? A criminal trial?

And then what?

Ride off into the distance with Eva at his side? Open a general practice in New Zealand? Become a veterinarian?

And what about Marie? Dear, brave Marie. What would she do? What could she do?

The timer rang.

Paul heard the hamster jump in its cage and squeal. Hopkins rarely used the laboratory at night. The animal was used to an undisturbed night's sleep. Paul walked slowly to the bench, stacked the trays in order, and carried them to the inverted-phase microscope. He snapped the light on, slid Marie's tray under the lens, and put his head to the eyepieces. Starting with A-1, he examined the wells one at a time for the percentage of dead cells killed by the antigen in each. He noted each score in a HL-A tally sheet fastened to his clipboard. Each time he took his head from the microscope to note a result, it took a full minute for his eyes to readjust to the glare of the microscope's lamp. There were sixty wells in the tray. It was twenty past two in the morning before Paul completed Marie's HL-A tally, the definitive profile of her genetically determined histocompatibility with other human organisms. It told who she could donate organs to and from whom she could receive them without rejection. And it told, without a doubt, to whom she was related.

Paul finished tallying David's tray at three-thirty. And at a quarter to five, he noted the score in the final box of the fetus's tally sheet.

Paul snapped off the light on the microscope and carried the trays and his clipboard to Hopkins' desk. He turned on the desk lamp, released the tally sheets from the clipboard and spread them in front of him. He read them.

It was no worse than Paul had expected. It was, in fact, precisely what he had guessed.

It was the most bizarre phenomenon he had ever seen in his life.

FOUR FORTY-EIGHT.

Marie watched the "8" melt like lava to be replaced instantly by a "9" on the clock-radio. David was nestled in the crook of her shoulder, the side of his face resting against her breast. He looked serene, happy. He had eaten two large slices of the chateaubriand, finished the bottle of Château Neuf du Pape, allowed his wounded thumb to be ministered to and kissed repeatedly. He had wanted to make love after dinner. Marie would have liked to also, tenderly, for absolution. For love. But if she had bared her scratched and bruised body, the questions would have started. And they would have never ended. She had asked for a rain-check. A queasy stomach, she had said, truthfully. Tomorrow.

All three digits melted away. Five o'clock.

She eased herself toward the side of the bed, slipping a pillow under David's head just as it rolled from her bosom. He made a gurgling sound, like an infant, but his eyes did not open. Marie swung her feet over the side of the bed and got up. She tip-toed to the living room, closing the bedroom door behind her. She sat down in front of the phone.

The first rays of morning light were glowing on the window pane. She walked to the window and looked out. There was already some activity in the street. Pre-breakfast joggers. A young woman with a mink stole over her evening dress strolling toward the canopy of the building next door like the dancer in *Lullabye of Broadway*. A short-haired boy sitting glumly on a bench against the park wall. Homosexual, probably.

She could wait if she wanted to. Meet Paul for breakfast as planned. Hold his hand if it became difficult, if the news were bad. She could wait forever, in fact . . . if the baby could wait forever.

She turned and walked quickly back to the phone table. Hopkins' number was on the inside of the matchcover in the ash tray. She dialed. It only rang once.

"Marie?"

"Yes. Are you done?"

"Yes."

Marie shut her eyes tightly. She gripped the side of the phone table.

"Tell me, Paul. Quickly."

Paul did not answer.

"Please, Paul." Oh, God! God! God!

"The baby's fine," Paul said in a monotone. "Perfect as far as I can tell. It's a girl."

"What?" Marie was on her feet. She was laughing and there were tears cascading down her cheeks. "I don't believe it, Paul! I don't believe it! A girl! A perfect little girl!"

"Yes."

"A perfect little girl?"

Silence.

And then a chill shot down Marie's spine. Frigid. Immobilizing.

"What, Paul? What else? There's something else, isn't there?"

"We'll talk later, Marie. At breakfast."

"Now! Tell me now, damn you!"

"Please, Marie. I have to explain it to you . . . in person."

"Why?"

"Because it's complicated, Marie, and I—"

"I'm coming right now!" Marie slammed down the phone.

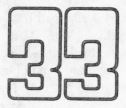

"I'VE NEVER been very good at good-byes."

Paul was leaning at the waist, eye-to-eye with the hamster. The hamster yawned.

"Yes. Well, tally-ho then."

He straightened up and returned to Hopkins' desk to finish packing his briefcase: the Typ-Jul trays, the HL-A tally sheets, the fetal cell slides, the karyotypes, his notebooks. The entire story in a battered leather briefcase. The evidence. He zipped it shut.

Paul looked at his watch. Quarter past five. Ideally, he would explain it all to Marie in the laboratory. Show her the slides, the trays, the tally sheets. Take her through every step of the process. Diagram it on the blackboard. Hope that she would anticipate the conclusion before he came to it, while the chalk was still in his hand. The academic's retreat. The coward's way.

He lifted the briefcase off of the desk. No, not with Marie, of course. He would take her back to his apartment. Make coffee. Sit her down on the sofa, take her hand, and tell her. Tell her everything straight away. Everything. The entire bizarre truth. Paul turned toward the door.

The knob was silently revolving.

"Marie?"

"Uh, huh."

"Good Lord, that was fast. I was hoping to catch you out front."

Paul took a ring of keys from his pocket and walked to the door. He unlocked it. Opened it.

"Hello, my friend."

Paul stepped back, his face reddening.

"Eva! What on earth are you doing here?"

"Is that all the greeting I get? Not even a kiss?" Eva smiled sadly.

Paul leaned toward her and kissed her cheek. It was damp, salty. She had been crying again.

"I was going to call you today. I thought we might have lunch. I've been rather busy, Eva."

"I know." Eva stepped into the room, closing the door behind her.

"I was just on my way out." Paul smiled nervously. "How in heaven's name did you find me here?"

Eva looked at him silently for a moment, then bowed her head shyly. "You never really answered me yesterday, Paul. What is going to become of us? What are we going to do now?" Her words came slowly, softly, her Nordic cadences more pronounced than usual.

"I . . . I really don't know, Eva. This is . . . well, it's a difficult period for me just now. Some problems have come up. Something serious." He stepped toward her, taking her arm, trying to turn her toward the door. "I'll tell you all about it at lunch, all right?"

Eva shrugged her arm free and walked away from him to the window. She looked down without saying a word, then turned back to him, the early morning light tracing the delicate contours of her face; it glowed, like a melancholy Vermeer maiden. "Do you think we could be happy together?" she said. "Do you think we could make a go of it someplace together?"

Paul could see the tears gathering in the corners of her eyes. She was certainly the most exquisite woman he had ever seen, he would most likely ever see. But no, he could never be completely happy with her. Not permanently. He had probably known that all along. He set down his brief-case and walked to her, wrapping his arms around her waist. "Oh, Eva, Eva," he murmured in her ear. "I don't think I could have gotten through these last months without you."

"We could leave now," Eva said. "Leave New York. The States. We could go anywhere you wanted." Her arms encircled his neck.

"Let's talk about it later," Paul said softly. Not once had he expected this from Eva, not from laughing, bawdy Eva in his blue pajamas and winter hat. He reached his hands back and gently tried to loosen her fingers. "I am very sorry, Eva, but I really do have to leave now."

"Don't you want to live with me?"

"Please, Eva. I'm meeting someone."

"Who? Marie Preston?"

Paul stiffened. He pulled his head back, but Eva held onto him tightly. "Whatever made you say that? What do you know about Mrs. Preston?"

"Oh, Paul, why can't you just leave it all as it is? It won't do the Preston woman any good to know. They're all really so much happier not knowing."

"My God, Eva!" Paul grabbed both of her forearms and wrenched his neck free. He began backing away from her, a rush of fear rising inside him. "That was you the other night, wasn't it? Hiding in the laboratory. Contaminating the amnios."

"You don't really understand, Paul. You can't possibly understand—"

"My God, how could you get involved in something so ugly?"

"Please, Paul." Eva stepped toward him, tears flowing down her cheeks, her hand reaching for his chest. "We could go away. We could start a new life."

"No, Eva! Never!"

And then Paul felt it. The circle of cold steel pressing into his ribs. His heart hammered in his chest.

"You don't understand," Eva whispered, forcing him back. "They're my babies. My very own little babies."

The hamster squealed with delight as the fresh cold air from the suddenly opened window ruffled the hairs on its back.

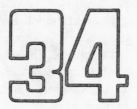

"YOUR PASS, please."

"My what?"

"Your identification pass," the guard said. "I'm sorry, ma'am, but this is the first time I've seen you."

Marie set her handbag on the reception desk and bent her head over it, trying to hide the color that was rising in her cheeks. She took out her wallet and began going through it meticulously.

"Oh, Christ, and I thought I was being so good getting here early on my first day. Dr. Hopkins gave me so many—"

"You working for Dr. Hopkins then?" The guard watched as Marie turned her handbag upside down, emptying the contents on his desk.

"Yes. Lab assistant." She looked up at the guard. "What exactly does it look like? The pass, I mean."

"It's got your picture on it," the guard drawled. Marie's lipstick rolled toward him. He caught it and handed it to her, smiling. "Why don't you just sign in for now."

"Oh, thanks." Marie scooped up her belongings and dropped them into her bag. "I'd hate to have to go all the way back to Queens for it."

The guard handed her a pen and she signed her name and the time on the sheet, where he pointed.

"Thanks a lot. I promise I'll have it tomorrow."

"It's the last row of elevators."

"Yes. Thanks."

Marie strode quickly to the elevators. One was open. She entered, pulling the matchbook from her coat pocket. "Hopkins—1606." She pressed the button for the sixteenth floor. The elevator did not move. She swung her pocketbook back and forth in front of the door's electric eye. The machine was fooled, the doors closed. She stood in the back of the elevator, resting both her arms on the rails. As it started to rise, she felt the baby twirl inside her.

Her baby girl. Her perfect little baby girl.

What in the name of God could be wrong with a perfect little baby girl?

The elevator coasted to a halt and the doors slowly slid open. Marie stepped out. The hallway was dark except for a shaft of yellow light jutting toward her from the right. She looked up. The door to the stairwell was slowly swinging closed. Someone was on the stairs. A glimpse of golden hair. Somehow familiar. The door clicked shut. Darkness. And silence but for the faint ring of footsteps on the metal stairs.

Marie paused a moment, waiting for her eyes to adjust to the darkness. Then she started down the corridor, her own footsteps resonating loudly on the tile walls. The laboratory doors were closed, dark. "1624," "1620," "1618."

Marie stood perfectly still. A sound from the far end of the hall. A bang. A rattle. Then a shrill, high-pitched wail. Like a baby. Again, the bang. The rattle. The squeal.

She wanted to run back to the elevator.

She ran toward the sound.

The door to "1606" was open, slamming against the inside wall. Rattling. Slamming again.

"Paul?"

Again, the slam. The rattle.

"Paul?"

She stepped inside the laboratory, feeling the wall beside her for the light switch.

"Paul?"

She found the switch, snapped it on.

The squeal pierced the air so suddenly that Marie screamed, stumbling backward. She sank to her knees, shaking, grabbing at the wall.

Again, the squeal. Ear shattering. Wild.

And then she saw it. The hamster. Its furry head pressed against the mesh of its cage. Staring at her, its mouth still open.

"Oh, my God . . . Jesus, God."

Marie slowly stood up, still trembling. She dug her hand into her pocket and pulled out the matchbook. "Hopkins—1606." She looked at the door. "1606." At the desk. The nameplate. "Dr. Lloyd Hopkins."

"Paul?"

Her eyes searched the room. No one. She turned back to the door. She had just missed him. He was waiting for her in front of the hospital. She started for the door. And then a blast of cold air slammed the door against the wall. Marie turned around. The laboratory window was open, the wind gusting through it, rattling the test tubes in their racks. She strode quickly to the window, pulled it shut, and turned back to the door. She stopped, hesitated one second as a shadowy image took shape in her mind, and then walked slowly back to the window and looked down.

Sprawled like a child's doll flung from a playpen, a figure lay face down on the roof of the west wing of Hebron hospital some twelve floors below. Paul.

Marie did not scream. Nor did she faint or even stagger, overcome with dizziness. It was as if the feeling of wretched sickness and despair that swept through her the moment she saw Paul lying lifeless on the rooftop could not find a response equal to it and instead something inside of her separated, cutting itself off from the rest of her emotions, from the rest of her consciousness. What remained—

precise, brilliant, unafraid—rushed her out of the door, down the corridor to the elevator.

She punched the "Down" button. If Paul's murderer—she had no doubt who it was—if Paul's murderer had taken the stairway all the way to the ground floor, Marie could still catch her by taking the elevator. If it came right away.

It did. Marie leaped inside before the doors were fully open and flung her palm against the "Mezzanine" button. The doors closed immediately and the elevator began its descent. She stood, poised on the balls of her feet just behind the doors, taking deliberate deep breaths like an athlete preparing for a jump. The elevator came to a stop with a slight bounce. The doors opened and Marie was out, bounding to her right, yanking open the door to the stairwell. No one. She listened. No footsteps. Nothing. She spun around and raced toward the entrance.

"Hey, lady, where you going now? You got to sign—"

Marie slammed her hands against the glass of the revolving door and spun through, out onto the steps, colliding with a group of orderlies sharing a carton of coffee.

"Fuck all, woman. Watch your ass."

She looked to her right. Three nurses, all dark-haired, sauntering toward the hospital. Beyond them, a man with a dog. To her left, two doctors in whites, bare-headed, stethoscopes dangling from their necks like medallions, coming toward her. And just in back of them, her golden hair bouncing prettily in the new day's light, the woman paced hurriedly down Fifth Avenue, something swinging in her hand. Paul's briefcase.

Marie darted around the doctors, then abruptly slowed to an easy walk some twenty paces behind the woman, keeping as close as she could to the hospital wall. From just the back of her perfectly shaped head, Marie knew where she had seen the woman some four months ago. And she knew with equal certainty where she was going now. Where they were going.

Ninety-eighth Street. Ninety-seventh. Ninety-sixth.
Marie kept pace with the woman, step by step, alert to her
every hesitation, every turn of her lovely head. A young
man tugged by three Great Danes came between them at
Ninety-fifth Street, but he crossed to the park side of the avenue at the corner. At Ninety-fourth Street, the blond
woman came to a halt and turned. Marie ducked into the
glass-doored entrance of an apartment building. The doorman approached her, but she kept her eyes fastened on the
woman who was looking up the avenue, apparently searching for a taxi.

"May I help you?" The doorman.

"No, thank you."

She could see the woman's face in profile now. Delicate. Glowing. And something else. Something Marie faintly
remembered sensing about the woman that afternoon in
front of McPartland's office.

"Are you waiting for someone?" Again, the doorman.

"Yes."

No taxi in sight, the woman crossed the street and
turned left. Marie waited a second and pushed through the
door after her.

Madison Avenue. Park. The woman was walking more
briskly now, pulling a half-block ahead of Marie at Eighty-
fifth Street, then crossing just as the light changed at
Eighty-fourth. Marie crossed against the light.

At Seventy-fifth Street, Marie quickened her pace.
What would she do when the woman came to McPartland's
office? Let her enter and call the police? Stop her? But what
about her baby? Had she forgotten about her baby? Her
perfect little baby girl . . .

The woman crossed at Seventy-fourth Street, Marie
only ten feet behind her. The woman cut diagonally across
the sidewalk toward the street entrance of McPartland's
office. The light was on over the door. Marie stood still. The
woman continued walking right by the office door. At the

entrance to the apartment building just beyond it, she turned left and entered.

Marie took ten quick steps and was at the door of the apartment building. She could see the blond woman inside the lobby, now turning, disappearing into a corridor to her left. A tall uniformed doorman stood directly in front of Marie.

"Yes?"

Marie stepped around him and pressed against the door. Locked.

"Madame, who do you wish—"

Marie turned and glared indignantly at the doorman.

"Would you please help my mother with the wheel-chair? I'll get the elevator."

The doorman nodded apologetically and buzzed the door open before heading for the curb.

Marie pushed the door and ran through the lobby to the corridor. At the far end, the blond woman was pulling a key from a large open door, now turning her back to Marie and letting the door swing slowly closed behind her. Marie sprinted toward the door, her arms stretched out in front of her. She caught it just as it was snapping shut.

For a moment, she stood still, her chest heaving, her hands holding the door open a crack. She listened. The woman was walking away from her, her heels clicking on the floor. She hadn't heard Marie.

Bracing the door with her shoulder, Marie slipped off one shoe, then the other. She put her ear to the crack in the door and again listened. A woman's voice. Muffled. Crying.

"No. Of course you don't want to hear about it, do you, Raymond?"

"Please, Eva."

McPartland's voice. Gentle. Always gentle.

Marie slipped in through the door, knelt and slid one of her shoes between the door and the jamb. She stood. She was in the hallway of McPartland's offices.

"What should we talk about then, dear Raymond? Genetic purity? Platonic beauty? The family of man?"

The woman's voice broke into a sharp, bitter laugh.

"Eva, Eva, please. We can talk about it all later. I have a patient waiting."

Marie could hear them both quite clearly now. They must be in McPartland's consultation office directly across from the examination room. And the operating room. Marie flattened herself against the wall. The operating room! Where it all began. Where she had to go now.

She slid her left foot sideways, then brought her right foot alongside it, moving up the hall like a dancer.

"Why don't you take a rest now? Alice will give you something to make it easier."

Marie looked up. She saw two shadows jutting from McPartland's office. They were coming into the corridor. She placed her palms against the wall in back of her, shoved, and skidded in her stockinged feet across the width of the hall through a half-opened door into a dark room. She pressed the door closed behind her.

"Try not to think about it. It's over. You did what you had to do."

McPartland and the woman called Eva were walking in Marie's direction. She could hear the woman sobbing softly.

"You're a special person, Eva. One in a million. You have to remember that. We wouldn't be doing all of this if you weren't."

They stopped directly in front of the door, only inches away from Marie. The knob was turning.

"There's a free bed in here. I'll send Alice right in to you."

Marie backed away from the door, her hands stretched out blindly behind her searching for a closet door. A screen. Anything to hide behind.

Oh God!

Marie snatched back her hand and covered her mouth,

stifling her scream. She had touched a face, a human face directly in back of her. Upturned, warm, immobile.

"I don't want to be alone, Raymond. Not now. Not now, please."

Marie held her breath. The knob stopped turning.

"Of course. You can wait with Dr. Langerfeld. I just have to change. I'll be right with you."

Marie waited until the footsteps receded to McPartland's office before she removed her hand from her mouth and let out her breath. Then she pried the door open an inch, letting in the light from the hallway. She turned around. Lying in front of her on a rolling stretcher was a woman with an I.V. tube taped to her wrist. Her eyes were closed and a faint smile turned up the corners of her mouth. Marie thought she recognized that smile: The woman was dreaming about her baby.

Marie turned back to the door, pulled it open, and peered out. No one. She slipped through the door and again pressed her back against the wall. She was only ten feet from the examination room. She edged toward it, crablike, passing the door to the waiting room, the bulletin board with the baby pictures, McPartland's office. She could hear him humming behind the door.

The door to the examination room was open, the lights on, the sound of running water coming from inside. Craning her neck slowly around the doorframe, Marie peered into the room. A woman was lying in an open smock on the examination table, her eyes fixed on the ceiling. And at the far end of the room, her back to the door, Miss Gold was standing in front of the sink.

Marie didn't wait. She sucked in her breath and raced on the balls of her feet across the room and through the open door on the opposite wall. She was in the operating suite. It was empty and only dimly lit by the light emanating from the examination room. Suddenly, the sound of running water stopped. Marie didn't move.

"Hold still. I have to shave you now. This will just take a minute." Miss Gold.

Giddy, nervous laughter.

"Please, Mrs. Browning. I don't want to cut you."

"I'm sorry. I'm a bit on edge, I'm afraid."

"That's understandable. But please do hold still."

Marie had only seen this room before upside down. She remembered the two large hemispheric arc lamps suspended over the operating table in the center, the sink where McPartland had scrubbed up, the clock behind her. She looked at the wall opposite her. Jutting from the wall, almost obscured in the dim light, was a wooden locker the height of the room with a rubber-rimmed door and a small window at its center. She remembered hearing that door open and close.

"Do you think you can get onto this without any help, Mrs. Browning?"

"I think so."

Marie started for the locker, sliding her feet one after the other over the tile floor.

"Hold still now. I'm just going to open a vein for Dr. Langerfeld."

"Gee, I never imagined this was going to be so complicated."

"It's just routine."

Marie pressed her face against the window of the locker door. It was totally dark, impossible to see anything.

"Hello, Clara. How are you doing this morning?" McPartland.

Marie froze.

"Okay, I guess. Is it morning already?"

McPartland laughed. "Just about. Well, let's get going, shall we? When she's in a good mood, Miss Gold lets me do things I haven't done since medical school."

Marie heard the soft rumble of rubber wheels on the floor coming toward her. Her eyes darted around the room.

No other doors. No windows. She stepped back from the locker. The corner where it met the wall was totally hidden from the operating table. In one second she was there, hunched over with her arms wrapped around her knees, her buttocks just touching the cold floor.

The arc lights flashed on and the stretcher rolled into the room. Marie could see nothing. But every click and rustle of the movements going on just three yards away from her resounded in her ears as if amplified.

"Now, we'll just get you onto the table and the hard part will be over."

Marie stared at the floor, a maze of tiles intersecting one another at right angles. They seemed to form a design of interconnecting crosses, then that image suddenly dissolved and she saw only a labyrinth, an endless labyrinth. More footsteps entered the suite, two pairs, Marie guessed.

"Ah, Dr. Langerfeld. You've met Mrs. Browning, haven't you?"

"Yes."

"And this is Ms. Persson. She'll be assisting me this morning."

Stretched taut from squatting, Marie's thighs were already beginning to tire. And her belly, tucked against her knees, was starting to ache. Silently, she rolled backward and rested her back against the wall. She had only one purpose now. She waited.

"All right, Mrs. Browning, let's just roll over on our left side like this . . . that's good. Now pull up your knees and curl forward . . . very good. Now hold still while I insert the syringe."

As Marie heard the antiseptic squirting onto the patient's back, she remembered exactly how that splash of cold liquid felt on her skin, the helplessness of waiting for the jab of the needle, the numbness that immediately followed it. And her trust, her unflagging faith in the men and women in white coats and rubber-gloved hands. Her saviors. She heard a sphygmomanometer bulb pumping, then the soft whistle of air escaping from the valve.

"One twenty-five over seventy-five." Dr. Langerfeld.

"Good." Footsteps. "Can you feel this, Clara?"

"No."

"Fine. Now we're going to do some acrobatics. Miss Gold will help you. First, turn to your right . . . good . . . now tuck your knees up under your chest. All the way. Make them touch. Good."

"This arm over here. And that one there. Stretch it out, Mrs. Browning. Good." Miss Gold.

"Hold steady now, Clara. I'm making the incision."

Marie could feel it, the warmth of the blade slitting the top of her vagina as she sprawled on the table, her buttocks in the air. Whatever you have to do, Doctor. Just let me get pregnant. Please, help me have a baby.

"Adhesions of the left tube, inner edge . . . right tube clear."

A wet sound, almost sexual.

"Just hold still a few minutes longer, Clara, we're almost finished."

And then Marie heard the footsteps again, padding on the tiles. Coming toward her. She rocked forward onto her knees, hesitated a split second, then crawled to the corner of the locker. The footsteps stopped. She held her breath. The snap of the door latch, the soft whoosh of air as the heavy door swung open, the click of the light switch. Then footsteps entering the locker. Marie slowly rose to her feet. She slid her head along the wall of the locker to its edge. Then beyond the edge. She turned her head and looked.

Dr. McPartland stood just inside the locker, a small covered glass dish in his hands. And beyond him, taped to the inside of the locker door, was a hand-printed sign.

CAUTION! STERILE HANDS ONLY!
LIVE HUMAN EMBRYOS

"CHRIST! WHO'S THERE? DOCTOR!"

A rubber-gloved hand pointing at Marie.

"STOP HER!"

Marie cut directly in front of the locker, smacking against McPartland's arm. The dish hurled from his hands and shattered against the wall. The woman on the operating table screamed. Miss Gold was already at the door and Eva was stalking toward Marie, something metallic glinting in her hand. Marie suddenly shot to the foot of the table where Dr. Langerfeld stood stunned, her arms folded across her chest. Marie seized her by the waist and flung her stumbling against Eva's outstretched hand. Langerfeld yelped, like a wounded dog. And Marie was racing for the door, her hands in front of her, adrenalin coursing through her veins. She grabbed Gold's smock in both her fists and yanked her toward her, bringing up her knee to the nurse's solar plexis. Gold bent over, gagging and Marie was through the door running across the examination room into the hall and toward the door where she had entered, footsteps now pounding behind her. Gaining on her.

"Stop! Damn you!"

A hand grabbed at Marie's coat as she flung herself against the door. She skidded through the opening, then spun around catching the door handle in her fingers and smashed the door closed against her pursuer's hand. She rushed down the hall into the vestibule, then slowed as she came to the outside door.

The doorman pulled the door open, staring at her shoeless feet.

"Ralph! Stop that woman!"

But Marie was already on the sidewalk, waving her arms wildly at a passing cab.

"Thief! Thief! Stop that woman!"

From the corner of her eye, Marie saw Eva coming through the door after her. She leaped off of the curb into the street. Something sharp bit into the sole of her foot and blood immediately began filling her stocking. A limousine screeched to a halt as she raced in front of it and across Park Avenue, each step grinding the pain deeper into her foot and shin. She made it to Fifth Avenue without stopping, then raced alongside the park wall searching for an opening, not daring to look behind her. The thought flashed in her mind that she should find a policeman, protection, but no, she could not stop now. Not yet. One block. Two. Dirt clung to her blood-soaked foot, but most of the feeling was already gone. The sidewalk had begun to fill with men and women leaving for their offices, depositing their children on buses. They stepped aside politely, allowing this shoeless, wild-eyed pregnant woman to pass in front of them, tolerant New Yorkers.

Seventy-ninth Street was just a few strides ahead of her, cutting into the park to her left. She took the corner without slowing, her knees pumping under her, the soft thump of feet running behind her, gaining with every step. Faster. Faster.

And then just in back of her, the sudden squeal of brakes screamed in her ears.

"Marie! Is that you?"

Faster!

"Marie! It's me. Tom. What's wrong?"

Marie spun around. Tom was out of his car, walking quickly toward her, his eyes wide with concern. For a split second, a man and a woman in matching sweat suits came between them, then jogged past Marie. No one else. No Eva. No Gold. No McPartland. Just Tom. Good, wonderful Tom. And Marie was laughing, tears cascading down her face, sputtering, quaking, falling into Tom's outstretched arms, clinging to him, now bawling, her head tight against his shoulder.

"Oh, Marie. What's wrong? What's wrong? You poor woman. What's happened?"

"Tom . . . Tom . . . Oh, God, Tom . . . take me home
. . . Please, take me home."

She leaned against him as she hobbled toward the car,
her body suddenly empty of all strength, exhausted.

"Marie, you're hurt. You're bleeding. I think we'd better get you to a hospital." Tom braced her limp body
against his hip and reached for the handle of his car door.

"No, Tom. Just take me home. Just take me home."

He opened the door and eased Marie onto the seat,
then closed the door and walked around to the driver's seat.
He got in beside her and released the brake. Marie was crying softly.

"It's all right now. Everything's all right." Tom turned
the ignition key.

"No . . . no, it's not, Tom . . . It's horrible . . . horrible."

Tom pulled slowly away from the curb. "What's horrible, Marie?"

Marie stared out the front window, the sunlight catching in her tears, splitting it into pinpoints of color. She
couldn't think about any of it yet. Not yet.

"You don't have to talk about it now if you don't want
to," Tom said.

Marie looked over at Tom, touching the sleeve of his
coat with her hand. "Thank God for you, Tom. You're always there."

They were coming to the edge of the park. The light
was red at the intersection of Central Park West and Tom
coasted to a halt. He looked in his rearview mirror.

"I'll . . . I'll tell you everything later, Tom. You and
Bonnie."

Suddenly the car was lurching to the left, Tom yanking
the steering wheel as he turned the car completely around,
now accelerating as he entered the east-bound lane.

"Where are you going? Tom! Where—"

"Don't spoil it, Marie. Not for Bonnie. Not for Adam."

"STOP, TOM! Let me out! Let me out!"

His hand shot in front of her and suddenly the door slammed open and Marie was out, sailing through the air, spinning, her mouth open in a soundless scream as she whacked face-down against the pavement.

THEY WERE the most exquisite roses Marie had ever seen. Their brilliant-red color reflecting on the dew drops that clung to the petals. When Paul presented them to her, he bowed deeply, like a courtly dancer. Marie selected the most beautiful of them and handed it back to him. Grinning, he placed the stem between his lips and twirled away. Now Marie turned and handed a rose to David, then one to Bonnie, and she gave the largest to Franny, who tucked it in her hair. Someone said that lunch was coming. All the guests gazed up the long, fern-lined pathway where Tom and Eva walked slowly toward them, their arms outstretched carrying a magnificent silver-covered dish. The sunlight glinted in it, dazzling Marie's eyes, blinding her.

"She's conscious, Doctor."

A pinpoint of light shined in Marie's left eye. She tried to blink it shut. A finger held the lid.

"Very good, Miss Bailey."

The finger withdrew, her eye shut and Paul danced toward her, the rose dangling from his lips. He was pointing at something. He opened his mouth. Blood poured out of it.

"I believe she's trying to move, sir."

"Just tighten the straps, nurse. She's not going anywhere today."

Marie opened both her eyes. Faces hung over her,

masks suspended from the ceiling. She closed them. The guests had gathered in a circle around Tom, pleading with him to lift the cover from the silver platter. Finally, with a magician's flourish, he whisked it away. Lying inside, like a plucked bird, was the baby.

Marie snapped her eyes open.

"Well, how are we feeling, Marie?"

A mask was smiling down at her. Dr. Raymond McPartland's mask. In an instant the dream completely vanished and Marie remembered everything.

She bolted upright. Something slapped against her arms and ribs. She fell back, limp. She had barely risen an inch.

"Easy does it, Marie." Dr. McPartland's face hovered over hers. "You've had yourself quite an accident."

Marie's eyes darted around her. She was in Hebron Hospital, the Ultrasound Room. A nurse stood next to her.

"Help . . . me . . . please . . . help . . . me."

Marie screamed each word. But the sounds wafted out of her mouth as softly as whimpers from another room.

"Let her have something to drink, nurse. She must be parched."

"Help . . . me . . . plea—"

A glass straw jammed into her mouth against her tongue.

"Thank you, Miss Bailey. That will be all for now."

Feet padded in back of Marie. A door opened and closed.

She was alone with Raymond McPartland.

"Listen to me carefully, Marie." The doctor leaned his face so close to hers that she could see the row of soft hairs along his cheekbones, the web of tiny laugh lines in the corners of his eyes. "We have a very important decision to make."

Using every bit of strength she had, Marie spat the

straw from her mouth. It grazed McPartland's cheek and shattered on the floor.

"Please, Marie. We don't have time for that kind of behavior. Not anymore." His head pulled back, disappearing from her sight. "We don't have much time at all anymore."

Again, Marie tried to raise her body and again it snapped back onto the table, pain shooting along her spine with a knifelike edge. She couldn't move. She couldn't scream. It was over. She knew it was all over.

Suddenly something cold touched her between her legs.

"Now listen to me, Marie. We have to decide what to do about your baby."

Something was sliding up inside her. McPartland's hand.

"You're lucky she's still alive after all you've put her through so unnecessarily."

The hand turned. She could feel his fingertips poking her cervix.

"You're still bleeding. I hope we can save the baby. Don't you, Marie?"

The hand withdrew quickly. Footsteps walking away from her. She tried to raise her head. Impossible.

"She could be a wonderful little baby, Marie. A wonderful little baby girl. You can't imagine how much you would love her."

A cabinet door clicking open. A metallic ring. A kisslike sound. His footsteps came toward her again. She saw his head bobbing from the corner of her eye. He was putting something on the table just in back of her. Then his hands appeared over her and dropped from view under her bosom.

The skin on her belly, raw with lacerations, stung as he ran his fingers over it. Marie welcomed the pain. Nothing mattered anymore. Nothing. She hoped he would do it quickly, whatever it was. She closed her eyes.

"Did you feel that Marie?"

For the first time since she had regained consciousness, Marie felt it. Pushing back against McPartland's hands. Kicking. Curling inside of her.

"Whose . . . baby . . . is . . . it?"

"It's yours, Marie. It's inside you. Part of you. Nourished by your own blood. She's fighting for her life, Marie."

"Whose . . . baby . . . is . . . it?"

McPartland abruptly lifted his hands.

"Enough, Marie. Enough questions. Look what all your questions have gotten you. What they got Mrs. Hollander. It's so much better if they don't know. It makes it so much easier to be a family."

"Please . . . tell . . . me!"

McPartland walked toward the window.

"They found him right out here, you know. He landed right out here. I'll never understand what drove him to jump like that. Didn't he realize I was only doing what they all wanted? All these geneticists. I'm doing their work for them now. I'm giving them exactly what they want. What all of you want, Marie."

McPartland's voice drifted to her from across the room. Low. Gentle.

"You have a perfect baby, Marie. A perfect baby girl. She has a perfect pedigree on both sides. Genetically unflawed. A perfect mind and a perfect body. What a shame to end all of that now."

"Whose . . . baby?"

Silence.

"Whose?"

"They made it my responsibility. They singled me out. And I vowed that it would never happen again. Never again would Richard Monroe give the world a genetically defective baby. An impure baby. I've made sure that would never happen again."

"Please."

McPartland's footsteps came slowly toward her.

"Dr. Bouchard advised me to terminate. That's what he put on your admission chart. 'Prostaglandin termination recommended.' It's hospital policy. The safety of the mother comes first. No one ever sues over a therapeutic abortion."

He stopped in back of her, picked something off of the table, then went to the foot of the table.

"This will just take a minute, Marie. It actually hurts less than real childbirth."

His fingers spread the lips of her vagina.

"Do you know what they do with the p.c.? That's what they call the baby, the p.c.—product of conception. Not a very personal way of putting it, is it? It's supposed to make it easier, I suppose."

His hand was in her vaginal canal.

"They burn it," he said. "Like trash."

He withdrew his hand.

"There. You'll feel your first contraction in less than an hour."

Marie felt something start to melt inside her.

"Please . . . God . . . tell . . . me."

"Does it really matter now, Marie?"

"Please!"

She heard McPartland sigh.

"Your ovum donor is Swedish," he said. "She has a re-markable genealogy. Flawless. But she gave you more than that, Marie. She gave your baby that critical gene that keeps the baby developing perfectly inside you. She's a uni-versal donor. Quite rare. We were all very lucky to find her. You have no idea how lucky you are. How lucky you might have been."

McPartland paused a moment. Marie could hear voices coming from outside the room. She thought she heard David.

"And it's funny about your sperm donor," McPartland

went on. "None of us have actually met him. His pedigree is well documented though. Perfect. Absolutely gene perfect. He's Dutch."

McPartland came beside Marie. He smoothed a strand of hair back from her forehead and smiled down at her.

"We thought one of our fair-haired babies would fit quite nicely into your family," he said. "We have other donors for our olive-skinned and brown couples."

Marie looked straight back into McPartland's eyes.

"How . . . many?" she murmured. "How . . . many . . . brothers . . . and . . . sisters . . . does . . . mine . . . have?"

McPartland abruptly lifted his head.

"I don't know exactly," he said impatiently. "Two hundred. Perhaps three. I don't keep those kind of figures in my head. But each one is different, Marie, just like brothers and sisters in the same family. And they are in the same family. The family of Man. Spread out around the whole city, the whole country. The perfect family of Man. I'm sorry you don't want to be part of that family, Marie. You could have been a credit to it. All three of you."

His hand pressed against her belly.

The baby kicked back.

"David? . . . Does . . . David . . . know?"

McPartland walked behind her. A switch clicked. Then another.

"No," he said. "David doesn't know. None of our parents do. Except Dr. Roundtree, of course."

Now the doctor appeared on Marie's left side, a long metal instrument extending from his hand. He touched it to her abdomen. Something flashed over her head.

"I don't see any reason why he should know, do you, Marie?"

Marie strained her eyes toward the top of her head.

And she saw the baby! God, yes, she saw her! Her little

arms waving, her feet kicking, the perfect oval head wagging back and forth, its features already defined. Beautiful. Incredibly beautiful.

"What a strong baby you have in there, Marie. What a perfectly healthy little baby girl. We can still save her, Marie. It would only take a second. We can still save her."

He slid the ultrasound sensor to another point on Marie's belly.

"She's your baby, Marie," Dr. McPartland said quietly. "It's a miracle. You're irreversibly infertile—I knew that without a doubt the first time I saw you—and she's your baby. The only baby you could ever have."

He reached down and gently brushed away the tears from Marie's eyes.

"It's really just a question of how badly you want to have a baby, isn't it?"

The infant's head turned on the screen. It seemed to be smiling at her.

"My . . . baby."

Marie was sobbing uncontrollably.

"I . . . want . . . my . . . baby."

AFTERWORD

EMBRYO IS a work of fiction. Yet every medical event in it could happen. And probably has.

The age of embryo implants and transfers has long been with us. In livestock breeding, embryo transfers from prize cows which have been fertilized by prize bulls into the wombs of less genetically gifted "host" cows is fast replacing artificial insemination as the most efficient way to build a superior pure-bred herd. Saved the time-consuming burden of nine-month pregnancies, a prize cow can thus produce up to eighty calves a year as compared to the six calves she would normally be expected to engender in her entire reproductive lifetime.

Human breeding is not lagging far behind. Since the first official "test tube baby" live birth in England, *in vitro* fertilization and embryo implantation in the womb of the genetic mother has become a viable option for infertile couples. (One in six American couples have infertility problems.) Embryo implantation into a "host" (non-genetic) mother is the coming alternative. Reportedly, this procedure has already been completed successfully in New Zealand, and for infertile couples, it has added advantages. For a woman who is able to produce eggs but who cannot hold or sustain an embryo in her womb, a "surrogate" womb provides a perfect solution; and for a woman who cannot produce eggs but who has a "friendly" womb, it can provide the experience of pregnancy and birth if not genetic motherhood.

But embryo transfer has uses which go far beyond solving fertility disorders. In a front page story of a recent issue of the *National Catholic Reporter* one doctor argued that embryo transfer should be considered as a morally acceptable alternative for women who would otherwise have abortions. And in some quarters the procedure has been offered as an option for women who want children but who, for professional or emotional reasons, do not wish to go through with a nine-month pregnancy. The ethical and legal problems involved in "wombs for rent" are already being avidly debated with the most pressing question being, what if the "host" mother decides she wants to keep the baby she was commissioned to gestate for the genetic mother?

The availability of amniocentesis and therapeutic abortion to the growing number of couples who want small families has clearly created a climate of consumerism in the business of human reproduction. It is no longer just a question of selecting out genetic abnormalities like Downs Syndrome. A large number of couples are now preselecting their offspring's sex—"A boy for you and a girl for me"—and, as prenatal diagnosis becomes more specific, may soon be choosing which fetuses to keep on the basis of their genetic disposition toward high intelligence, size and even beauty.

The legal principle of "Wrongful Life"—a gynecologist being held liable for failing to advise a patient that she was at risk for giving birth to a genetically defective child—was upheld in two recent decisions by the New York State Court of Appeals. Hailed as a victory by most geneticists, the ruling is expected to dramatically increase the number of therapeutic abortions counseled by doctors. This will undoubtedly include the abortion of healthy fetuses in low-risk cases as the physicians' only alternative to the threat of costly liability.

Finally, in answer to the question of whether an embryo transfer could be done without the knowledge of the "mother," I turn to a landmark event in medical history that occurred nearly one hundred years ago:

In 1884, using sperm donated by a medical student, one Dr. William Pancoast effected the first successful case of artificial insemination on a woman who lay anesthetized on a hospital operating table. *Neither the woman nor her husband had any idea what had been done.* Only after the child was born did Pancoast confide the truth to the husband. As reported by the doctor, the husband was undisturbed and only asked that his wife not be told.

D.M.K.
Southfield, Massachusetts